I0564911

BEAT IN HER BLOOD

VOLUME 1 OF THE HEAVY METAL QUARTET

J.K. Ullrich

For my sister, the real rock.

PLAYLIST

PRELUDE

Iodine stained her hair the color of rust, an ironic prelude to forfeiting her machinehood. One flick of the scalpel re-opened the scar near her ear; it seemed almost a shame to unravel her body's deft pink stitches. Skin folded back in soft petals, revealing a silver gleam. Funny that such a tiny object could have such tremendous consequences.

Filaments spread across her skull, almost melded with the bone. Forceps could barely pluck them out with the boat yawing underfoot. Trying to remove the device now might only make things worse.

Maybe there was another way. An ugly way, but it might ultimately turn out better for everyone.

Waves hammered the porthole, demanding an answer.

Shivers crawled down her spine despite the stifling heat. This would require more anesthetic.

1. MISS MYSTERY

Water sprayed up from the ambulance wheels, and a hard brake hurled Jonathan Rowell against his seat belt.

"Smart car, my ass. Someone is dying, and it's worried about wet rims!" He jabbed the dashboard controls, but the autopilot's hazard alerts continued their shrill duet with the siren. Rising in his seat, he assessed the route ahead. Floodwater transformed the cobbled streets of Fells Point into frothy canals. "If this is why you were late for your first shift, Evans, I forgive you."

"I told you the storm last night made a mess of the roads!" The trainee squelched her shoes in the passenger footwell. Sodden synth-leather spoiled her new Baltimore City EMS uniform. "I don't remember the weather being this bad when I lived here as a kid, except when that hurricane ruined the aquarium."

"Once the rest of those ice sheets melt, the whole city will be an aquarium. Even machines should learn to swim." Switching to manual control, Jonathan pressed the accelerator. The ambulance lumbered forward. Tires skidded against the flow of oily water and trash.

Evans clutched the grab handle. "Is this standard emergency response protocol?"

"Sometimes lives outweigh laws. Replay the call," Jonathan ordered the auto-dispatcher. The voice that had summoned them from the station a few minutes earlier filled the cabin. Traces of a sunken-South accent didn't soften the woman's brisk tone.

"I need an ambulance at Henderson's Wharf. There's a woman with a head injury on the boat *Wind of Change*. It's not bleeding much, but she won't wake, and she's barely breathing."

"She doesn't sound very upset about it," said Evans, frowning at the dashboard. "People on the training calls are so panicky you can hardly understand them, but this one might as well be a robocall."

"It's all the information we've got. This is your first practical lesson—use transit time to anticipate what you might find at the scene, and prepare for nasty surprises." Jonathan veered around a plastic bin lid adrift in the alley-way, holding his breath until the hydroplaning tires steadied. "What do you think might have happened?"

"Someone chugged too much on a party boat. Or came out to check on their yacht after the storm, and slipped on the deck. Or got in a fight with a sea monster."

"You don't get to joke until you're off probation."

"I'm not joking."

The marina emerged from the drizzle. Vessels bucked on the choppy water. Halfway down the jetty, someone leapt into the prow of a weather-beaten power yacht, with a massive attacker close behind.

Jonathan squinted at the name and home port embla-zoned on the boat's stern: *Wind of Change, Baltimore, Maryland*. Dread slithered through his veins. "Okay, then. At least I'll already be wet when Davy Jones there throws me overboard. Stay here while I de-escalate. There's no point in both of us getting soaked until we can access the patient. Or until I become one." Alarm widened Evans' eyes, so he eased the dark humor with a smile. Tugging up his windbreaker hood, he grabbed his jump bag and hopped down from the ambulance. Tepid water soaked the shins of his six-foot-plus frame. He sloshed to the floating wharf, where the yacht's foredeck had become a boxing ring.

"This business is already going broke without you chucking thousands of dollars' worth of gear overboard," the big man roared, swinging a cinderblock fist at a woman half his size.

She dodged, high-top soles screeching across the fiberglass. "We can get more hardware! Mechanic can't get a new body."

"Wanna bet?"

"Dammit, Steel, I'm not gonna watch another shipmate die!"

"Then let me help," Jonathan called up. The woman spun toward his voice. In the distracted instant, her opponent seized her arm and hurled her over the rail. Reflex opened Jonathan's arms to slow her fall. She slammed into him with twice the force he'd expected for her small body. Staggering, he slipped on the wet dock and fell backward. Aluminum clanged against his skull. Comets shot across his vision.

Crap, that's a grade-one concussion, and mandatory medical leave if anyone finds out! Can't afford that. Get up, quick, and don't act dizzy.

He tried to rise, but the woman atop his ribs pinned him down. Bright citrus scents swirled into his lungs, mingled with a hint of ozone like overworked electronics. "Are you hurt?"

"I hurt every damn day," she muttered into his shirt. It was the voice from the dispatched call, with its distinctive blend of long vowels and impatience. Lifting her head, she appraised him through a tempest of dark bangs. She looked about his age, early thirties, but metallic tattoos on her temple gave her a youthful edge. Wet eyelashes blinked away the rain, and her left pupil gleamed red.

Jonathan sat up with a gasp, catapulting the woman off his chest.

She tumbled backward, but converted her momentum midway and landed in a crouch, ready to retaliate. "Everybody quit throwing me! If you two wanna play catch, what's left of Camden Yards is over there." Standing, she shook water off her clothes: jeans, a hoodie, and a pair of cotton work gloves. The layers looked suffocating in the humid late-summer air. No skin showed except her face. Both eyes matched the stormy sky again.

Must've just been a reflection from the ambulance lights. Or I hit my head harder than I thought. Taking the woman's outstretched hand, Jonathan hissed at the sight of her limp left arm. "Your shoulder…"

"Can wait." She pulled him to his feet. "It's my friend who's hurt bad."

"She'll have company if you bring him in here," Steel rumbled from the aft deck, towering over them. "We agreed never to get uniforms involved. You broke the code making that 911 call, Rock."

Rock? It seemed a more appropriate name for Steel than his petite companion. But she didn't even blink when another punch missed her chin by inches.

"What was I supposed to do? Let her bleed out?"

"Maybe that's what she deserved."

"No one deserves to go without medical attention," said Jonathan, palms open in a placating gesture. Rock made a skeptical noise, but he focused on the colossus between him and the patient. "I don't care what else you've got going on in there. I just want to get your friend to the hospital."

Raindrops slid down Steel's pate to grease the mechanical gears tattooed on his neck. "I'm not letting in any cops."

"You need some new eyes installed. This is a paramedic," Rock replied. Sirens echoed from Fells Point, and she snapped up her hood. "*Those* are cops."

Blue light refracted through the raindrops. A squad car squealed up in a wake of spray.

Oh, hell, that's the last thing we need. Jonathan scrambled for his dropped bag, calculating the supplies he'd need for the average police confrontation. He let out a tense breath when Corporal Latoya Duke stepped from the car. *At least it's one of the good ones.*

"Got a call about a live-action pirate movie playing down here," called Duke, strolling over. Her casual tone belied the shrewd glance she cast Steel. One hand rested on her holstered taser. "You two fighting over sunken treasure?"

"Something like that." Steel hefted a bulging gym bag that lay beside the rail and tried to disembark. Rock jumped into his path. He swung the bag to knock her aside, and she gave it a vicious kick. Strained nylon tore with a crunch, disgorging its contents.

Jonathan yelped as a disembodied hand grazed his ankle. Biomedical products spilled across the dock, prosthetic limbs flopping like bizarre metallic fish.

Smaller items in containers skittered all the way to Duke's shoes. "Give me a medical opinion here, Rowell," she said, addressing Jonathan by his surname as if he were her newest rookie officer. "Is this what I think it is?" She tossed over a plastic bag. It held a metal cylinder the length of a finger. A similar, crimson-glazed piece flashed through Jonathan's memory.

Shuddering, he tossed it away and wiped clammy fingers on his shirt. "If you think it's an implantable hemofilter, yes."

The corporal pinned Steel with a look that made even him flinch. "You want to explain why you've got a whole hospital's worth of bionic implants wrapped up in your stinky socks?"

Steel glanced over the miniature black market scattered at his feet. "I don't know what those are. Never saw 'em before," he said flatly, stepping off the yacht. Boards quaked under his tread. "Must belong to my business partner, on board."

"Why, you lying…" Rock grabbed one of the chains that festooned Steel's thick neck. A flick of his wrist sent her sprawling. Azure shot through the gray dawn, and the corporal's taser electrodes landed on Steel's back. His limbs flailed in a jerky dance.

Jonathan stepped forward, assessing in an instant what injuries the big man might incur when he collapsed. *Concussion, wrist fracture, dislocated knee caps…*

But Steel didn't fall. Swearing, he tore off his shirt. A sweat-stained harness lay beneath. Cables twined around his arms and waist merged between his shoulder blades, where electrodes sparkled on a large battery pack.

"You don't own any illegal bionics, huh?" Duke snorted. "I'll need to see your industrial operator's license for that contraption."

"He left it in his other powered exoskeleton," said Rock, smirking.

Steel's twitches could have been rage, or just aftershocks of an electrical surge in his suit. He cast a murderous glance at Rock, then barreled up the pier. Vehicles blocked his path; he vaulted over the squad car and landed on the ambulance's hood. Metal groaned. Evans, gaping through the windshield, let out a muffled shriek. Steel pulled a face at her, then jumped into the flooded street and took off downtown faster than any man his size should have been able to run.

Duke waded to her car, snatching a radio from her belt. "Unit four seven six, requesting backup, we've got a 10-57 foxtrot…" She whizzed away in pursuit.

Jonathan splashed back to the rig. "Move, Evans, that patient's been waiting too long already."

She winced when she hit the water, but helped him carry the stretcher to the dock. "I admit, that's not what I anticipated from the call."

"You never know what you're getting on a screws cruise."

The rhyme made her giggle. "A what?"

"Medical tourism charters that sail outside territorial limits, where a doctor can cram people full of black-market bionics without breaking the new HPM laws."

"What's HPM?"

"Human performance modification. Biohacking. Tricking out your body with machine parts. Whatever you call it, it's illegal, but that doesn't stop anyone." Jonathan flicked one of the strewn gadgets into the harbor with his heel: one fewer bionic device meant one fewer butchered patient. "Half the calls we get these days are from wannabe cyborgs with a kitchen knife halfway through their cerebral cortex, realizing their so-called upgrade isn't as easy as that internet how-to video made it look."

Evans navigated the minefield of robotic limbs and implants around the yacht. "Where does all this come from?"

"Smuggled through the port. Maritime trade and easy access to the big Eastern cities makes Baltimore the biohacking capital of the Atlantic."

"The city needed a new tourist draw after the crabs died out," Rock said dryly, trying to tug her limp arm back into the socket.

She should be writhing on the ground with a dislocated shoulder like that! But only tight lines in her face betrayed pain. Jonathan kept his tone friendly, demonstrating for Evans how to build rapport with a reluctant patient. "You should come to the ER with us and let someone look at that shoulder, Rock."

"Don't call me that! It's just a stupid nickname." She hesitated, massaging her eye tattoos. "My real name's Petra."

Linguistic ghosts from old medical school texts stirred in Jonathan's head. *'Rock' in Greek.* He bit back a smile and eased the stretcher aboard. "I'm Jonathan, and this is…er…" Embarrassed heat crawled up his neck. Despite being introduced at the start of their shift, Evans' first name had already evaporated from his mind.

"Elizabeth," she reminded him with a reproachful glance, and turned to Petra. "What happened here?"

"I don't know. I just captain this tub—was up in the pilothouse the whole trip. Found her unconscious after we docked." She led the paramedics into the salon. Nothing about the yacht's living quarters looked suspicious. A small galley and dining booth occupied one side of the space; on the other, a sofa faced an entertainment center. The master stateroom, just visible through a cracked door, presented no greater offense than an unmade bed. Innocuous items dislodged in the storm rolled around the deck.

"What were you doing out in such rough weather?" Jonathan tried to sound impressed, fishing for confessions about the cruise.

Petra didn't bite. "I've sailed through worse."

"Someone else hadn't." Evans coughed as they passed the head, rank with bile.

"If that bothers you, don't come back here," said Petra, sliding back another hatch. The smaller second cabin had been converted into an operating theater. Boxes of gloves and steri-strips tumbled from open cabinets. Packets of generic antibiotics spilled from a drawer. Jonathan took a step forward and skidded on loose bone screws. Kicking them aside, he approached the metal table where the bunk should have been. A young woman lay motionless.

Air vanished from Jonathan's lungs. "April?" The face he looked forward to seeing every day in the ER, alight with energy, shone pale beneath the surgical lamp. She still wore yesterday's rumpled scrubs. Jonathan squeezed her fingernail beds, but she didn't respond to the basic consciousness test. *This is not how I pictured holding her hand!*

"You know her?" asked Evans, hooking up the pulse oximeter and blood pressure cuff.

Jonathan had to swallow twice before he could speak. "Dr. April McCormick. She works in our ER." *What is she doing on an illegal surgery boat?* The obvious answer sent cold tendrils of dismay down his spine. He turned to Petra. "You found her like this?"

"Yep. Something must've hit her when the storm knocked us around." She indicated the side of April's skull, wrapped in bloody gauze.

Pulling on a pair of gloves, Jonathan gently combed aside hair stuck to the wound. Iodine darkened the amber waves that haloed April's face when she leaned over a stretcher to reassure one of his patients. "Not even a flying scalpel would've sliced down to the bone like that."

"Well, it was a helluva blow." Petra took a lozenge from her pocket. After a moment struggling to unwrap it one-handed, she tore the plastic with her teeth. Citrus collided with the miasma of dirty water and disinfectants.

Jonathan stared at her. *How can she scarf candy with someone bleeding in front of her? Maybe Evans had a point. She's no hysterical bystander. I guess she* has *seen worse... or this injury doesn't surprise her at all.* He applied a fresh bandage to April's head. "Did you dress this?"

"Yeah."

"Good first aid," he acknowledged grudgingly. "But you should hold pressure on a wound like this to stanch the bleeding."

"I was a little busy." Petra maneuvered her injured arm inside her sweatshirt's opposite sleeve for a makeshift sling.

"Busy throwing all those illegal implants overboard?"

She froze, cradling her arm. Suspicious eyes searched Jonathan's face, and he could have sworn the left one flickered scarlet again.

The diagnostic machine's beep turned his attention. Evans hissed at the readout. "Pressure or no, a gouge like that shouldn't put her into respiratory depression."

"There might be brain trauma. We need to get her imaged and find out what's wrong." Placing the oxygen mask over April's nose, Jonathan ran a finger down her cheek. "You're going to be okay."

In reply, the heart rate monitor began to scream.

"I've got this," Evans announced. Grabbing a scalpel from the nearby tray, she sliced open April's scrub top and placed defibrillator pads on her chest.

Jonathan tore them off. "You never defib someone at a biohacker scene! If they've got implants, the devices could short out, or amplify the current like on that exoskeleton back there. You might kill your patient."

"Then how do you resuscitate them?"

"She keeps adrenaline somewhere, in case her patients code during a procedure." Petra yanked open one of the supply drawers. Pre-filled syringes rattled inside. "Dammit, these are the anesthetics!"

She? Her patients? April is running this operation? "You owe me some answers when you pull through," Jonathan whispered to April, starting chest compressions. He chanted an old song under his breath to maintain optimal cardiac rhythm: "Too many of you dying...everybody thinks we're wrong..."

"...But who are they to judge us?" Petra's voice joined in the next lyrics. The monitor resumed its erratic cadence, and she cast Jonathan a relieved look. "Do you always sing to your patients?"

"Only songs with the right tempo for CPR. That one's less tacky for medical applications than *Stayin' Alive* or *Another One Bites the Dust*."

They exchanged tentative smiles, but a gasp snapped both their heads back to the table. Shallow breaths seethed between April's teeth. Green eyes fought open and roved around the cabin.

"Hey, April, it's me!" Jonathan cradled her head. Heartbeat pings accelerated. "Take it easy, you're safe now."

She reached up to touch his face. Blue-tinged lips moved soundlessly; he leaned in to hear, shivering when they brushed his ear: "Don't trust her."

A shudder racked her body, and she slumped in Jonathan's arms.

2. SCENE OF THE CRIME

The ambulance siren bored into Petra's sensitive ears. Gritting her teeth, she strained to parse Jonathan's words beneath its drone.

"This is way beyond the usual summer-smog respiratory problems." He widened the valve on the oxygen tank, but April's chest barely stirred beneath the emergency blanket. "Did you notice if she had any trouble breathing before this happened?"

Petra shook her head. "Her lungs were in good enough shape last night to yell across the marina."

"At who?"

"Dunno. I heard an argument outside while I was prepping the boat—she was shouting at someone to leave her alone. I came on deck to chase whoever was pestering her, but they were already gone. And she sounded fine on the crew headset when I told her we needed to cut short the cruise."

"Why was that? Something wrong?"

"Yeah, the whole damn climate. Storms never used to change course that fast. It tracked right for us, and I had to race back before we ended up as more ocean trash." Petra flexed her right hand, stiff from clenching the yacht's controls in the face of foam and fury. The left one hung like an anchor, dragging her sideways under its limp weight. "I'm surprised more people didn't get hurt."

"So there were others on the boat?" Jonathan pounced on the implication, and Petra silently cursed her exhausted brain for letting the clue slip. "Who was with April besides you and Steel? Passengers?"

"I told you, I just pilot the yacht. I didn't see anyone."

The paramedic's hard expression reminded Petra of a historic Baltimore row house, a brownstone face bearing weary witness to the city's ruthlessness. "It's pretty obvious why you all were out in the storm last night, but prosecuting bionic butchery isn't my job. Healing it is. And I can't heal April unless I know what happened to her."

"Well, I don't know, either," said Petra. *But I have a good damn guess.* The object shoved into her pocket jabbed her hip. She leaned back on the molded bench, widening the space between her and Jonathan as much as the ambulance's close interior permitted.

"Twelve hours ago she was asking me if she could throw her brother a birthday party at the diner, and now..." He clasped April's hand with desperate tenderness, fingering the recycled-aluminum bangle around her wrist. The gesture triggered Petra's memory: the doctor humming an upbeat tune while the two of them restocked supplies in the yacht's surgery cabin:

"Practicing for your first metal hardware, Mechanic?"

"Oh, we pass these out in the pediatric clinic when kids cooperate with shots. One of my co-workers gave it to me."

" Id'a thought doctors could afford nicer jewelry."

"He's not a doctor, he's a paramedic. And it was just a joke. The department head was giving me a hard time again —my daily dose of bureaucracy—so he gave me a kiddie prize to make me laugh."

"And blush pinker than the Gulf in a red tide."

"We're not like that. We can't be. He'd never talk to me again if he found out about this business."

"Then he's a narrow-minded jerk, and he's not good enough for you."

"Speaking of not good enough, your blood work results came back today. Our treatments haven't improved things much. I really wish you'd consider surgery..."

Petra shook away the rest of the conversation, much as she'd brushed off her friend's suggestion. *Jonathan must be her work friend. No wonder she wrote him off—nosy luddite! But I promise not to tease you about it, Mechanic, if you just wake the hell up.* Salt stung her eyes. She squeezed them shut and focused on the heart monitor, trying to find a song in its rhythm, but no melodies emerged from its irregular chirps. A lurch betrayed the ambulance's halt, and Evans came around from the cab to open the back doors.

"Did she make it?" she asked nervously.

"Yes, but she hasn't regained consciousness again, and her respiration rate is getting worse," said Jonathan, easing the stretcher free. Petra tried to help him, but her dead arm interfered. "Just stand back, we've got it."

No, I'm pretty sure you don't get it at all. But it's better for everyone that way. Especially Mechanic.

Gripping the stretcher rail, Petra let it half-drag her into the emergency department.

Cold indoor air prickled on her skin. Figures swarmed around her; instinct tensed her muscles for a melee. A television tuned to twenty-four hour news shouted across the waiting room, irony echoing on the tile:

"This week, Congress will debate new legislation to crack down on illegal human performance enhancement. Concerns about so-called biohacking made headlines last year when a university student was caught developing a controversial brain implant..."

A sharper voice sliced through the broadcast, and Petra jumped, recalling delivery of orders under fire:

"Tell the lab techs I don't care how understaffed they are. We need faster turnaround on test results. And if we can't improve patient wait times...."

Petra caught her breath in her teeth. *That's the voice I heard arguing with Mechanic on the wharf last night!* She tracked it to a doctor at the triage station. Grey-streaked hair twisted in a chignon at the nape of the woman's neck. She turned when the stretcher approached, revealing a familiar profile against the stark wall.

Ingrained signals flashed across Petra's synapses: *enemy sighted, take cover, do not reveal position!* Feigning a misstep, she ducked behind Jonathan.

The doctor frowned at the paramedics. "Beds are filling up already. How serious is this one?"

"We found her unresponsive on a screws cruise," Evans replied with relish, then whimpered when Jonathan stepped on her foot to silence her.

Scowl lines carved the doctor's brow. "She should go to the back of the line, then."

"It's April, Dr. Bhagat," said Jonathan grimly.

Bhagat's eyes flew wide. She shoved Jonathan aside and pressed her stethoscope to April's chest. "I should have known. Bring her, now. I'll take this case myself." She marched toward the trauma bay, mud-spattered pant cuffs swishing. Jonathan raced the stretcher after her. Petra managed to slip through the doors unnoticed in his wake.

"Probable biohacking case. Once she's stable, I want x-rays to check for embedded devices that might have malfunctioned," Bhagat told a nurse as they transferred April to a bed.

"She's not a biohacker," Petra interjected, clapping a hand over her pocket. *At least, I didn't think she was.*

The doctor didn't even glance her way. "No visitors allowed in here. Rowell, get her out."

Jonathan cast an anguished glance at April, but took Petra's good arm and steered her back toward the waiting room. "If she's not a biohacker, what was she doing on that boat?" he asked beneath Bhagat's barked orders: *"Get a blood specimen to the lab, stat—I want a full drug screen."*

Petra shrugged her functional shoulder. "Lots of doctors have yachts."

"Not with custom-built surgical suites. I've pulled injured people out of enough basement operating theaters to know a biohacking setup when I see it." A shiver passed from Jonathan's bones into hers. "I just don't believe April would do that. She's a good doctor."

"Which is why she'd do anything to make sick people better."

"Oxygen is still dropping. We might have to intubate."

"Cutting patients open and stuffing them full of electronics isn't medicine." Jonathan deposited her outside the trauma bay. "Our healthcare system is strapped enough without people injuring themselves on purpose."

"Yeah, y'all are real busy charging everyone a fortune just to walk in the door." Petra jerked her chin at the packed ER. "We need more Mechanics, trying to keep people out of the hospital."

"And breaking the law?"

"Since when is survival a crime?"

"Pulse is crashing—we're losing her!"

A machine's monotone scream severed their argument. Blanching, Jonathan charged back inside. Petra leapt after him, but the bay doors almost clipped off the end of her nose. She slapped her palm against them.

If my shoulder weren't busted, one good punch would destroy this thing...along with any chance Mechanic has of keeping her name clean.

Her breath on the glass blurred the scene into a macabre kaleidoscope. Screens blinked. Needles flashed. Figures whirled around the bed, then went abruptly still. Dr. Bhagat flicked off the heart rate monitor. Jonathan sank into a crouch, reaching toward Mechanic's limp fingers.

"No!" Petra pounded on the door, and he raised his head. Accusatory eyes bored through the barrier. "Don't glare at me when you're the one sitting on your ass! Help her, do something, do *anything...*" *Just don't leave me stranded again, watching my crewmates die!*

A polar blast from the air vents blew down her back. Suppressed tears burst free in a torrent, and Petra fled the ER. Pneumatic doors spat her onto the street. Humidity's thick blanket felt almost comforting after the hospital's sterile chill. Her sneakers pounded across city blocks, puddles splashing her legs. Each step shot pain through her joints, but it barely registered against the agony of loss.

Should I have told them about the device? No—that would have just made it worse. They'd have pushed her down the priority list, like they did with me before.

Air fetid with exhaust sawed through her lungs. Traffic poles became wet tree trunks: Patterson Park's labyrinthine trails unspooled through the mist, but Petra's knee threatened to collapse. She sank onto the pagoda's bottom tier. Rain on the roof evoked gunfire a decade distant.

I can't believe it's happening again. How did this *follow me here, after all this time?* Petra extracted the bundle from her pocket. Folding back blood-freckled layers of gauze, she exposed the metal shard she'd pried from Mechanic's skull before the ambulance arrived. The chip's filaments—each tipped with a fine needle—trailed across her palm like the tentacles of a tiny jellyfish. A surge of old panic sent her heartbeat skittering. *At least now I have more than fading memories to follow. I can finally hunt this thing down, and stop it from hurting anyone else.*

Galvanized with an objective, Petra stood. Her sluggish right leg refused to come along, and she lurched into the pagoda wall. "Dumb-ass," she chastised herself. *Dashing off like that burned too much energy. Now I can either go back to the hospital and make up a story for the docs about what happened to Mechanic, or clean up all the evidence on the boat. But not both.* She massaged her hip until the limb begrudgingly responded. *Can't do much for a dead woman. She'd want me to cover for her patients. Besides, I'd rather not deal with Bhagat again!*

Limping through the park, Petra entered the first cafe she passed. An advertisement over the counter invited her to *'trade fever for flavor—mosquito season is back, and so is our iced lemongrass latte, with all-natural botanical repellants!'* She ordered the biggest lemonade on the menu, then slipped into the bathroom and locked the door. Peeling off her damp long sleeves, she examined the injured shoulder.

"Guess I've gotta be my own Mechanic now," she told the mess in the mirror. Wedging her left hand behind the toilet tank for resistance, she jerked back as hard as she could. Pain blazed through her nerves. Another merciless yank popped the ball back into the socket. Nausea crashed over her, and she crumbled against the porcelain.

A knock rattled the door. "Just a minute," Petra called, adding in an annoyed whisper, "you can change your underwear more easily than I can change my limbs." Forcing down a few deep breaths, she flexed her fingers until sensation flowed again. Tendons squirmed beneath the diamond-shaped tattoo inside her right wrist. The color seemed darker than usual.

"It's just the heat. You're fine," she told herself. Splashing water over her flushed face, she pulled her shirt back on and stalked out to claim her drink.

Sugar and citrus infused new energy into her body. By the time she'd walked back to the marina, her hand had stopped rattling the ice with tremors. *That's better. I'll be fine once I take my meds…if I can get to them.*

Yellow tape cordoned off the end of the dock. Police milled around the *Wind of Change,* collecting Steel's lost merchandise. Petra pulled up her hood and crept onto the adjacent vessel. Concealed behind the pilothouse, she focused her ears. Stiff breeze carried the officers' conversation:

"Corporal Duke, I got a call back about the boat. It's registered to an April McCormick. Previous owner had the same surname—probably a family cruiser."

"My family cruiser is a twelve-year-old hatchback," replied the woman who'd tased Steel earlier. "Though a yacht is better for getting around Baltimore these days. What about my warrant?"

The cop squirmed. "Since the boat doesn't belong to your suspect, HQ says there's not enough evidence of illegal activity to justify a search."

"What about all this?" asked Duke, slinging the last of the gym bag's contents into an evidence crate. Petra did a quick visual tally of the merchandise and chewed her paper straw into pulp. *That's a few grand worth of hardware, easy. Steel's gonna have a fit.*

"I sent them pictures, Corporal, but they said we technically found it off the vessel, with no proof any of it is linked to the owner."

"Why do they bother making these high-profile new laws if they don't let us enforce them?" Duke huffed. "We'll just have to cross our fingers for EMS."

"To do what?"

"Mandatory reporting. They're required to notify us if they spot a biohacking operation during a call, but they're so busy it takes them weeks to file. Luckily I know the guy who was on-scene today. I'll call him and ask for a favor." Hefting the box, Duke headed back toward her car, but halted when a tinny guitar ringtone shredded the stillness.

"Al'ama!" Petra cursed, pawing her phone from her pocket. The caller's number almost made her toss the device in the harbor. Pressing it to her ear instead, she hissed, "Your robotically supported ass had better be halfway back to Pittsburgh, because if I ever see it again—."

"I overreacted, okay?" said Steel, exasperated. "I was just messed up after seeing Mechanic like that."

"You think I wasn't?" Petra peered around the bulkhead. The corporal scanned the slips with narrowed eyes for the source of the noise.

"Didn't act like it."

"Why, because I tried to save her life instead of having a meltdown?"

"Not all of us left our feelings in a combat zone."

"And not all of us put on an HPM demo for the BPD."

"Funny you mention that." A long sigh shuddered down the line. "My battery died a few miles from the marina. The fuzz caught up and seized my suit. I'm at the goddamn police station."

Petra laughed, scaring seagulls off the pylons. "I'm your one phone call?"

"Not my top draft pick, believe me. I need Mechanic to write a doctor's note and get back my suit on medical grounds, but she wasn't answering her phone. Is she up and talking yet?"

Heat swelled in Petra's throat, a searing contrast to the icy words on her tongue. "No. She's dead."

Bellows shook the receiver. Petra held the phone away until the staticky roars disintegrated into snivels. "...Stuck me with debts and now cops, too..."

"Do you care about anything besides yourself?" Petra snapped.

"Sure, I care about the business. What am I gonna do without Mechanic bringing in customers? You don't know how bad things have gotten."

"I know they're a lot worse now," said Petra, risking another glance. Duke did a last sweep of the dock, then headed off with her subordinate in tow. "I just watched Charm City's finest haul away your stock."

Thunderous profanity rattled her skull, punctuated with a distant thud where Steel's fist hammered the nearest flat surface. "That was fresh merchandise! No way I'm gonna make bail now. You've gotta spot me, Rock."

"After you tore up my shoulder?" Petra flexed the joint and winced. "I need the money myself to get it fixed."

"Money can't buy what you can't find for sale."

"You're not the only supplier."

"You wanna go explain your situation to somebody new? I'm all you got, if Mechanic is gone." Stunned silence hung for a moment before Steel spoke again. "What even happened to her?"

"I was hoping you'd know." The police car vanished into the flooded streets, and Petra hopped across to *Wind of Change*. "What went on belowdecks last night?"

"Nothing weird. We only had three passengers. The first two were basic installation and maintenance—didn't even need to put 'em under—and the last one never got to surgery, since we turned around early."

"What about on the return trip?" Sliding back the salon's door, Petra almost gagged on the reek of bile.

Steel stifled a vestigial retch. "All I saw was the inside of the toilet."

"Which I now have to clean, along with everything else. An operating room on a yacht is bad enough without the cops finding it ankle-deep in blood."

"You throw out any more merch, Rock, and I swear…"

"Are you sure you want to discuss future assaults before your bail is set?" Petra smirked at the stammering reply. "Send me the price tag after the arraignment and I'll see what I can do. Until then, don't start more trouble."

"That's your department."

"Yeah, I know," Petra muttered, touching the parcel in her pocket as she hung up. The salon became a different ship's interior, one cold enough to capture her breath in clouds. Stark corridors. Swift, shadowed movements. A scream. Petra started, and the memory shattered like it always did, leaving her alone on the empty yacht.

"If I have to be stuck in a loop, why can't it be a fun one?" she grumbled, turning to the entertainment center. The frayed sleeves of vintage records whispered under her fingertip. She slid a disc onto the turntable. Metal music from the previous century shook the bulkheads. Once the upbeat cadence had steadied her heart rhythm, Petra held her breath and grabbed her medicine from the bathroom cabinet. A solo note rattled inside the jar.

Shit. Where am I going to get these with Mechanic gone? She promised to bring me a refill this week...maybe she left it in the cabin somewhere.

Swallowing the pill and her panic with the last gulp of lemonade, she entered the operating room. The morning's discovery replayed in a gruesome flash.

Mechanic, pale and unresponsive. Silvery gleams amid the blood. Recognition. Revulsion. Resolve. Snatching up a scalpel, then a bandage. Hesitant fingers at the phone—*it's her license or her life!* Three numbers. Evidence overboard. Steel chasing her into the rain to relive a frantic fight on deck with another overmatched opponent, and another dizzy tumble overboard...

Plastic crunched underfoot, disrupting the replay: the empty barrel of a pre-filled syringe.

Mechanic never leaves sharps lying around! As Petra threw it into the dispenser, the label flashed toward her. *Propofol—that's a heavy anesthetic. Steel said none of the clients last night needed that. So who got this one?*

She turned to the metal cot where the doctor had lain a few hours before. "If you're gonna extend my list of people to avenge, you'd better extend my life, too," she told Mechanic's ghost. Fetching the doctor's personal bag from a cubby, she searched for her promised medicine. Breathing masks. A spiral notebook filled with illegible scrawl. An employee badge for Ripken Memorial Hospital. Petra ran a thumb over the laminated photo. "If I'm going to find out what really happened to you, I need someone who knew Dr. McCormick, not just Mechanic."

She unzipped the bag's last compartment and extracted a folded prescription slip. Hope sank once she deciphered the words. Instead of her medication, Mechanic had written a cryptic note: *Dapọ Diner, Pigtown. J knows owner—can arrange K's birthday party. Karaoke!*

Petra chewed her lip. *This must be the place that paramedic recommended. He said 'the diner', like there was only one. Maybe there is, in his world.* Pulling out her phone, she found the restaurant's website and grinned. "Alright, Jonathan. I hope you like rock music."

3. A MAN I'LL NEVER BE

Jonathan's feet knew the walk home without assistance from his eyes, freeing twelve hours' worth of withheld tears. A hectic shift had allowed him to dodge Dr. Bhagat's questions, Evans' worried glances, and the horror of the day's first case. Now his mental bulwark cracked. Double shocks hit him with almost equal force: April dead, and April moonlighting as a biohacker surgeon.

She saw how much stress those freaks are putting on healthcare workers! How could she commiserate with me in the ER, then turn around and do it herself? No way her head wound was accidental. But I just can't see her resorting to that. Not after all the awful DIY surgery cases we worked on together. God, we'll never do that again, will we? She made it bearable, and now…

Dusk and grief darkened the world around him. A lone beacon emerged at the end of the street: the sign for the Dapọ Diner. Pausing in front of a shop window, Jonathan composed his expression. A sleeve dried his cheeks, but couldn't erase the haggard lines.

"You can't worry about dead people when there are still live ones who need you," he said sternly. The reflected man gave a curt nod. With a bracing breath, he went into the diner. Chimes on the door sang out his entry. An atmosphere of stout beer and nutmeg embraced him.

"Jonathan!" Grace Njoku's Rubenesque form sailed through tables of slurping customers to greet him. Her radiant smile faded as she pressed a palm to his forehead. Although she was barely old enough to be his mother, that had never dissuaded her from adopting the role. "You look more miserable than the weather. Are you sick?"

"Sick of sick people," Jonathan told her with a thin laugh. "I had a terrible shift, that's all."

"You need to eat." Steering him onto a barstool, she bustled into the kitchen. "Ayodele! Bring Jonathan a bowl of peppersoup!"

"I'm not hungry," he insisted, but Del had already emerged. Lithe as their mother was curvaceous, they maneuvered the tray with a girl's quick step, a boy's broad hands, and enough self-assurance for both together.

"She still thinks this can cure anything." Del tossed back their long braids with adolescent disdain. "Like I'm not enough evidence to prove her wrong."

"I thought your new inhaler was helping," said Jonathan.

"Yeah, but the stupid insurance only covers one per month. If I go outside every day, I'll burn through that in like a week." Laying a tablet on the counter, Del flicked aside a list of dinner orders and stared wistfully at a live video stream. Teenagers on skateboards and rollerblades gamboled beneath an overpass, smashing through puddles of water that poured off the bridge above. "Everyone else went skating after school, but Mama said the air was too bad and wouldn't let me go."

"So you hacked into city surveillance cameras again?"

"If they don't want people watching, they should patch their system more than once a decade. I'm not stealing anything or hurting anyone! I just want to see more than what's outside the window——." Del broke off in a wheeze and leaned on the counter.

Jonathan dropped his spoon with a clank. "Are you okay?"

"Yeah...just need...a drink." Reaching for one of the pitchers nearby, a spasm wracked Del's body. Their elbow overturned the vessel. Ice cubes clattered across the floor.

Jonathan vaulted over the counter and grasped Del's thin shoulder. "Where's your inhaler?"

"Have to save it..." One hand clutched at an apron pocket. Peeling away desperate fingers, Jonathan extracted the medicine. Del gave a resentful yowl. "No! Don't waste... need it for...going..."

"If you don't use it, the only place you're going is back to the hospital." Jonathan shoved the plastic mouthpiece between Del's strained lips, the way he had when they were a small child, and depressed the canister.

Erratic breath drew the spray into Del's lungs. Slowly, their ribs stopped heaving. At last they croaked, "I hate you."

"That's fine, as long as you have enough breath to tell me so," said Jonathan. Del punched his shoulder, then snuggled under it like a fond younger sibling. He hugged back. "Why's the asthma so bad if you've been staying in, huh?"

"Lots of chilis in the peppersoup today."

"And you probably still put hot sauce on yours. That's not it." Jonathan held Del at arm's length. "You snuck outside last night, didn't you?"

A smirk spoiled their innocent expression. "Is it sneaking if no one's around to stop me?"

"Your mom got a second job to pay for your treatment, not to give you opportunities for making yourself sicker. Do I have to park myself outside your bedroom as a guard, like when you were little?"

"No need. My inhaler is my jailer," Del replied in a bitter singsong. Cramming the medicine back into their apron, they retrieved the tablet and expanded another internet window they'd been browsing between customers. "But not for long. I've been researching new treatments. You know about the vagus nerve, right? It's the longest one in your body."

"Technically it's two nerves, a left and a right." A smile tugged Jonathan's mouth for the first time all day. "Have you been poking through my old med school textbooks?"

"No—biohacking forums."

"What?" Jonathan snatched the tablet. Selfies of people with crude stitches studded the comment threads. Product pages displayed gadgets alongside all-caps caveats disclaiming any liability. "Why are you looking at this junk?"

"It's not junk, it's a vagus nerve stimulator. Fibers from that nerve run into your lungs and affect airway function."

"That hasn't been medically proven."

"Only because no one wants to test it. If it worked, it'd be like having a permanent inhaler!" Hope lit Del's brown eyes. "There's a tattoo parlor right here in Baltimore that does something called a skinterface—touch-sensitive metallic ink that overlays wires from a bionic device. All I'd have to do is tap a control panel drawn on my arm, and I could breathe!" Taking the tablet from Jonathan, they pulled up the parlor's website. Jagged letters advertised *Heavy Metal Tattoo & Piercing - custom ink and implants by SoulSteeler.* A dour headshot of the proprietor glared at Jonathan.

That's the guy with the exoskeleton from this morning! He must be selling all that black-market bionic gear out of his parlor...and filling my ambulance with patients when they malfunction. I hope Corporal Duke picked him up and put him away. Corralling the scattered ice cubes, Jonathan clenched his hands around the frigid fire. "Promise me you're not going to get mixed up with biohacking, Del."

"Ugh, you sound just like Mama." Del grabbed a dish towel and mopped up the spilled water. "I told her I don't take medical advice from someone who still uses a mortar and pestle."

"Then take it from someone who ferries amateur surgeons to the ER every day."

"I'm not going to give myself a lung transplant with a butter knife! It's just a little chip."

"That's what the kid in that university scandal said last year." Sensational news tickers from the ER television scrolled across Jonathan's mind: *Graduate student develops implant to hack human brains! ... State withdraws university's funding over secret HPM research! ... Student expelled, biomedical engineering program suspended after brain-chip controversy!* He blinked the headlines away. "Remember how the media tore into him? 'It's just a little chip', he said. As if it didn't have huge consequences!"

"It did for him, getting expelled from such a prestigious school." Del scrubbed the wood until it squealed. "Now the poor guy probably can't get any engineering job, other than repairing fast-food robots. Although even that's better than taking online classes all day and waiting tables all night because you can't get enough medicine to step out the freaking front door."

"I'll get you some extra inhalers from work," Jonathan promised, then yelped as the cold, wet cloth draped around his neck.

Tugging the ends of the dishrag, Del pulled his face level with theirs. "I don't want you to keep stealing for me, Jojo."

"It's not stealing. You know how much asthma medication the hospital goes through these days? They give out inhalers to kids like lollipops. Getting spares is easy." *At least, it was when April was on duty. I can't picture Dr. Bhagat writing prescriptions for imaginary patients so that real ones can get medicine. I'll have to figure out something else.* Jonathan disentangled himself. "The important thing is that you get what you need."

"What I need is new lungs. Hey, I wonder if SoulSteeler has those..." Del laughed at Jonathan's horrified face and squired him into the kitchen. "I'm just kidding! Hank, was he always this uptight?"

"Not that I recall." Jonathan's father, perched on a stool beside the sink, looked up from peeling yams. "How was school today, son?"

"I think I flunked a test," said Jonathan, too fatigued to challenge the chronic misalignment in the old man's memory. He laid a hand on the bony arm, an affectionate gesture that concealed a diagnostic squeeze. Beneath the usual shakiness, Hank's pulse felt strong.

"What subject?"

"Chemistry."

"That's a tough one. Do you get another chance?"

Not when she's lying in the morgue. "I don't think so."

"Well, you know the joke—the guy who graduates at the bottom of his med school class still gets called 'doctor'."

"These are the only knives I'll ever be licensed to use," said Jonathan, grabbing a dirty cleaver. *Although that would still make me more qualified than the average bionic butcher. Did someone use a thing like this on April?* Animal blood glistened on the blade. He threw it into the sink and started scrubbing every item in reach, but couldn't scour away the image in his head.

Once dinner service ended, Grace grabbed her purse and turned to Del. "I'll be home after midnight. Don't wait up—you need your sleep."

"So do you," Del retorted. "How are you going to survive night shifts after running a restaurant all day?"

"People get used to it, don't they, Jonathan?" Tension stiffened the corners of Grace's smile, and she didn't wait for a reply. "Can you please take Ayodele upstairs?"

The teenager groaned. "Mama, I'm not a baby, I don't need my fake big brother to tuck me in."

"Then I'll just check your window latches," Jonathan muttered, earning a slap on the arm. He walked Grace to the bus stop, then escorted his two charges out the kitchen's back door. Del scampered up the metal stairs to the Njokus' apartment over the diner while the men descended to their basement rental unit.

Hank placed both unsteady feet on each step going down. "I don't need help," he grumbled when Jonathan hovered a hand beneath his elbow.

"That's what Mom used to say, and look what happened."

"She also said not to skip meals." A gnarled finger poked Jonathan's ribs as he unlocked the door. The mat squished underfoot, soaked with floodwater that had trickled down from the street. "No wonder you're doing poorly on tests—you never take the time to feed that brain! How about I dig up some leftovers for dinner?"

Jonathan glanced from the twitchy old man to the appliances. *Can I trust him in the kitchen?* Weariness overcame wariness, and he let Hank poke through the fridge while he mopped up the vestibule. Peeling soggy envelopes off the floor, he distributed them between two piles of unopened mail on the table: medical bills and insurance claim denials. Large numbers glared through the damp paper.

"Maybe I need a second job, too," Jonathan muttered, then flung the notices aside at an outburst of violent coughs. "Dad? Are you all right?"

"Damn milk's spoiled." Hank rinsed his mouth in the sink.

Jonathan seized the jug and swore. "That's vinegar!"

"What the hell is it doing in the fridge?"

"That's not the fridge, it's the pantry."

"Well, they're too close together. Anyone would grab the wrong handle now and again. Doesn't mean I'm losing my marbles." Hank buried his face in a dish towel and dried it much longer than necessary.

At least it wasn't bleach, like last time. Jonathan checked that the cleaning supplies were still on the top shelf, out of his father's reach. "How about you go put on a movie, and I finish making dinner?"

"Forget dinner," Hank snapped, then attempted a chuckle. "Grace has me tasting so many dishes that I get ten meals a day. I'm tired, anyway." He shuffled toward the bathroom.

Jonathan scrutinized his father's bedtime routine even more closely than usual, but tried to sound cheerful when he powered up the small speaker on the nightstand. "Who do you want to hear tonight?"

"Surprise me. I'll be asleep before the chorus anyway."

Jonathan picked a favorited playlist at random—there were no bad choices in a lineup of classic rock and roll icons —and adjusted the volume. "Come wake me if you need anything."

"Can't a man even sleep without being fussed over?" Hank pulled the covers up to his beard and turned away.

Sighing, Jonathan left the room. Music murmured through the door, a woman's voice reminiscent of April's. Their last conversation drifted through his mind:

"...My brother's birthday is coming up. He's hardly left his laboratory since moving in with me, so I want to take him out to celebrate. Something low-key and fun. Your neighbor's restaurant has karaoke, right? How many drinks would I have to buy you before you'd sing for me?"

The request moved Jonathan toward the dusty guitar in the corner. Tuneless, neglected strings bit his tender fingertips. He set it back in its stand with a desultory clang.

Maybe I'd be able to practice music, or study for a less exhausting job, or go on a date somewhere other than the hospital cafeteria if I didn't have to spend every night playing nurse for a senile old man! Revolted at himself, Jonathan clawed the harsh thought from his mind, but couldn't dislodge its bitter seed. Walls seemed to contract around him. Tightness gripped his chest until he ran through the list of heart attack symptoms in his head. Desperate for distraction, he texted one of the few numbers in his phone's contact list: *Are you working the graveyard shift tonight?*

The reply pinged back a few minutes later: *If you think that's funny, you need to get some sleep.*

Not after the day I had. Can I come over?

Siempre! I've got company, but she won't mind.

Checking that Hank was asleep, Jonathan slipped back out into the dark. A mile's walk brought him to the familiar glass-striped building. Operatic music beckoned him down empty halls to the autopsy lab, its door illuminated by a small digital sign: *Pathologist on Duty—Dr. Ciro Iglesias, Deputy Medical Examiner.*

A stocky figure in scrubs stood at the sink, humming along with the aria. He looked up when Jonathan entered. "If I didn't know better, I'd think you were my next case," said Ciro, appraising him with concern. "You look half-dead."

"That's fifty percent better than I feel." Jonathan caught his reflection in the long row of body freezers. Metal distorted his features into a human Rorschach blot; anything and nothing, negative space.

"You're still doing better than her." Ciro nodded at the autopsy table. Pale toes peeked from beneath a cloth. At the other end, like a doomed crocus poking from January snow, gleamed a wisp of strawberry-blonde hair.

Jonathan's throat clenched until he could barely form words. "Is that...April McCormick?"

"*Sí.* Her brother came in a little while ago to identify her. Then some pushy ER supervisor at Ripken called in a favor to bump the line for post-mortem, and—." Ciro gasped, fingers dripping into the sudden silence. "*Ay, dio*, that's your bad day, isn't it?"

"She was the first call I got this morning. I restarted her heart," Jonathan whispered. "It wasn't enough."

"I doubt anything would have been, with that much propofol on board." Drying his hands, Ciro swiveled his computer monitor to show Jonathan a screen full of test results. "Toxicology turned up high concentrations in her blood."

"Why the hell would she be sedated?"

"In the right amounts, propofol can make you feel rested. I knew an anesthetist who dosed himself when he only got a short break between rotations," said Ciro. "April might've tried the same thing. You're always telling me how everyone in the ER is overworked."

Especially if they stay up all night running a surgical side hustle. Jonathan lifted the shroud's corner. "Can I...?"

"Have a good, snotty cry?" Ciro offered him an economy box of Kimwipes. "Absolutely."

"I already did that. I just don't want my last glimpse of her to be in the trauma bay."

"And this is better?" Overhead lights bleached April's face, her once-lively features stilled in a waxen portrait. "Try to remember the last time you were with her alive, instead."

"That wasn't great, either."

"Why? Was there a fight?"

"Not with me." Under his friend's patient gaze, Jonathan let the last brick in his cognitive wall crumble. "The last patient I brought in that day looked like another malaria case, but when we took the guy's shirt off, we found a horribly infected bionic implant. April wanted to admit him, but Dr. Bhagat said we didn't have bed space for biohackers who'd caused their own problems. She told April to give him antibiotics and send him home. And April just...snapped."

"It's a tense environment. Why do you think I prefer the morgue?" said Ciro, patting April's head. "ER doctors must disagree about treatment all the time."

"Yeah, but April never loses her cool. Her arguments are rational—she rarely even raises her voice. It's one of the things that makes her so good in trauma care. But yesterday, she lost it. She started yelling at Dr. Bhagat, accusing her of discrimination in patient care. Even threw the damn stethoscope at her!"

"What happened?"

"I took April out of the room before Bhagat called security, and just held her until she stopped flailing. I didn't know what else to do. I'd never seen her act like that." Jonathan rubbed the bruises inside his arms from trying to restrain her. How could that enraged form lay so still now?

"Did she say what upset her so badly?" asked Ciro.

"I tried to ask once she'd simmered down. She insisted she was fine and ran off. I figured she might be ready to talk about it today. But the next time I saw her was on that damn screws cruise!" A lump swelled in Jonathan's throat. "If I'd have gone after her and found out what was wrong, maybe she'd still be here."

"You can't think like that, *amigo*. You'll make yourself crazy," Ciro murmured, clasping his shoulder.

"Spare me the pep talk. I've lost patients before."

"But not someone you liked."

"Who says I liked her?"

"Your face. I haven't spent so much time examining dead people that I've forgotten how to read live ones. At least, not specimens I've been studying for a decade."

"Okay, I...I *admired* her. New doctors usually end up at Ripken for lack of better options, but she chose it for a residency in social medicine." Jonathan touched his sleeve, feeling April's fingers on his arm as they sat helpless beside a patient who'd died en route to the hospital, young face still damp from a new mosquito-borne fever. *"Climate change and poverty are the real diseases, Jonathan—we have to do more than just treat the symptoms!"* He swallowed hard and continued. "She'd do just about anything to help the community stay well. Even got the hospital to participate in some clinical trials for kids with respiratory problems, before the new department head shut it down. She did what I wanted to do, but failed at."

Forceps poked him in the side. "You did not fail!"

"I dropped out of med school, Ciro."

"You changed priorities. No one says you can't change again someday and finish the degree."

"Are you kidding?" Jonathan rubbed at his bleary eyes. "I could barely hack it back then."

"Only because you were working full-time to pay for it," said Ciro, tying a scrub cap over his glossy ponytail.

"I couldn't remember all the terminology, no matter how often you assaulted me with flashcards."

"Memorizing a bunch of Latin words doesn't make you a good caregiver. Not when AI does most of that work." Ciro waved at the complex computer station beside the autopsy table. "You've got something that robots—including the Ivy League prigs in our cohort—will never have."

"Yeah, an unfinished medical degree."

"Compassion. You get people. You see the hurts that don't show up on a scan or a blood test."

"That's not a skill," muttered Jonathan.

"No—it's a gift. If I had it, I'd be working in some cushy private practice, instead of being a city pathologist on the nightshift." Shrugging into his protective apron, Ciro spun so that Jonathan could tie the strings in the back. "But I don't have the patience for people's whining. I just want to understand why our magical meat machines malfunction. *Qué lástima*—I was looking forward to your late lady friend's thoughts on that."

Jonathan drew the sheet back over April's face. "What do you mean?"

"She was going to talk about biohacking at a law debate sponsored by Tae's alma mater. It's the first time I've wanted to attend one of his panels for the topic, not just the buffet. Now they'll have to find someone else for a medical perspective." Latex-gloved index fingers aimed at Jonathan. "Hey, they should ask you!"

"It'd be a short discussion. I can sum up biohackers in two words: *selfish* and *suicidal*."

"At least it would be a short lecture," said Ciro, chuckling. "You should come hang out with me, so I don't have to ravage the hors d'oeuvres alone while Tae schmoozes. We can count it as continuing education hours. It'll be just like med school again!"

Jonathan shook his head. "If I had time to go out, I might've asked April to something other than a coffee break."

"Then do it in her honor. Don't lock yourself away while you've still got a heartbeat. We're all going to end up alone in a box soon enough." Ciro nodded at the freezers, then donned a face shield to begin the autopsy.

Nausea twisted Jonathan's insides. He bid his friend a hasty goodbye and hurried out of the lab. Cold smells of death and steel clung to his clothes; once he got home, he tore them off and stepped into the shower, not waiting for the water to warm. Numbness seeped through skin, muscle, and bone. He willed it to penetrate his heart. Tears swirled down the drain. The metal grate shone up at him like Petra's tattoos, flashing accusations through the trauma bay door.

For all the candy and cagey answers, she seemed genuinely upset when April coded. So why did she run?

***

The next day brought another parade of chest pains, breathing troubles, and minor injuries. Routine reassured Jonathan's work at each scene, but patients that required ER transport plunged him into a dizzy nightmare. April haunted every set of scrubs, every hurried footstep, every stricken face in the trauma bay. When a woman called Jonathan's name, he jumped and almost toppled an empty stretcher Evans was guiding back to the ambulance.

Dr. Bhagat, who had hailed him, frowned. "Is something wrong? You don't look well enough to be on duty."

"I'm fine," he lied, waving Evans ahead.

"In spite of what happened yesterday?" Glancing around for eavesdroppers, she went on: "The hospital is conducting an internal investigation into Dr. McCormick's death. They'll want to ask you some questions about how you found her."

Jonathan stared at a crack in the floor tile. "There's not much to tell."

"It will still need to go on record, especially given the preliminary autopsy results. Weeks away from our departmental inspection, and I have to disclose that one of my doctors was abusing surgical drugs!" Bhagat pinched the bridge of her nose. "It looks terrible. I should have suspected it, given McCormick's habits."

"What habits?"

She shook her head, tossing light off her gold earrings. "I shouldn't say anything that might color your report. I'll arrange an interview in the next day or two, before you forget the details."

As if I'll ever forget! Limp weight in his arms, hair matted with blood, eyes forever dulled of their passionate spark.

Bhagat's orthotic shoes clunked away down the corridor like fading heartbeats.

"What was that about?" Evans asked when he returned to the rig.

"Yesterday."

She shot him an anxious look. "I thought it was an accident. What's there to say?"

"That it wasn't the hospital's fault, Dr. Bhagat is a competent manager, and the compliance office checked all the right boxes," Jonathan muttered, jabbing the dispatch map.

"It's still terrible to make you talk about it. I mean, you obviously liked Dr. McCormick."

"She was one of the most dedicated doctors here. Everyone liked her."

"That's not what I meant."

Jonathan started up the engine. "There's nothing romantic about healthcare."

"That's not true. I met my husband when he took a lacrosse stick to the face in a college practice. Blood everywhere. It freaked out his teammates, but I'd seen way worse in my nursing program, so I bandaged him up with my scarf and took him to the clinic. Ten stitches later, he asked me out to dinner. I fed him french fries through the gauze." Evans waggled her finger, showcasing two diamond-encrusted rings. "Once you've seen someone raw like that, you can't help feeling close to them."

"Yep, that's why I joined emergency services—every night is like speed dating." The siren howled with laughter as they sped off to the next call.

By the shift's end, exhaustion and sorrow left Jonathan hollow. Harbor breeze swept him down the sidewalk with the discarded paper face masks. He pushed open the diner door, desperate for its cheerful warmth.

Sound waves slammed into his skull. Lights spun over a tiny dais in the corner, where a woman swayed with a microphone.

Ugh! I forgot it was karaoke night. Grace's recent attempt to increase weeknight business brought in customers, sold beers, and gave Jonathan migraines. Ignoring the stage, he found his father.

"Let's go, Dad." He had to shout twice before Hank glanced up from sorting utensils, placing each piece in time with the beat.

"You don't want to hang out and listen awhile?" he asked, eyes a little brighter than usual.

"If you want music, we'll put on one of your playlists. These drunk belters are always terrible."

"Always?" Hank peered over the bar at Jonathan's feet. One worn boot tapped on the floor. The rock song, carried by a strong mezzo-soprano, moved his body independently of his mind. A pitch-perfect high note drew every empty glass behind the bar into a reverberating chorus.

"Okay, she's pretty good," Jonathan admitted beneath raucous applause from the tables. He glanced over his shoulder at the singer and froze. Grey eyes locked onto his. Disco lights glazed the left one red.

What the hell is she *doing here?*

Replacing the mic in its stand, Petra sauntered through the tables toward him.

4. ONE WAY OR ANOTHER

The diner door opened when Petra hit the second chorus. *'Tall, dark, handsome stranger.' Right on cue.*

Jonathan didn't even glance toward the stage. Hands in pockets, he went straight to the counter and addressed the old man who'd been shuffling along with the music since a frail teenager had fired up the karaoke machine. Petra sang the rest of the number with her eyes on the paramedic's back. When the final riff crashed down, he turned. His mouth fell open at the sight of her.

Tactical surprise. I've got the advantage, at least for a few minutes. Setting the mic reluctantly down, Petra wended between the crowded tables and leaned on the bar beside Jonathan.

A sideways glance betrayed his discomfort. "If you want me to look at your shoulder, too late. I'm off duty."

"I already got the treatment I needed—booze and blues." Petra pulled Mechanic's note from her pocket and smoothed it across the polished wood. "My doctor prescribed this place. She heard about it from some guy she liked at work. Figured I'd look him up and share memories of her over a drink. It's on me. Just don't assume that because I'm short, I can't drink my half of a pitcher." Grabbing a menu, she scanned the beverages.

"I have to go." Jonathan patted the old man's arm. "Come on, Dad."

"Where? To microwave dinner and watch TV?" A gnarled hand waved away the idea. "That'll still be there in half an hour. When was the last time you chatted with a good-looking girl?"

Pain twisted across Jonathan's face, fleeting but unmistakable. "Dad, I just finished a long shift. I'm tired, I—."

"Del! Get Jonathan a drink! With caffeine!"

"And one of those hibiscus juice things for me," Petra called, and the older Rowell beamed her a vacant smile. *He's not all there, is he? Guess that's why his son picks him up after work like a kid from daycare.* She tugged Jonathan's sleeve a little more gently than she otherwise would have. "Let's get a table."

Shoulders hunched in defeat, he followed her to a corner spot beside the stage. Bass buzzed in the condiment jars. "I won't be able to hear a word," he shouted beneath the next singer's off-key screech.

"Neither will anyone else." Petra slid into the chair nearest the speakers. Sonic waves purred through her spine.

"I thought we were reminiscing about a mutual friend, not plotting a heist," Jonathan grumbled, dropping down across from her. "How do you know April at all?"

"She hired me to pilot her boat. Apparently she scored it from a relative, but didn't know how to sail. With the ocean getting so unpredictable, she wanted someone experienced at the helm."

"And you just advertise in the yellow pages? Screws cruise captain, part-time nights and weekends, scarification guaranteed?"

"We met at the hospital." Petra fiddled with a seam in her glove, teasing out threads of the story along with those in the fabric. "I had a medical problem a few years back. Tried to fix myself with a biohack, but I botched it and landed in the ER. When the triage team figured out what I'd done, they bumped me down the priority list."

"Good."

"It was, because they stuck me with a resident who wanted to help me, not just punish me," Petra retorted. "She said that if I needed treatment in the future, I should go straight to her. After a while, I referred a few friends, and she started running a private clinic out of her house. Just stitches and antibiotics, but it made a big difference. She became our community Mechanic."

Jonathan mouthed the nickname, exploring the slant-rhymed syllables. "Is that her connection to SoulSteeler? Judging by his product display yesterday, I'd guess his piercing parlor does a lot more than nose rings and tongue studs."

"Yeah, but he doesn't have the facility or the training for advanced upgrades," said Petra, jabbing a demonstrative fork into her elbow. "Partnering with Mechanic on bigger operations—literally—made him one of the top biohacking suppliers on the East Coast."

"She really *was* in business with that guy?"

"More of a part-time volunteer. She refused to charge for her share of the work, no matter how much Steel bitched about profit margins."

"Is that his idea of a complaint?" Jonathan nodded at Petra's shoulder.

"If Steel wanted to hurt Mechanic, he'd have busted a few bones, not cut a neat little hole in her head. But I think I know who would." Petra leaned forward, preparing to share her hypothesis, but straightened as the server approached.

"Cherry soda for JoJo, *zoba* for his date." The kid placed two drinks on the table and turned a smug smile on Jonathan. "Are you gonna introduce me?"

"Not now, Del," he replied in a gentle growl.

"My Southern daddy would roll in his grave if I let manners lapse like that." said Petra, extending a hand. "Petra."

"You were awesome up there!" Del's manicured fingers squeezed hers with unexpected strength. "Where'd you learn to sing like that?"

"I have terrific teachers. Pat, Joan, David, Axl…"

"Dead rock stars who were big when my dad was born," Jonathan explained to Del's blank face. He shot Petra a wry glance. "One of them even wore a glove like that."

"Wrong hand." Petra tugged down her sleeve, even though the cuff already stretched to her knuckles.

"He's just jealous because he never wears anything cool." Del jammed a napkin in Jonathan's collar like a child's bib. "I hope you sing again before you go, Petra."

"You do carry a mean tune," Jonathan admitted, removing the napkin the moment Del departed. "Is that why people call you Rock?"

"No." Ice cubes bobbed in the hibiscus juice, evoking bergs in a bloody pink sea. A sip left Petra's mouth even dryer than usual. "It's my old military nickname."

"Ah, I figured you were a soldier. Which service?"

"U.S. Coast Guard Seventeenth District, freezing for freedom in the Arctic." Pulling down one side of her collar, she flashed the emblem tattooed on her right deltoid. "What gave it away?"

"Not many people are that calm when someone is dying in front of them. First responders. Medical professionals. Veterans." Curious eyes surveyed her over the tumbler rim.

"Is that how you know Dr. Bhagat? April told me she transferred in from a military hospital."

Wet glass squeaked against Petra's tightening glove. "Who says I know her?"

"You hid behind me when we saw her in the ER."

"You're pretty sharp for someone who looks like he hasn't slept in a week," Petra muttered. "Yeah, that's how I know her. It's also how I know *this*." She drew out a pill container tucked inside her jacket and shook its contents onto the table. Disco lights shone across the chip's tiny chrome needles.

Jonathan pinched it in his fingernails, studying it close to his face. "Is this some new bionics trend?"

"An old one. It looks just like a...a piece of matériel I saw in the field years ago. I about had a heart attack when I found it here in Baltimore." Petra rubbed her chest. *And the damn thing gives me enough trouble already.*

"Where'd this come from?"

"April McCormick's skull."

The singer missed some lyrics, leaving a gap in the music that framed Jonathan's speechless pause. He dropped the device, wiped his hand on the discarded napkin, and took a long draught before he could speak. "You said she hit her head in the storm."

"I said *probably*," Petra corrected him. "Just like you *probably* wouldn't have made her a priority case if I'd told you she had an upgrade."

"So you carved open her cranium?"

"No! I found her unconscious in the operating cabin after we docked, with this chip sticking out of her." *Just like the first one I saw—bolts through blood and bullet holes.* Shuddering, Petra forced the image back down into her mind's submarine trenches, that uncharted darkness full of trash and monsters.

"So she tried to put a bionic device in her own head, and messed up," Jonathan speculated.

"Not in that weather. Mechanic wouldn't operate on anyone in those conditions. Besides, she never wanted upgrades, no matter how many freebies Steel offered her."

"You think he forced this one on her?"

"No. But someone did."

"Who?"

"Dr. Bhagat."

Jonathan choked on his drink.

Between his splutters, Petra explained: "She was the one Mechanic argued with at the marina before that cruise. I recognized her voice as soon as I heard it in the ER."

"Bhagat knew about the cruises?" Jonathan wheezed.

"She must have! If it came out that one of her staffers was doing illegal surgeries, it would ruin that big inspection Mechanic said she was counting on for her promotion," said Petra, offering him a napkin. "So she snuck on board and cleaned up the problem, making it look like Mechanic was a patient rather than the doctor. Your uniformed pals love to prosecute people who perform biohacking operations, but never ask many questions about the ones who die doing it themselves."

"I don't think murder is Dr. Bhagat's style," said Jonathan. "If she wanted to get rid of someone, she'd build a paper trail."

Petra propped her chin on her hand, smirking. "Think you could follow it for me?"

Sardonic laughter scattered bubbles across the surface of Jonathan's soda. "I am not going to spy on a hospital department head! Even if I had time between calls—which I don't—I could lose my job. I can't afford that." A look over his shoulder revealed the reason why.

"I'm guessing your old man needs a lot of attention," Petra murmured. "Alzheimers'?"

"Something like that."

"You must care a lot about him."

Jonathan glared at her. "Is that a threat?"

"Envy. My family died years ago. Mechanic was the closest thing I had. And obviously she was more than just a casual co-worker to you, too."

Settling his glass in the coaster's damp ring, Jonathan spoke with quiet resignation. "I deal with the dead all the time, Petra, and every one of them was important to somebody. Pretending a person's death was exceptional is just a way to avoid the reality that they're gone."

"Don't you want to know what happened?"

"That won't bring her back."

"It might save others."

Jonathan pressed his palms flat, as if the table were another stilled heart, and leaned toward her. His voice dropped to a harsh whisper. "The medical examiner says April died of a drug overdose. She probably took it to pull extra hours, so she could patch up you transhumanist freaks after her hospital shift ended. You want to save people? Stop playing god and wearing out the angels."

Annoyance seethed through Petra's veins. Standing, she leveled her eyes with Jonathan's and dangled the brain chip between their noses. "Your angel had a device that makes demons."

Confusion wrinkled his brow. "I don't know what you mean."

"Hopefully you never will." Petra dropped the node back into its jar. "If you won't give me information, at least give me time. Wait a few days before telling the cops about the setup on the boat."

Jonathan sat back and folded his arms. "I'm not going to break the law for the sake of a few biohackers."

"Mechanic did."

"And it got her killed."

"No, it got her *murdered*. Last I checked, that was a worse crime than giving local biohackers a few sutures and scrips." Petra waved Mechanic's note, a crumpled white flag of truce. "Maybe she wasn't as perfect as you thought, but I guarantee Dr. Bhagat's got much dirtier secrets under her starched lab coat. Watch her this week. When you realize I'm right, call me." Snatching the pen clipped to Jonathan's breast pocket, Petra jotted her phone number on the back of the paper, then returned to the karaoke machine. She flicked through the selections, one eye on the screen and the other on Jonathan. He slouched at the table, prodding his drink with a straw.

You could make things a little easier for me, you self-righteous organic, but I sure as hell don't need you. I'm going to solve this, one way or another.

She chose a song and took the mic again. Across the diner, Del gave her a thumbs-up. When the music began, Jonathan crammed the prescription into his pocket and steered his father out the door without a backward glance. Petra raised her voice, singing her vow to Jonathan and whatever faceless killer lurked in the shadows beyond:

"*...I'm gonna getcha.*"

5. INTO THE FIRE

"I need a spacesuit to walk on my own damn planet!" Jonathan gasped, wiping sweat from his forehead as he stumbled across the potholes. Orange vests clustered around a figure on the curb. He called out to them, but spume from the asphalt paver erased his words. "Give him some space, please. I said, space! Can you turn that thing off?"

"Gotta finish this repair before the next storm rolls through," the road crew boss yelled back. "All the rain has put us weeks behind schedule. These crazy seasons are killing the roads."

"And the people who maintain them." Jonathan knelt beside the stricken man. Dilated pupils mirrored the blazing sun. *It doesn't take advanced medical training to figure out what happened here. But it's good practice for Evans—she'll see plenty of cases like this.* He beckoned his trainee to take the lead.

"What's the trouble, sir?" she asked the patient in a chipper tone.

"Thought it was just a headache from the tar smell. I get those a lot. But then my eyes blacked out, and...I must've swerved." He pointed a shaky hand at the road roller. It had rammed into a traffic pole, which now leaned over the street with its signals dark.

"I warned you about having too many beers the night before a shift," said the boss with false joviality.

The man scowled. "I been sober three years."

"I'm going to insist you drink on the job—water," said Jonathan, handing over a chilled bottle from his bag. "We need to bring down your core temperature."

"Let's see how far you need to go." Evans clicked the infrared thermometer a few times and made an exasperated noise. "How can the battery be dead already?"

"It's the heat." Jonathan jerked a thumb behind him. "There's a backup mercury thermometer in the rig."

"I've got my own," the man whispered as Evans trotted to the ambulance. Pushing up his sleeve, he showed Jonathan a number line that ranged between ninety-seven and one hundred and four, tattooed on his inner arm.

Looks like one of those bionic control panels Del mentioned—what was it, a skinterface? This guy must be one of Steel's customers! Forcing his voice to stay neutral, Jonathan asked, "What is that?"

"Body temp indicator. I got it when I quit booze, to keep tabs on my fatty liver. A little biofeedback monitor under my skin makes the ink darken when my temp goes up." The man pressed a chipped nail into the blot near the spectrum's far right end.

Jonathan grimaced. "You don't need a biohack to know you've got heat stroke."

"Heat stroke?" The boss wheeled around at the diagnosis. "No way. We take all the legally required precautions against that."

"So, almost none."

"We provide water!" An adamant finger pointed to a battered cooler on the back of a truck.

"What about shade? Or air conditioning breaks? Or just calling things off when the weather gets too hot?"

"If we did that, we'd have to suspend road work between May and October." The boss placed a hand on Jonathan's shoulder and drew him aside. "You drive an ambulance—you must know better than anybody that Baltimore needs its streets! We can't lose the city highway contract because one unhealthy guy with a hangover says he overheated. It's better for everyone if you leave those claims out of your report." Opening his wallet, he offered several large notes.

Heat shimmer warped the digits into reflections of over-due doctor's bills on Jonathan's kitchen table. His finger twitched, but he contained it in an empty fist. "Save it for your workers' compensation fund," he growled, and stalked back to the patient.

Evans crouched beside him, squinting at the glass ther-mometer. "Fever, for sure. Good thing you keep this retro backup equipment, Rowell."

"Sometimes low tech is the way to go. It's certainly the best treatment for heat stroke—a cool environment and some fluids." Jonathan helped the patient toward the rig. "We'll have a doctor check your heart, just to be safe. You might even feel better by the time we get there. The ambulance has good AC."

"I'll test that out," the man replied with a weak grin, and held up his tattoo.

Evans examined it with interest. "Ooh, how does that work?"

"Not diagnostically relevant," Jonathan chided her, but someone hailed him from down the sidewalk. Shoving cold packs into Evans' hands, he strode over to where Corporal Duke directed traffic through the dead light. "What do you need, Latoya?"

"A snowstorm," she replied, dabbing her face with a cuff.

"Yeah, they should start calling this *griddle*-lock. Those mobile ovens will roast their passengers while they're stuck here." Metal roofs paved the street with a blistering mosaic, and Jonathan shaded his eyes against the glare. "Want me to send over an ambulance crew on standby?"

"Only if you volunteer for it yourself. Sitting around will give you time to write up my report on that screws cruise from the other day." Duke glanced at her watch. "We have to release our suspect this afternoon."

"Steel?" Jonathan asked without thinking, and the corporal's arched eyebrow demanded an explanation. "That woman he injured mentioned his name. You got him?"

"Yeah, when he tried to jump a ten-foot fence and discovered my taser had fried his batteries," said Duke, chuckling. "We impounded that crazy suit, but he claims it's a medical assistive device."

"So you have to give it back?" Cartoonish images spooled across Jonathan's imagination: Steel bending prison bars to escape and flinging police cars into the harbor.

"Not until I get written documentation from his doctor. Which won't be any time soon—I tried to contact her, and turns out she's dead."

Jonathan's tongue turned to cement. "Not April McCormick, at Ripken?"

The other eyebrow jumped. "How did you know?"

"She was the emergency patient on that yacht." Aches constricted his ribs. "She died in her own ER."

"There was a doctor on board? Make sure you include that—it'll help support the case against this guy. Right now all we've got is possession of some black-market bionic hardware. Half of Baltimore is guilty of that. All it'll get him is a few fines." A shrill blast issued from Duke's whistle, and she jabbed a finger at a motorist who'd tried to cross out of turn. "We need to get creeps like him off the street. If we can prove intent to distribute, or unlicensed medical practice, that's jail time. But since he doesn't own that boat, we can't investigate it without a formal tip about something shady."

"Keep these commuters from cooking in their cars, and maybe I'll have a chance to do it before the deadline," said Jonathan, turning back to the ambulance before the corporal could see his grimace. *It's bad enough I couldn't save April's life. Do I have to trash her reputation after death, too, by reporting how I found her?*

His brooding brain projected April in a dozen places the moment they entered the ER. New sweat broke out on his skin. "You're still in charge," he told Evans while they wheeled their patient across the busy floor.

She beamed like he'd given her a raise and marched up to the triage station. "Forty-eight-year-old man suffering from hyperthermia. He's got a temperature of one hundred and three, dyspnea, tachycardia, visual disturbances…"

She might be a little overeager, but she knows her stuff really well for a new paramedic. Maybe I can get her to write up that report. Paperwork is good practice. And then I don't have to relive that horrible scene again.

"Mr. Rowell!" Dr. Bhagat swept over to him, ushering a heavyset woman with a tablet. "Excellent timing. This is the investigator following up on the…incident earlier this week. She'd like to speak with you about what happened."

So much for not reliving anything. "I'm sorry, I've got a patient." Jonathan indicated the road worker, who already looked better.

"I'll take care of him. Go answer a few questions—it won't take long. You can use my office." Bhagat commandeered the stretcher and introduced herself to the victim. Helpless, Jonathan trudged after the investigator to a tidy closet-sized space just large enough for a desk. The flimsy plastic chair creaked underneath him.

Donning a pair of eyeglasses on a beaded chain, the investigator read a legal disclaimer aloud with all the tonal variation of a heart rate monitor. "Now, how long did you know Dr. McCormick?"

"About four years, since she came to Ripken for her residency."

"To your knowledge, did she ever use any controlled or illegal substances to alter her performance, or for recreational purposes?"

"No."

"To your knowledge, were there any stress factors in Dr. McCormick's life that might have precipitated the taking of such substances?"

"She worked in the emergency department. We're all stressed, all the time."

The investigator blinked and made a brief note. "Please describe how you found Dr. McCormick on the morning of her death."

He repeated it all again, every scrape of the stylus picking away the tender scabs in his heart. *It's just like with Mom —describing the horror a hundred different times for a hundred different people. Will this one loop forever, too? My own morbid playlist of untimely deaths?*

"Thank you, Mr. Rowell. I think we have all we need."

"That's all?" Jonathan stood to let the investigator waddle past. "What if there was a good reason she dosed herself with anesthetics? Or…or if someone else did it to her?" The possibility slid out before he could catch himself. *Ugh, that paranoid Petra got to me!*

"I know these tragedies are difficult to process." The woman gave him the sort of patronizing smile dispensed in the pediatrics ward. "But promising young doctors often think medical training exempts them from the damage of prescription abuse."

"So your report is going to say that April was just an arrogant addict who signed her own death certificate?" Jonathan asked through clenched teeth.

"The committee will review all the evidence," said the investigator with a sanctimonious nod, but her voice left no doubt about the conclusion.

This isn't an investigation at all—it's a cover-up! Bhagat wants everything sterile and neat, scrubbing April out of the ER's history like bloodstains from a bedsheet.

Beads on the investigator's eyeglass chain caught the light as she turned to leave: silver and pink, Petra's eyes studying him over a glass of hibiscus juice. *"If it came out that one of her staffers was doing illegal surgeries, it would ruin that big hospital inspection Mechanic said she was counting on for her promotion."*

Reckless resolve pumped through Jonathan's veins. He pretended to retie his shoelace in the hallway, and once the investigator disappeared, he ducked back into Dr. Bhagat's office. Stillness amplified the sound of his nervous breath. Pulling on a pair of latex gloves, he probed the desk drawers: tea, office supplies, and a glossy brochure advertising a new surgical treatment. The shelves lay bare except for a few dusty medical tomes and a photo of a Persian cat.

What am I even looking for? Riffling a stack of folders, Jonathan's wrist nudged the computer mouse. The login prompt flared, and he repeated his own answer from the diner: "A paper trail."

Sticky notes lined up on the monitor offered no password clues. Jonathan peeked under the keyboard, but Dr. Bhagat wasn't amateur enough to tape her login information there, either. The cat watched with a reproachful expression uncannily like its mistress.

"Wanna give me some hunting tips?" Jonathan asked it, then leaned closer to the frame. An ornate collar, half-buried in lush fur, bore the pet's name. He typed it into the password box.

Login failed.

He replaced select letters with numbers and characters.

Welcome, Nalini Bhagat!

The computer desktop mirrored the physical one for order; no obvious icons stood out. Jonathan searched the email inbox for messages from April and opened the most recent entry. A long thread unwound from his cursor, beginning with a note from Bhagat the previous month.

Dr. McCormick:

Attached are the documents I referenced in our conversation earlier today: the hospital's conflict of interest policy and our ethical pledge. You signed both when you were hired. Please reacquaint yourself with them, and we will consider the matter closed.

April's reply, without greeting or sign-off, radiated haste and annoyance. Jonathan pictured her typing fast between patients, tousled hair spilling into eyes alight with rage:

nothing in those documents says i can't volunteer in the community. there's no MATTER at all. i'm not doing anything wrong.

Even if your activities could be classified as pro bono work—which I would strongly contest—there's the question of legal statutes.

i'm going to do what's best for patients, even if it's not traditional. if you keep harassing me about this, i'll get the hospital ombudsman involved.

By all means. Let the ombudsman judge your appalling professional conduct, since my cautions seem to have no effect. You're a skilled doctor; it would be a shame to damage your young reputation with formal censure.

the only reputation you care about is your own. these ridiculous emails prove my point. every minute I spend arguing with you is a minute away from patients. stop being a dictator and start being a doctor again.

That's a rich remark from someone flagrantly disregarding her Hippocratic oath. Stop what you're doing, or there will be serious consequences.

like shutting down my clinical trial? you already did that. dismissal? you can't afford to lose anyone from the er, especially with your big review coming up. unless you want to take this to the board and show what a selfish bureaucrat you are, there's nothing you can do to me.

We'll see about that.

Bhagat's final four words raised the hair on Jonathan's arms. *She just means some kind of official warning. She wouldn't hurt one of her own staff...would she?* He opened the word processor and skimmed the recent documents. *Ha, I knew it—McCormick_Misconduct_Report_Draft.*

The incomplete letter only contained a few lines:

I have reason to believe that Dr. April McCormick is involved in illicit activities that violate not only the hospital's conflict of interest policy, but possibly several federal laws. Her conduct endangers both our patients and the reputation of our fine institution.

She must've found out about April's side hustle with the biohackers! But how? Footsteps outside froze Jonathan's hand on the mouse. He held his breath until they faded again. *I don't have time to go through the whole hard drive to find out. Bhagat could be back any second.* Pulling up the computer directory, he searched for the word *bionic*. A single result popped onto the screen. He opened it eagerly, but hope deflated at the document's date, almost ten years ago. The letterhead bore the emblem of a Bethesda military hospital. Jonathan's keyword appeared halfway through Bhagat's rebuttal to a complaint:

Indulging the patient's request to explore experimental bionic devices for rehabilitation, without first exhausting proven conventional treatments, would be medically irresponsible. The patient displays classic characteristics of post-traumatic stress disorder. While this is understandable in the sole survivor of the Sedna *incident, I believe it compromises her judgment.*

Did this have to do with why Bhagat left government service? Jonathan skimmed to the aggrieved patient's biographical details: female, born a few months before him, holding a rank that sounded low even to his minimal knowledge of military command structure. He spoke the name aloud, because pixellated text couldn't quite convince him it was real. *Who else could it be?*

The knob rattled, launching Jonathan's pulse into overdrive. He locked the computer and vaulted over the desk just as the door cracked open.

"—Did my best to cover it up, but it's an utter mess. It needs to be dealt with immediately, before the situation gets worse." Bhagat's low, tense voice preceded her into the room. Catching sight of Jonathan, she took the phone from her ear. A dent on her cheek remained where she'd pressed the device hard against her face. "Why are you still here, Rowell?"

"Er, I was looking for some paper to jot down the investigator's contact information, in case I thought of anything else to tell her," said Jonathan, cramming the latex gloves into his pocket. "You were right—she didn't ask very much."

"She reports for compliance committees, not tabloid news feeds," said Bhagat, turning off her phone. "I may not have always seen eye to eye with Dr. McCormick, but I have no desire to tarnish her name."

"Or the hospital's," Jonathan added pointedly.

"No. And I don't think Dr. McCormick would have wanted that, either, despite her constant flouting of its rules."

"Is that what you were arguing about, just before she died?"

Disapproving fissures carved the doctor's brow. "I take it she mentioned our disagreement to you. Typically indiscreet of her. It was a hospital matter, and no concern of yours. EMS's role here is to deliver patients. I suggest you get back to it."

"At least one of us should," Jonathan retorted under his breath as he strode out of the office. Pausing at a waste bin, he dug out the gloves to discard. A scrap of paper tumbled free with them. He unfolded it: *Dapọ Diner, Pigtown. J knows owner—can arrange K's birthday party. Karaoke!*

April's handwriting scrawled fresh pain into his ribs. *She wasn't a junkie, or a corrupt black-marketeer. Just someone who tried to make people feel better, whether that meant fudging some prescriptions or arranging a break for her workaholic brother.* He traced the paper's edge, longing to fold it into his breast pocket, where April had slipped dozens of identical sheets with a conspiratorial whisper.

"Here—Del might need this, since our new ER overlord axed the asthma study. I can't believe she'd let patients suffer, just because she's biased against biotech! There must be other ways...but this will have to do for now."

Phantom pressure over Jonathan's heart marked where her fingertips had lingered. He touched the spot, but met only fabric rather than a warm, chapped hand. *She's gone. Others are still here.*

Sighing, he pulled out a pen. Loose strokes approximated the name of a brand-name asthma medication. Prescription clutched in his damp palm, he headed for the pharmacy.

The dispensing assistant was behind the shelves, so Jonathan smoothed the paper on the counter, trying to make it look less secondhand. More ink flashed up at him from the back side: Petra's number.

Maybe her idea about Dr. Bhagat wasn't crazy after all. Almost unbidden, Jonathan's fingers extracted his phone and punched in the digits. He typed the last one an instant before the pharmacy assistant snatched up the note.

"All this medical technology, and docs still want to scribble on slips. I swear they make it illegible on purpose," he grumbled, retreating into the aisles again.

Time slid to a guilty halt. Jonathan posed himself the way he might position an injured patient, arranging his limbs to look casual even though tension prickled his every nerve. Cabinets clicked. Paper rustled. At last the assistant emerged with a stapled bag. Jonathan reached for it and—

"There you are!" Evans came over, frowning. "Where'd you disappear to, Rowell?"

"Had to answer some questions." Jonathan stuffed the bag into the deepest cargo pocket of his uniform pants. "About Dr. McCormick."

"What kind of questions?"

"The kind they've already decided the answers to," he muttered, handing over the ambulance keys.

Evans patted him on the arm. "Well, now you can move forward. If you spend too much time looking back, the past can creep up and get you."

Get you, get you, get you. Petra's song echoed in Jonathan's head, a musical threat drifting over his shoulder as he'd left the diner.

She did exactly what she said. While his trainee accepted a new assignment from the AI dispatcher, Jonathan tapped out a text message. *Let's hope she keeps all of her promises so well.*

6. POLAR NIGHTS

"Hey, Rowell! We're gonna grab burgers for dinner," a boisterous male voice rang from the fire station's open vehicle bay. "Fisher needs a protein fix—he tore open that car wreck today like a freaking superman! Wanna join?"

Petra's long shadow did a dance step on Eastern Avenue. *Guess I haven't lost those GEOINT skills from my drone-running days!* After she'd savored triumph at Jonathan's message requesting to meet in Patterson Park, a quick scan of internet maps had showed her the area's EMS posts. Determining his probable work site was a simple matter of triangulation between the park, marina, and hospital. *He's got a lot to learn about operational security. Now I get to do a little recon first.* Pretending to be absorbed in her phone, she strolled past the station.

"Why do you always invite him? He never comes," a second man added nastily. "He runs straight home like a good boy. Does daddy put out cookies for your after-school snack, Rowell?"

"Nah, I'm a pretzels guy," said Jonathan dryly, without looking up from the ambulance's supply cabinets. Petra began to whistle his CPR song. His head snapped toward the street. Startled eyes found her face, and he almost dropped an oxygen tank on his foot.

She bit back a smile. *Ambush.*

The trainee appeared through the inner door. *What was her name again? Better if I can't remember—no need to drag a rookie into this mess.* Petra shook her bangs over her face and crossed the road before the other woman recognized her. Jonathan's voice, tenser than before, drifted in her wake. "See you tomorrow, Evans, I need to run."

Waiting at the corner, Petra feigned interest in a store's window display. New-model gadgets glittered up at her. Eyeglasses, wristbands, and headsets promised to integrate the wearer with the digital realm.

And Steel has to smuggle his gear around in hockey bags. Devices glowed within the reflected outlines of Petra's body. *Wear bionics outside, it's a commodity. Wear 'em inside, it's a crime.*

A shadow appeared in the glass beside her. "Shopping for the parts Dr. Bhagat wouldn't let you have?" asked Jonathan, scowling at the electronics. "I learned a few things about her and April today, including that they shared a patient. When you told me you knew her, you didn't mention that she treated you."

"She didn't. She would have left me a cripple when I was barely old enough to buy a beer," said Petra, challenging his gaze in the window's mirror. "I suppose she gave you the same bull she told the medical review board—that I was a traumatized kid, unfit to make decisions about her own body."

"That was the implication." Jonathan shoved his hands into his pockets, hunching his lanky form in discomfort. "She also mentioned something called Sedna. What's Sedna?"

"An Inuit sea goddess." Petra stalked away toward the gentle curve of the Eastern Avenue Bridge. Leaning on the rail, she wiggled her toes between the posts. Storm-swollen water churned high enough to speckle her soles. Two scuffed work boots appeared beside hers, evoking combat boots on the edge of an ice floe. That image pried truth from her tongue. "It was also the name of a U.S. Coast Guard ice-breaker."

"I remember hearing about those, years ago. An Arctic standoff seemed exotic to a kid from Baltimore, so I followed all the news for a while." Jonathan broke into a guilty geek's smile. "In pre-med, I even wrote a paper on how human physiology responds to extreme cold."

"Too bad you didn't know me back then. I could've given you a lot of firsthand reports." Petra waggled her left hand in front of his face. "Frostbite cost me a few fingers."

He winced. "Now I'm sorry I teased you about the glove."

"Don't be. At least most of me is still here to tease." She kicked a piece of flotsam back into the canal. It joined the garbage flotillas blockading the current. "You think it sucks to transport biohackers to the hospital during rush hour? Try busting through acres of pack ice to free a container ship that got greedy and tried to run the polar lanes too late in the season. Half of 'em weren't even legit freighters—they were poaching seabed claims, trying to steal our pathetic deposits of rare-earth minerals."

"They did a thorough job of it. My dad used to work at a semiconductor factory, and when the Arctic didn't turn up any new resources, raw materials costs drove the company bankrupt." Jonathan glowered at the oily water, lips pressed together as if sealing off the rest of the story. "Wasn't the military supposed to be defending our territory from that sort of thing?"

"With half a dozen leaky old icebreakers to cover a thousand miles of coastline?" Petra waved an arm toward the harbor behind her. "I might as well assign a single ambulance to handle emergencies for all of Baltimore."

"That must've led to some incidents."

A bitter laugh scraped her throat. "Is that what Bhagat called it? An incident?"

"What would you call it?"

"A massacre." Petra's next breath carried the stale metallic tang of a control room, and the watch officer's voice whispered in her ear:

"What do you mean 'there's no one aboard', Rock? No crew would be suicidal enough to abandon ship and try crossing the ice on foot. It's not the lost fucking Franklin expedition, just some late-season fishermen, looking for anything the Chinese trawler fleets left behind."

"I'm just telling you what the sensors say, sir. There's no sign of life on that ship out there."

"Maybe because they're all dead. Could've been sitting out here for weeks and we just never got a distress call."

"Aerial recon from yesterday has nothing at these coordinates, sir. I checked."

"Probably just didn't pick it up. Ice on the drone lens again."

"Not on my drones, sir."

"Still nothing on comms?"

"Not even a ship identifier."

"Well, that's not suspicious at all. Hey, Gunny! Get a boarding team together..."

"*Sedna* came across a stranded ship—an unflagged old tub, didn't even look ice rated," said Petra, peeling a flake of paint off the rail. "She wouldn't return hails, so we broke a channel to reach her and went aboard to look for survivors."

Jonathan leaned against one of the old lamppost plinths. "A ghost ship?"

"Not ghosts…."

"Nothing on the bridge, sir."

"Did you check the cabins? The head? Maybe they all got the runs from too much of that machine-room hooch the Russian sailors trade around."

"Sir, do you hear that?"

"All I hear is your redneck mouth running, Rock."

"That clicking sound. Reminds me of the thing belugas do. What's it called? Echolocation."

"Echo-NO-WAY-tion. There hasn't been a wild beluga up here since before your skinny little ass landed on my deck. You spend so much time wearing headphones that you're hearing thi—."

"Sir, behind you!"

Pale blurs swooped past. Petra jumped, but it was only seagulls fighting over a choice bit of trash. *"Tuniit."*

"You should be used to off-key seagulls," said Jonathan, glancing at the birds.

"Not 'tune it'. *Tuniit*. Creatures from Inuit folklore, a species of giants that lived peacefully alongside humans until some punk kid killed one of 'em. They ran into the wilderness, and take their revenge on intruders." Whispers from the dank corners of Alaskan pubs still raised hair on Petra's neck. "Miners and loggers in port used to tell some freaky stories about encounters. Made me glad to get back on *Sedna*, where I'd be safe at sea. Or so I thought."

Medically trained eyes scanned her for some outward symptom of insanity. "You expect me to believe that you boarded a ship full of these mythical things?"

"It's the best word I have to describe them. They moved fast and quiet, all in sync like a school of fish. Cut down half the boarding team before we could even open fire. No guns, no knives, just blood on the bulkheads." *Pull off the gloves, pull on the trigger, pop pop pop flash-blind too many fall back fall back...* Petra's feet scuttled away from the bridge, obeying the useless order ten years too late. Traffic noise turned to shots and screams.

Jonathan's voice filtered through the chaos. "Sounds like some kind of cutting-edge battle robot."

"That's what I thought at first. They sure looked like machines, with armored uniforms, and helmets that covered their faces. Then I shot one point-blank while trying to cover our retreat. Brains everywhere." Phantom spatter seared Petra's cheek; she scrubbed it with the back of her glove, but that only made the nerves burn worse. "It was human, but crazy strong. Knocked me overboard onto the floe while its friends swarmed *Sedna.*"

"A handful of boarders captured a military ship?" asked Jonathan, skeptical.

"We were glorified security guards! The most action we saw was chasing off ice poachers or playing hide-and-seek with automated submarines. The brass insisted that none of the Arctic nations would risk their new polar money machine with serious conflict, and ignored any intelligence reports that suggested otherwise. Including mine." Petra clutched the rail to steady her shaking.

"Then who proved them wrong?"

"I told you, I don't know. There were no flags or insignias. None of the attackers spoke, so I didn't hear any language. Even the ship was just a repurposed old bucket that could've been bought cheap in any port."

"It almost sounds fake."

"The slaughter was real enough." Petra turned her ear toward the rushing water, but it didn't drown out the agonized voices. "You know how far screams carry across open ice? I must've heard them for miles as my little frozen raft drifted away. They were still ringing in my head when a patrol picked me up two days later."

"You were stranded on an iceberg for two days?" Jonathan stared at her. She couldn't tell if he was incredulous or impressed. "How did you survive?"

"I had another body to keep me warm." Weathered metal turned to stiff flesh under Petra's palms. She shoved away and moved off the bridge, heading up President Street. "The enemy thing I'd shot landed on the ice with me. Its face was blown off, so I never knew what it looked like."

"No dog tags, or whatever high-tech identifiers the military uses now?"

"Just a numbered patch on the uniform. Seventeen." The number tasted like a malediction. "That, and a scrap of metal embedded in the side of its head."

"Your bullet?" Jonathan nodded at the Phoenix Shot Tower ahead.

"No. A little chip, with wires spread out like a spider web across the skull."

Alarm stiffened his shoulders. "Like the thing you found on April?"

Cold crept down Petra's spine. "I've come across a lot of weird stuff on the biotech black market, but she was the first time I'd seen that chip since *Sedna*."

"What does it do?"

"I've cooked up a hundred theories over the years. My best guess is that it affects neurochemicals or synaptic patterns to make better soldiers. Crank up their aggression, maybe, or enhance their senses."

"Or increase their stamina?" asked Jonathan, pausing on the sidewalk. "April used to struggle through her long shifts —we'd grab coffee together almost every day, and I'd still catch her napping on her lunch break. A few months ago, that all stopped, but she always had energy."

"Could be all those things, or something worse. I'm sure as hell not watching it spread all over Baltimore to find out." The crowded street suddenly teemed with sharp teeth and hostile eyes. Seizing Jonathan's elbow, Petra hauled him into the shot tower's shadow. Brick at her back reassured her enough to speak. "You think there's a public health crisis now? Twenty fighters with this chip slaughtered six times that many people on *Sedna*. Imagine hundreds of biohackers getting one, and turn 'em loose downtown. I hope you restocked that ambulance real well."

Jonathan chewed his lip, watching oblivious pedestrians stream past. "How do we stop that from happening?"

'We.' So he'll help me...at least for now. Petra released his arm, and her held breath. "First we figure out where Mechanic got it."

"What happened to the one you found years ago?"

"I thought it was locked in some classified filing cabinet. Politicians wanted to avoid declaring actual war in the Arctic—that would've been too expensive—so official an-

nouncements said *Sedna* went down in a storm. And my reports were dismissed after my wonderful doctor branded me
a basket case. The whole thing was wrapped up tighter than a
catfish line. Not many people know what really happened."
I'm not even sure I do anymore. Petra corked the last confession with a citrus drop, giving her molars something to gnash
besides their own enamel.

"Did Dr. Bhagat know?" Jonathan asked, in a less dubious tone than he'd used the night before.

"Why do you think she refused my request for bionic
treatment options? She thought I was trying to relive my
trauma or some shit, turning myself into the thing that attacked me."

Astonished white rimmed his eyes. "So planting a military chip on April might frame you for her murder."

"That was the real reason I thought she might be behind
it," Petra admitted with a grim nod. "If she found out about
Mechanic's side hustle, she might've recognized me, too."

"She definitely knew something." Jonathan related the
senior doctor's email feud with April as they walked along
Jones Falls. Suspicions spun through Petra's head until she
felt dizzy; when they reached the War Memorial, she leaned
against one of the art deco horse sculptures for support.

"We'll see about that?" she repeated the quote, but it
sounded no less ominous in her own voice.

"I think it was a threat against April's job, not her life,"
said Jonathan. "I still can't picture Dr. Bhagat physically
hurting anyone."

"You couldn't picture April McCormick performing illegal surgeries, either."

Stiff shoulders confirmed the guess. "That's another
thing. If April was attacked on the boat, Bhagat would've

had to have been on board with you. Wouldn't you have noticed?"

"No. I spend the whole trip at the controls. I don't deal with customers." Petra shook the last static from her vision. "Besides, they always wear hats and hoods to avoid the city surveillance cameras."

"They must take them off for surgery. Would your buddy Steel remember any faces?"

"Only one way to find out." City Hall's arched windows stared from across the plaza; Petra marched beneath their imperious gaze, humming a defiant old rock song. "You can come if you want," she called to Jonathan over her shoulder.

"Where?"

"Prison."

Steps skidded behind her. "What?"

"Not as inmates." She flashed him a devious smile. "At least, not yet."

7. STEELER

"This building always reminds me of a car accident I saw once," said Jonathan, after blocks of silence compelled him to conversation outside Baltimore City Detention Center. "A sports car hit a municipal bus and the two sort of fused together. A total mess, like the modern extensions grafted onto this Gothic monster. The city should've just built a whole new structure."

"Sometime you have to work with what you got." Petra rubbed her left arm and winced. A stiff denim sleeve didn't hide the limb's awkward movement.

"Whoever set your shoulder didn't do a very good job. It should be immobilized..." Jonathan began, but a flick of grey eyes made it clear who would be immobilized if he continued. He changed topics. "Why are you posting bail for someone who beat you up?"

"Because like any good bond agent, I'll charge him a hefty fee. In this case, information. He's my lead witness for what might've happened to Mechanic."

"Maybe your lead suspect, too."

"I still don't think he did it."

"Why not? You said he and April had been arguing about money—that gives him motive. Working her in the surgery cabin would've given him plenty of opportunity. And your shoulder demonstrates his preferred methods of conflict resolution."

Petra glared over her jacket's upturned collar. "You sure you're not a cop?"

"Positive—BPD reminds us lowly paramedics of that constantly when we're on the same scene," said Jonathan, rolling his eyes. "But I've picked up a few things about police procedure."

"Like bigotry? Having some upgrades doesn't make Steel any more likely a killer than anyone else."

"No, but it gives him an advantage if he tried."

Taking quick steps to the detention center door, Petra whirled to block Jonathan's way. "You wanna go in?"

He skidded to a halt before he collided with her. "I thought that was the point."

"Just shove on through, then. You're a lot bigger than me."

"That doesn't mean I want to plow you over."

"No, but it gives you an advantage if you tried." Her point made, Petra marched into the detention center's utilitarian lobby and addressed the clerk. "Hi. I'm here to pay the bail for Eddie Bukowski."

"That's his real name?" Jonathan tried—and failed—to stifle a laugh. "No wonder he goes by a handle. Did he pick SoulSteeler because he thinks he's armoring people's spirits with all his gizmos, or does he extract their essence during biohacking procedures and use it for the dark arts?"

"Neither," said Petra, filling out a form. "He's a die-hard football fan from Pittsburgh."

"Oh. That's not nearly as cool."

"Cool has nothing to do with it. It's a scrap of identity protection in a controversial industry." Petra jabbed the stylus toward the jail's inner door, indicating the risks of discovery. "Most people involved use an alias."

"Like Rock?"

She ignored him and pulled up her banking app. The payment system pinged.

"Mr. Bukowski will be out in a moment. You can have a seat," said the clerk, waving them toward a row of plasticized armchairs. Jonathan collapsed into the nearest one and stretched out his legs, sighing as pressure came off his feet for the first time in hours. He watched Petra through half-closed eyes, curious whether she would sit beside him or leave an empty chair between them.

She didn't sit at all. She paced. Each step measured one floor tile. Eight tiles comprised each lap before she spun and retraced her path. Folded arms gave her posture an anxious rigidity, but didn't affect the metronomic beat.

Imaginary guitar strings coalesced under Jonathan's fingertips, and he began tapping out a melody line on the chair's arm. Petra's ear cocked toward him. She embellished her walking rhythms with a heel-toe flourish at each turn. Jonathan replied with a more complicated lick. An irresistible smile tugged at his cheek; when Petra spun again, he caught a mirrored expression on her face.

The inner door's click interrupted their duet, and Steel lumbered into the lobby. A smaller man in a slim-cut suit trotted alongside him, muttering brisk commentary:

"Remember, if they can't prove you knew those bionic products were in the bag, much less that you distributed them, the most they can do is fine you for possession."

"What about my exoskeleton?" Steel rumbled.

"Send me your medical documentation and I'll sort it out."

"You could afford a lawyer, but you squeezed me for bail?" Petra glowered at Steel's svelte companion.

"Tae's a public defender," said Jonathan.

Tae-soo Kim glanced up at his name, and his polished demeanor dissolved in delight. He offered a warm handshake-turned-hug, which Jonathan returned. "What are you doing here, Jonathan? Did someone have a heart attack?"

"I will, when that charge hits my account," said Petra as Steel hunched over the desk. Her gaze flicked between Jonathan and Tae. "What kind of trouble made an uptight city paramedic pals with a court-appointed lawyer?"

"Love. Tae married my best friend from med school," Jonathan explained.

"Guilty as charged, and happily serving my life sentence." Tae spun his wedding band and smiled at Petra. "Has Jonathan finally recruited a partner in crime?"

She cackled, drawing a glare from the clerk. "We just met."

"And you're already getting him in prison-worthy mischief!" Cupping a palm around his mouth, the lawyer addressed Jonathan in a stage whisper: "I like this one."

Jonathan sighed. "We're following up on a patient's case."

"Ooh, I'm afraid I can't help you there. Attorney-client privilege."

Petra planted a hand on her hip. "What about just-forked-over-thousands-of-dollars-in-bail privilege?"

"Makes up for all the discounts I gave you over the years." Steel signed the last form with a stab of the stylus. "I'll repay you, now that I can get back to my job."

Tae beamed. "Excellent—juries love a hard-working small business owner! You shouldn't have anything to worry about if your late partner was responsible for all the unlicensed bionics. I'll see you on your court date, Mr. Bukowski, and I'll see *you*," he told Jonathan, "at my bioethics panel. Ciro told me he invited you. He'll pout all evening without a non-lawyer for company. Two would be better." He winked at Petra.

Steel nodded at his attorney and shuffled out the door. Petra followed, taking three steps for every one of his. "I wouldn't have given you a goddamn dime if I'd known you rolled on Mechanic, you shameless son of a—"

"It's the least she can do after almost running our business into the ground," he growled. "Dead people can't pay fines or serve prison terms. Doesn't hurt her any."

"It hurts her memory, her reputation, and everyone who knew her," said Jonathan, catching up in a few strides.

Steel looked at him for the first time. Beady eyes blinked in recognition. "What is this joker doing here?" he asked Petra.

"Preparing to testify that he witnessed you throwing me overboard," she replied smoothly. "I'm going to press assault charges, unless you tell me what I want to know."

Heavy footsteps scraped to a stop. "You wouldn't do that. We've known each other for years. We do business together!"

"Which will not help your claims of ignorance if I mention it to the judge."

Cursing, Steel sank onto the bus stop bench. "What will it take to shut your dirty sailor mouth?"

"Tell me who was the last person in the cabin with Mechanic the other night."

"Me," said Steel, but sat up straighter when Petra and Jonathan stared at him. "Hey, that doesn't mean I attacked her! Someone else could've gone in while I was in the can."

"Were any of the passengers acting suspicious?" asked Jonathan.

Steel guffawed. "Brother, they chartered a boat into international waters to get their bodies tricked out with illegal electronic parts. They were all twitchy as hell. Mechanic goes through sedatives on our clients the way I go through six-packs on game day."

But who would use them on her? Jonathan pulled up the Ripken Memorial Hospital website on his phone and magnified Dr. Bhagat's stern face in the department leadership photo. "Was this woman aboard that night?"

Steel shook his head. "Both the clients I worked on were younger—some teenaged brat who brought along a cheap-ass secondhand implant instead of buying one of my certified products, and a guy about your age who wanted an existing implant calibrated."

"What about the third one?" Petra asked beneath the hum of the approaching bus.

"Never saw a face, since we had to cancel 'em. Mechanic wouldn't work on anybody once that storm blew up." The vehicle wheezed to a stop in front of them. Automatic doors folded back with a clatter, and Steel squeezed through the gap. Petra hopped up on his heels. Both waved hands over the ticket scanner, earning affirmative green blinks.

They must have removed the chips from their fare cards and embedded them in a fingertip instead. That's just gross mutilation, not to mention defacement of city property! Swallowing a faint ripple of nausea, Jonathan scrambled after them.

"Please present your fare card," the smart-bus' disembodied voice instructed him.

He fumbled for his wallet. "Hang on, I'm getting it."

"Please present your fare card."

Drivers' license, credit card, insurance card...where the hell is my bus pass?

"Please present your fare card."

"This is why I always walk," Jonathan snapped at the machine, swiping his card at last. The kiosk gave a sancti-monious beep. *Okay, a public transit biohack* would *be pretty convenient.* Hydraulics hissed underfoot, and the bus chugged along East Monument Street. Stumbling down the aisle, Jonathan passed Steel—who occupied a row to him-self—and sat beside Petra in the seats behind.

"What did number three say when you told them to reschedule?" Petra asked Steel.

"All I got was a nod. Poor sucker was probably trying not to puke, thanks to your crazy driving."

"If you talked to them, you must've noticed something. Height?"

"Everyone looks short to me, Rock."

"Build?"

"More layers than even you, and baggy to boot."

"Eye or hair color?"

"Not with a hood deeper than the Fort McHenry tunnel."

"You know how the hospital resolves identity mix-ups?" Jonathan interjected. "Billing. Money has to come from somewhere. And I get the impression you don't work for free."

"Unlike our Saint Mechanic, who couldn't say no to anyone who needed an upgrade." Steel snorted. "She'd have run it as a damn charity, but even those need funds. The whole thing would've sunk years ago if I hadn't been mind-ing the money."

"How do you manage payment?"

"Some cryptocurrency, some cash. I do all the bookings online through an anonymous darkweb portal."

"Passengers have to check in with a code he sends them. Otherwise…" Petra made a jerky heave-ho gesture and imitated a splash.

"Hey, we can't take chances on spies." Steel shot a dark look at Jonathan and punched the stop button with demonstrative relish. "It's a high-risk business."

"No kidding. It got Mechanic murdered."

"Murdered? I thought she just whanged her head." Lines deepened in Steel's brow, channeling sweat. "Why would someone kill her?"

"Maybe for this." The chip appeared in Petra's palm.

Steel swiped for it, but gloved fingers yanked it away. "How'd you get that?"

"How'd you know about it?"

The bus halted in a run-down McElderry Park neighborhood, and Steel hauled himself up with a groan. "I made it."

Petra froze for an instant, then dove across Jonathan's lap to reach the back door. He lunged after her, and they intercepted Steel at the curb.

"You're a lying bastard," Petra hissed as he disembarked. "I know you didn't invent that device."

"I never said I invented it." Steel shoved her aside and limped down the block of dingy shops. "I said I *made* it."

"From one of those amateur kits?" asked Jonathan, thinking of the jeweler's screwdrivers, suture glue, and poorly translated diagrams that often littered biohacker emergency scenes.

Steel shot him a glare. "Do I look like an amateur?"

No—you look like someone in serious pain. Each shuffled step made Steel wince. Although he couldn't be out of his forties, he moved like someone twice that age. *Like Mom.* Remembrance softened Jonathan's disdain. After a moment's hesitation, he offered Steel his arm. Watery eyes scanned his for sincerity. Then a massive hand landed on his shoulder, leaning on him like a crutch.

Jonathan locked his knees to keep them from buckling under the weight. "Bad back?"

"Sports injury. I used to play pro football. Not many people know that."

"Every barfly in Baltimore knows that," said Petra, jogging impatient circles around the two men. "You tell this story every Sunday between August and February."

Steel continued unabashed. "Defensive lineman, recruited straight outta high school. First play of my first game, *wham.*" He clapped Jonathan on the back, almost knocking him into the storm drain. "Four hundred pounds of offensive tackle fractured my spine. Surgical screws and a lot of rehab saved my legs, but not my career. Twenty-five years later, walking still hurts."

"I bet the suit eases things a lot," Jonathan gasped through winded lungs.

"Sure does. But you wanna know the funniest part?" Steel stopped at a door tucked between a shabby storefront church and a noodle house. Letters glimmered across the window: *Heavy Metal Tattoo & Piercing.* "Not long after I got hit, the league approved exoskeletons for player safety! Now even the damn kicker gets one, while the fuzz keeps mine impounded over a stupid license."

"Yeah, you're a real human tragedy." Petra's sarcasm dripped like the rusty AC unit on the second-floor window.

"Takes one to know one." Steel waved a finger over the digital door lock—a different one than he'd used for the bus

—and stepped into the parlor. Reclaimed wood floors whispered under Jonathan's boots. Vinyl cushions on the chairs gleamed with cleanliness. Flash art adorned the walls in fierce animals, flowers, and skulls. The whole place looked alarmingly normal.

Petra helped herself to a candy bowl on the jewelry case and caught Jonathan staring. "What, you were expecting a robot factory?"

"That's back here." Steel beckoned them past screened workstations to a door marked *Staff Only—Keep The Hell Out.* Behind it, the piercing parlor fused with a machine shop. A hydraulic tattoo chair stood over a floor drain. Counters ringing the walls held an autoclave, 3D printers, and tools. Electronic parts overflowed from every drawer.

"So this is the real business." Discomfort prickled the hair on Jonathan's arms. *How many people who stumbled out of here ended up in my ambulance?*

"It is these days. All the news coverage last year about that college kid's brain chip research got a lot of people interested in upgrading their bodies. I couldn't have made up a better advertising campaign!" Steel patted a full-size plastic skeleton that could have hung in one of Jonathan's pre-med classrooms, except for demo devices affixed to its bones. "Big tech companies are too litigation-shy to meet the demand, but not me. Bionics is the biggest untapped fortune since the Arctic opened up."

"Biggest exploitation of hapless grunts, too," muttered Petra, flopping into the surgery chair.

Jonathan examined the row of 3D printers. Delicate implants in various states of completion shone up at him. "I didn't know you manufactured so many of these things yourselves," he said, impressed despite the faint revulsion writhing through his insides.

"Where else are we gonna get unapproved, unregulated biomedical implants? Cyborgs 'R' Us?" Petra activated the chair's articulated leg rests so her knees mimicked robotic movement.

"Where'd you get yours?"

"Who says I have any?" She rolled onto her side and struck an exaggerated pinup pose, daring him to look. Layered clothes obscured all but the outlines of her lean anatomy.

Jonathan tore his eyes away. "You said a biohack landed you in the ER."

"I didn't say I was stupid enough to try it again."

"She's my favorite example of what happens to biohackers who order secondhand crap from countries with lax medical research laws," said Steel, chucking a few loose bolts back into organizer bins. "No quality guarantees there. If you want to be sure of what you're putting in your body, you've gotta make the parts yourself."

"What kind of parts are we talking about?" asked Jonathan.

"Whatever the healthcare system won't give you. I keep a stock of popular stuff people can buy off the shelf, like implantable glucose monitors and biofeedback units, but I do custom work, too."

"Like this?" Petra rattled the pill container with April's neural node inside.

"That was the most complicated piece I ever tried to replicate. Had to buy specialty filaments for my printer, design new molds for some of the components, order high-grade microprocessors that cost a fortune..." Steel eased himself onto a stool. "And after all that, Mechanic wouldn't let me sell the damn things."

Wrappers stopped rustling, and Petra gaped with a candy-stained tongue. "She *commissioned* that chip?"

"Yup. Brought me a blueprint a few months ago and asked if I could make her one. She was real cagey about it, too—made me destroy the templates and delete the files afterwards." Steel snorted. "All that work for one lousy prototype, and she selfishly stuffed it in her own skull."

Jonathan's knees faltered, and he sank onto the chair's wide bed beside Petra. "She embedded that thing herself?"

"No. I did it for her, right where you're sitting now."

April's ghost stirred beside him; Jonathan toppled out of the seat and leaned his trembling body against a wall instead. "You did *brain surgery* on her?"

"More like a fancy sub-dermal body mod. This chip uses a nifty kind of bone conduction for transcranial stimulation, so you can slip it right under the scalp without having to drill into the actual brain tissue." Steel traced an ink-stained nail around his own ear to illustrate. "Brilliant design."

"What did it do?" Petra demanded.

"Hell if I know. Mechanic wouldn't tell me. But based on how it was built, I'd guess it modulated brain activity."

"Did she say where she got it?"

"No, and I didn't ask. I figured it was some hot new treatment she'd smuggled out of the hospital—there was a watermark on the pages she brought in." Grabbing a tablet, Steel sketched on the screen. Precise geometric shapes formed under his thick finger.

Jonathan leaned closer. "Wow, that's good."

A smile dimpled Steel's jowls. "Well, I did my art in ink before I started sculpting meat and metal."

Or you know this particular graphic a lot better than you let on. The rest of the pattern emerged: a stylized caduceus that replaced snakes with circuits. Jonathan caught his breath. "That was on a brochure I saw in Dr. Bhagat's desk drawer."

"Steel, can you send me that picture?" asked Petra. Her phone chimed a moment later, and she ran the doodle through an image search program. "It's a logo. Some company called Biocinium."

"Biocinium?" The name seared an acid hole through Jonathan's tongue. "I didn't know they were still around."

"You've heard of them?"

"They owned the semiconductor factory where my dad used to work." He gripped the back of her chair, denting the vinyl. "What are they doing with blueprints for fancy bionics?"

"Pivoting their brand?" Petra pulled up the company's slick website and read the banner statement aloud: "*For decades, Biocinium manufactured chips for medical electronics. Now we are excited to apply that expertise toward bionics innovations that will enhance the health of our community.*"

They browsed the sparse pages, Jonathan reading over Petra's shoulder. A brief *About Us* paragraph touted Biocinium as a family-run enterprise; the *Research* page made vague promises about cutting-edge implants; vacancies for credentialed engineering and healthcare professionals promised exciting *Careers*.

"They don't even have products on the market yet!" Jonathan exclaimed. "How did April get blueprints for technologies that don't exist?"

"Maybe she didn't get them from Biocinium at all. I told you, this device looks too familiar." Opening the *Contact* page, Petra tapped the number for company headquarters.

"Are you going to call the customer service desk and ask about deals on ex-military research designs?" asked Jonathan, folding his arms.

"They're the customer." Someone picked up the line and Petra's voice turned silky, her eyes alight with schemes. "Good evening—I'd like to speak with your CEO about an endorsement opportunity."

8. BLINDED BY SCIENCE

And this is where they wanted to post me before the Coast Guard Yard went under!

Petra wrinkled her nose at industrial emissions creeping through the car's closed windows. Chemical silos streaked with guano jutted from the water where the river had chewed into the coastline. Flood barriers protected Curtis Bay's remaining refineries and trade yards, including the Biocinium semiconductor factory. Only two cars sat in the parking lot: a luxury SUV and a tiny electric hatchback. Pulling in between them, Petra hooked the handicapped tag onto her rearview mirror and approached the door.

A screen embedded near eye-level awakened. "Welcome to Biocinium Technologies," it greeted her in a smooth, synthesized voice. "How can we upgrade your life today?"

She looked straight into the concealed camera. "I have an appointment with Mr. Steven Simms."

The lens winked, capturing her photo, and an animated version of the caduceus logo spooled circuits around its staff. "Your meeting time is confirmed." Pneumatic doors opened into a sleek lobby. Frosted glass wall panels reflected Petra's movement in bright smears.

The auto-assistant's voice emanated from a metal column set where the reception desk might once have been. "Is there anything I can do to make your wait more comfortable?"

"Yeah—keep it short," said Petra, brushing a few wrinkles out of her suit pants. *These are falling off my ass! I must've lost a few more pounds since last time I had to wear them. Dammit, Mechanic, I need your help right now.* She slid a bobby pin from her hair—it was losing the battle against her bangs anyway—and clipped the waistband tighter around her hips.

"Ms. Arceneaux?"

Tugging her blouse back down, Petra turned. One of the panels had opened to reveal a ruddy-cheeked man with the look of an atrophied athlete. Broad shoulders still strained the expensive cloth of his suit, but his belt betrayed a slight paunch.

I bet he doesn't have to do field surgery on his pants with hair accessories! Petra leaned into her accent to ensure he'd underestimate her. "You must be Mr. Simms."

"Just Simms, please. My varsity years might be behind me, but I still like the feeling that I'm part of a team." He shook hands with a smile, crinkling the faint scar that bisected one eyebrow. "But I don't need to explain that to a military veteran. I was very interested to get your call! Please, come through."

He ushered Petra into an office redolent with fresh paint. Business trophies and framed photos cluttered the monolithic desk. Petra perched in a stylish armchair that still had plastic wrapped around its legs. *Lots of glitter, but no goods. How are they planning to pay for this shiny remodel?*

Simms sat across from her, swiveling back and forth in a chair that looked more suitable for a space station than an industrial park. "So you represent a veterans' healthcare group?"

Yeah—one living veteran, and a ship full of dead ones waiting to be avenged. "More of an advocacy network. I want future soldiers to have better treatment options for combat injuries than I did," said Petra, raising her gloved hand.

Awkward expressions skittered across Simms' face and settled on a sober pout. "I'm so sorry...ah...thank you for your service."

Petra interlocked her fingers in her lap, so she wouldn't punch him for the trite sentiment. "Recovery was my toughest battle. There weren't good bionic products available for what I needed." *Not legal ones, anyway.* For a moment the expensive desk became the registration counter in Ripken's emergency department, and a face haloed in red-gold hair bent to examine Petra's wounds.

"It must've hurt a lot, doing this yourself! Let's get you something for the pain first, then see about removing this implant. I don't know if I can save the device, but maybe I can save your eye..."

Petra swallowed to keep her throat open. "I found a solution, but others might not be so lucky, with all the new laws banning human performance modification."

"Don't get me started." Simms groaned. "The regulatory process has been a nightmare. We haven't gotten approval for a single medical trial."

"Why do you need one? Baltimore's so full of biohackers, it's like a citywide clinical study."

"Except that most of those people won't talk to corporate interests, no matter how well-intentioned. My wife—a former research nurse, now Biocinium's medical director—is liaising with the local user community, but it's a challenge." Simms smiled at a wedding photo tucked among his display.

"Especially since we have to overcome some unfortunate company history."

"What do you mean?" asked Petra, recalling Jonathan's tense remarks in Steel's workshop.

"Biocinium was founded decades ago, to cash in on the demand for domestic microchips. There was a lot of competition, but the CEO banked on an influx of rare-earth metals from the Arctic to drive down materials costs."

Petra indulged a thin smile. "Sorry we disappointed them."

"He was the disappointment, cutting safety corners to stay solvent." A practiced frown communicated Simms' official stance on that decision. "Karma bit him in the behind. His shortcuts exposed employees to dangerous chemicals, causing so many occupational health problems that they brought a class-action lawsuit against Biocinium. Settlements drove the company bankrupt. It couldn't even sell off assets because the industry bubble popped, so everything just sat around collecting dust."

"Doesn't sound like a prime business opportunity," said Petra.

Simms shrugged. "The missus and I acquired the place for almost nothing after the founder passed away last year. With her medical background and my business degree, we saw an opportunity to provide affordable consumer bionics. If the old Biocinium made people sick, the new one's purpose is to make them well."

Petra rolled her bad shoulder, and its audible pop made Simms jump. "That's a mission I can get behind."

"I'm relieved to hear it. Endorsement from veterans could help rehabilitate our brand, and show those stuffy regulators that our heroes deserve the best in biomedical technology!" Taking leaflets from a drawer, Simms slid one across the desk. "I hope you'll give us a chance to earn your group's support. It could mean the difference between Biocinium's second death, and a second life for people with unmet healthcare needs."

This guy could sell matches in a California wildfire zone. Petra unfolded the brochure. Sensational claims from the company website shone in glossy color. The inset photo froze the air in her lungs: a tiny chip strung with wires. Stifling a shudder, she stretched a smile across her face. "Maybe we could start with a look at some of your products."

"Of course! I should have taken you straight there, instead of rambling on. I'm so used to giving investment presentations that I've forgotten how to deal with people of action." Bouncing up, Simms ushered her back to the lobby, where another pair of glass panels revealed an elevator. He hit the button for the basement. "We have our own on-site R and D lab, state of the art. Hopefully our engineer is in today—he's just had a death in the family. If he's around, he can show you our flagship piece."

"What does it do?"

Eager teeth flashed in the full-length mirror. "I think a better question is, what *doesn't* it do!"

Doors opened on a dim, pipe-strung corridor reminiscent of an old ship passageway. Shadows took on humanoid shapes; skin crawling, Petra hurried after Simms. He swiped his badge to open a windowless cybernetics laboratory. Machine hums resonated in Petra's bones. Electronic components and energy drink cans left a trail across the workbenches, ending at a figure hunched over a micro-manipulator.

"Kade!" Simms' hearty hail turned waspish when he received no response. He strode over and clapped a hand on the other man's back. Kade spun, trendy sneakers squealing on the floor. He clawed a pair of audio buds from his ears.

"Dude! I've told you a hundred times not to do that when I'm working in the box. One wrong twitch and those fiber-optic filaments could…" Green eyes shifted to Petra, blinking at her through oversized glasses.

Mechanic's eyes! Oh, hell, this can't be…

"Petra Arceneaux, I'd like you to meet Kade McCormick, our chief biotechnology engineer," said Simms, in a tone that suggested the job title explained his employee's behavior.

"By 'chief' he means 'only'," said Kade. "Nobody else ever comes down here except the cleaning lady."

"Kade doesn't trust clumsy robots to bang around in a space full of sensitive equipment, so we bring in a custodian a few nights a week. It's one more example of how Biocinium is different from other companies—we're already giving back to the community by creating jobs for humans, not just machines! Just think of what we'll accomplish once we get enough preliminary data to justify a proper clinical study," said Simms, digging fingers into Kade's shoulder.

"If you want me to work faster, don't bring people in to distract me." Kade shrugged off his boss' hand and scowled at Petra. "Why are you here?"

"I'm evaluating how your products could help injured military personnel."

"Products? Plural?"

Redness deepened in Simms' face, and his showman's smile wavered. "He means we're currently maintaining a very focused portfolio."

"Translation—we've only got one thing." Kade tossed droopy hair from his forehead. "But it might be the only one anybody needs."

"Enough with the teasers!" Petra disguised her impatience with a laugh. "Do I get to see this wonder device?"

"Of course, it's…" A chime from Simms' pocket cut him off. He took out his phone, and the caller's number triggered a twitch in his cheek. "That's the other half of the enterprise. Kade, show our guest the Beat, will you? Excuse me, please —hey, babe! How's the market survey going?" The hallway swallowed the rest of his conversation.

Kade sagged in visible relief. Under the lab coat, he wore a graphic tee-shirt that showed silhouettes evolving from stooped apes to giant robots.

Like Mechanic's goofy taste in scrub patterns. A pulse of affinity toward the kid made Petra smile. "Your boss reminds me of a commander I had once. Always harassing us to 'impose cost' on our adversaries, even though he had no idea what that might actually involve. He just wanted his superiors to think he was doing something."

"Ugh, right? They don't get how complicated the work is." Kade patted the micro-manipulator. Stepping closer, Petra peered inside the box. A tiny chrome lozenge shone under the lights.

So that's what it looks like when it's not covered in blood. Revulsion and excitement quickened her breath. "This is…what did you call it? The Beat?"

"Short for Body Evaluation and Automated Therapy," said Kade proudly. "My most disruptive design ever."

Bull. This gadget powered the Sedna *massacre back when you were building solar matchbox cars for the high school science fair! No way you invented it.* Rubbing the tattoo on her temple, Petra turned from the Beat to its sup-posed creator. "How long have you been working on this?"

"Only about two months here at Biocinium, but I started development way before then."

"How'd you come up with the idea?"

"Would you believe it came to me in a dream?"

"No."

"Dang, that's a lot more epic," said Kade with a sheepish smile. "It just emerged out of theoretical work I encountered in my graduate program. A new twist on old concepts."

All that eye movement—he's lying about something. "What does it do?"

"'Restore the rhythm of life'." Kade traced an imaginary banner through the air. "Either that, or it's 'at the heart of your health.' I haven't decided on a slogan yet."

Petra crossed her arms. "Neither of those answer my question."

"Guess the military drilled out all your imagination." Heaving an exaggerated sigh, Kade reached for a pair of forceps. "It's a type of neural stimulator."

"Those have been around for years. Hardly cutting-edge."

"No, but I've improved the standard implementation. Instead of clunky pulse-generator discs, and batteries that need replacement or leak toxic chemicals, the Beat redirects current from your body's natural bioelectrical field. No more intrusive brain surgeries, either—these electrodes use bone conduction. Just insert them under the scalp." Picking up the device, Kade held it against Petra's ear to demonstrate its placement. She backed away so fast that she banged into a microscope; it wobbled on its stand. "Chill out, I just wanted to show you."

"So far all you've showed me is a fancy fishing lure." Petra slapped a hand on top of the instrument to steady it, and herself. "What does this Beat cure?"

"Depends on the brain region you target with the nodes." Kade indicated a dangling wire for each item as he listed it. "Psychological problems, nervous disorders, endocrine diseases…"

"…Adrenaline jolts to improve your speed or give you the edge in a fight." Frost-framed memories clouded Petra's vision, and she shook her head to melt them away.

Kade made a face. "Those things are hypothetically possible, but I hadn't planned to include them in the app."

"There's an app?"

"Duh. Putting patients back in control of their bodies is the whole point! After initial placement, they can modulate the Beat's function from a smartphone and manage their own therapy. Within parameters programmed by their health consultant, of course." Bounding over to the nearest computer, Kade pulled up an emulator and showed off a slick user interface. "The coolest part is an artificial intelligence component that lets the Beat adjust to your unique biological rhythms. If you've got something like epilepsy or asthma or anxiety, my algorithm learns the tiny physical clues that come before an attack, and takes preemptive steps to reduce severity."

"That's a lot of power for one little device," said Petra, poking the Beat with a finger. *And a lot of danger, if it's programmed the wrong way in the wrong heads.*

"Right? It'll be the biggest medical breakthrough since penicillin!" Excitement raised Kade's voice before it plummeted back to mumbled apathy. "At least, if we ever get it approved for use."

"Simms mentioned that you were having some trouble with that."

"Moronic review committees keep rejecting our applications for clinical studies. They claim it's because we haven't demonstrated a strong enough use case, but I think they're just afraid of new technology." Kade swatted an empty can off the desk. It clattered into a wastebasket full of identical siblings. "A bunch of unimaginative reactionaries, just like my old university faculty."

"What happened with them?"

"The Beat was my graduate research project, but my advisor…well, let's just say I wasn't about to get any grant money. I wanted to start my own company, but I needed capital, and all the investors I pitched were too squeamish about the anti-HPM legislation going around. No one wanted to take the risk, until my sister introduced me to Simms."

"How did she know him?" Petra's spine stiffened. *She never mentioned any biotech industry friends. Maybe she just didn't want Steel bugging her for prototypes.*

"She and Mrs. Simms worked on the same clinical trial a few years ago. When Mrs. S. quit to reboot Biocinium, she convinced April to help with the medical side of product development. But that stopped around the time I started working here. I guess April didn't want it to look like she was propping me up." Tears swam under Kade's glasses. "She always was my biggest supporter. Pulled me out of a hole after I left school, helped me find this gig, even let me live with her while I got settled in. I leaned on her for everything, and now she's *dead*." His sneaker lashed out at the wastebasket. Cans chattered across the floor like machine gun fire. Instinct threw Petra behind one of the monolithic instruments, pulse pounding in her throat.

"Sorry! I didn't mean to scare you!" Kade's flare of anger extinguished as suddenly as it had sparked. "I just lose it when I think that she's gone. It happened so fast that it doesn't even seem real."

"I know what you mean." Converting her cover move into a lunge for one of the cans, Petra began picking up the recyclables. "I wish I could tell you it gets easier, but the truth is you just get used to the hurt."

"Maybe I can configure the Beat to fix that."

"Fix what, being human?" Petra twisted a pull tab in her fingers; the bite of rough metal affirmed her flesh. "That's a terminal condition."

"Only until we invent a cure." Kade slam-dunked a bottle, cast Petra a confident grin, and turned back to his workbench. Taking the hint, she went back upstairs. Simms ambushed her in the lobby with handshakes and enthusiasm. She uttered non-committal assurances through a smile that felt brittle enough to crack her lips:

"Yes, very impressive." *Impressive that the kid downstairs managed to steal a classified military prototype.*

"Yes, relevant to veterans' interests." *It got dozens of them killed, and their own brass covered it up.*

"Yes, I'll be in touch." *Once I figure out how Mechanic was mixed up with your shady little company.*

Extricating herself at last, Petra fled into the afternoon heat. Her heart struggled to regain an even tempo. Rather than bake in traffic, she walked along the waterfront. Wind cooled her flushed face, but a headache blossomed as she dredged her memory for clues. No new treasures emerged from the neural sediment. She dialed her phone on the way back to the car.

"How'd it go?" asked Jonathan on the other end.

"More questions than answers." Unlocking the trunk, Petra shifted aside Mechanic's backpack—she hadn't known what else to do with her dead friend's potentially incriminating possessions—and dug through her own go-bag for a better-fitting pair of pants. "Got any police pals who might do you a favor?"

The drone of an automated dispatcher in the background added tension to the pause. "Why?"

"I need a look at some surveillance footage."

A relieved chuckle warmed her ear. "If that's all, I know just the person."

9. YOUNG BLOOD

"Hey, Rowell! We're gonna find a bar to watch the game tonight. Come with, so we can order pitchers."

"The only pitcher he'll drink is milk. Daddy's warming it up for him right now."

"Nah, he's stirring in the chocolate syrup," Jonathan replied without looking up from the ambulance's tires. The firefighters' predictable banter registered as ambient noise, like the thumping car stereo in the street outside the station and the muffled clatter in the rig as Evans restocked supplies.

She leaned around the vehicle's back door to peer at him. "Why do they tease you like that every day?"

Jonathan pried a tarry pebble from the treads. "Because my dad lives with me. He's got a lot of health problems and can't stay on his own."

"And they think that's a bad thing? I wish I could've spent that kind of time with my father. He died last year. Heart attack."

"Sorry to hear it. I know how hard it is to lose someone unexpectedly." *Although watching them leak away one memory at a time might be worse.*

Evans sat down on the bumper with a sigh. "It wasn't all that unexpected. He'd been fading for years, ever since his business went under. I think his spirit withered away with his work."

"What happened to his job?" The music's crescendo drowned Jonathan's question. Irritated, he stood up to confront the driver. A vintage coupe blocked the garage, graphite paint tinted ruby in the sunset. Dress boots swung out from the driver's door, followed by frayed jeans and a slim-cut oxford shirt buttoned all the way up to Petra's smirk.

She called over the song's falsetto screams. "Get in, Jonathan, I've got a more important job for you than counting band-aids."

The firefighters gawked. Jonathan's shoes seemed to have melted into the floor. Only Evans remained unimpressed. "What are you doing here?" she asked.

"Your partner wouldn't look at my bum shoulder when he was off-duty." Petra gave an exaggerated shrug and winked at Jonathan. His ears burned, remembering his remark in the diner. "So I thought I'd catch him on the clock."

Evans folded her arms. "We're not an emergency room."

"Doesn't mean he can't play doctor," Fisher snickered, eyes whizzing between Jonathan and Petra so rapidly that they blurred.

Jonathan ignored him and took Evans aside, scrambling for fragments of truth. "She was a patient of April's, but she...she doesn't like hospitals. Remember how she took off before getting treatment? I offered to help, for April's sake. Compassion is part of the job."

"Yes, she looks totally distraught." Evans glared at Petra, who had slid back behind the wheel and was using it as a drum kit.

"People grieve in different ways." Jonathan dove for the time clock before his coworkers could probe any further. He jumped into the car and didn't exhale until the station disappeared in the rearview mirror. "You shouldn't have done that," he told Petra.

"What, stop that jackass firefighter from harassing you?"

"I don't need you to rescue me from Fisher, thanks."

"Someone needs to, since you won't do it yourself. He was heckling you when I walked by the other day, too. Why do you let him get away with it?"

"It wasn't that bad until a few months ago. But he's got a sick kid at home, and has been picking up a lot of extra hours to cover the medical bills. He's probably so strung out on energy drinks that he doesn't even know what he's saying." Jonathan tapped the rim of a jumbo drive-through lemonade jammed in the cupholder. "The more he razzes me, the more I feel sorry for him."

Grey eyes flicked from the road to his face. "Was your med school program in psychiatry?"

"No. People just tell you a lot, when you stop listening to what comes out of their mouths."

"You should've come to Biocinium with me and analyzed those creeps. The CEO's oilier than the gulf after hurricane season," said Petra, poking out her tongue in disgust. "And then there's Mechanic's little brother."

"He works there?" Jonathan sat up so straight that his seat belt locked. "I never met him, but April mentioned he'd moved in with her after getting a job with a local tech company. What's he doing with a crooked operation like that?"

"Making a bid to earn his sister's nickname. He claims he invented this thing." Petra pulled a brochure out of the glove box and dropped it in Jonathan's lap.

He studied the cover. "This is the same flyer I found in Dr. Bhagat's office!"

"I bet Mechanic brought it to the hospital, hoping to promote her brother's career." Petra related her interview while rush-hour traffic crawled around the harbor. "Mechanic never mentioned anything to you about a side gig?"

"No, but she never mentioned playing doctor for Baltimore's biohacker underground, either."

"Because it was illegal, which makes me think that whatever she was doing with Biocinium was the same. Kade is hiding something, too."

"What makes you say that?"

"I'm good at reading micro-expressions," said Petra, a little too breezily. "Plus, he's younger than me, which means he was just a teenager when *Sedna* went down. He can't have designed that so-called Beat himself."

"Biocinium's owners must've stolen it, then exploited some desperate student to claim it was original. Another bid to screw over sick people." Jonathan tossed the brochure on top of the dashboard.

Petra tilted her head back and forth, considering. "I dunno. Simms strikes me as a mediocre corporate bullshitter, not a mastermind of industrial espionage."

"Then how did your classified technology become his flagship product? And how did it end up in April's skull?"

"I might be able to answer the second one, if you can get me surveillance footage from the marina," said Petra, pulling into the turn lane.

"You're going the wrong way for that."

"I thought we were going to see your police pals!"

"I'm not going to waste favors on something this easy." Jonathan pointed down the other street. "Head to the diner."

"Why, does the karaoke machine interface with Baltimore's traffic cameras?" The light turned green, and Petra cut across the intersection. Angry drivers leaned on their horns. One almost shaved off the coupe's bumper.

"*Al'ama!*" Petra launched a barrage of multilingual expletives out the window: English and Arabic seasoned with Louisiana French, and a few words that sounded Russian.

"What does that mean?" asked Jonathan, wavering between amusement and alarm.

"Literally, *blindness,* but the slang use is more like *dammit.*" She stilled the palm-shaped amulet swinging from her rearview mirror. "It was my Jordanian mother's favorite curse word."

"Was she a refugee from the river war?"

"No, a soldier in it. That's where she met my dad, the G.I. Joe. They were allied forces in the West Bank."

"Is that why they named you after the ancient city?"

"A name with the strength to survive droughts, floods, and earthquakes." Petra's words had the cadence of catechism, learned from the cradle. Laughter punctuated her recitation. "Thanks to climate change, I've checked off centuries' worth of natural disasters in about thirty years."

"Which one was the worst so far?" asked Jonathan, curiosity overtaking his annoyance with her.

Gloved fingers gripped the wheel. "The unnatural one."

Before he could ask anything else, the car purred into the alley behind the Dapọ Diner. Petra climbed out, then caught the door and clenched her eyes shut.

"Are you all right?" Paramedic habits brought Jonathan to her side.

"Just a little dizzy. Too much heat shimmer on the roads." She peeked at her right wrist, but yanked the cuff back down when Jonathan approached, and hurried ahead of him into the restaurant. Its proprietress bustled around the counter, orchestrating dinner service.

"Hey, Grace," Jonathan called. "Where's Del?"

"Napping. They went to school in person today! Came home exhausted, but happier than I'd seen them in weeks. They promised to help with dinner, though." Grace glanced up at the ceiling, radiance fading to worry. "I've tried calling and texting, but they don't answer."

"Probably just turned the phone off to sleep. I'll go wake them." Wheeling around, Jonathan went back out to the Njokus' apartment.

"I thought we were gonna get video evidence?" Petra followed him up the stairs at a distrustful distance. "If you're trying to pull a fast one on me…"

"No surveillance system is more watchful than a house-bound teenaged hacker," Jonathan assured her, unlocking the apartment with his spare key. Colorful textiles dazzled his vision after hours in the smog-greyed city.

"I take it this is the same Del who runs karaoke night?" Petra fingered a sequined jacket draped beside the sewing machine. "I liked that kid."

"Why, because they said you were cool?"

"Because they said you weren't."

"Little siblings can be big brats, even when they're not genetically related."

"Try having two." A chuckle caught in Petra's throat and she turned away, inspecting the empty kitchen.

Jonathan knocked gently on Del's bedroom door. "Del? Time to get up. Your mom needs you downstairs." He tried again, then peeked inside. A mussed but empty bed stood beneath the window. Del's laptop lay shut on the desk. "Dammit, they must've snuck out again! Let's try the skate park down the street, or the overpass by the stadium. The way you drive, we can still get them home before Grace—."

Petra's fingers gripped his elbow.

"What?" he asked. She tapped her ear in reply. Jonathan focused his own hearing: traffic outside, murmurs from the diner below, the air system rattling behind the walls. "I don't hear anything."

Petra crept across the room. Shifting into a defensive stance, she paused for a heartbeat, then kicked open the bathroom door. Another Arabic curse echoed off the porcelain.

Jonathan burst in after her and drew a jagged breath. Del slumped against the sink, a red-speckled washcloth on their shoulder. History held up a ghoulish mirror: blood smeared across the bathtub, stained towels draped over a limp form, fixtures amplifying a child's scream...

"Hey! Medic!" Petra's sharp voice yanked him back from the maw of memory. She crouched beside Del, fingers pressed against their neck. "Help me, or call someone who can."

Training took over. Jonathan knelt and ran through the usual checks. A strong but erratic pulse fluttered under his fingertips. The teenager's thin chest shuddered with each rise and escaped in weak murmurs. "How did you hear that over all the background noise?"

"I have very sensitive ears. Looks like Del does, too." Petra held up a crimson-stained glove tip. Dark liquid dripped from beneath Del's hair wrap.

"They must've had a bad asthma attack, fallen, and cracked their head," said Jonathan.

"With all this padding?" Unwinding the turban, Petra exposed a patch of gauze around Del's ear, where the long braids had been shaved away. She peeled back the bandage and hissed. Ointment shone around a line of neat stitches. A slight bulge hinted at something beneath the skin.

Jonathan fought the urge to pry it out with his fingernails. "Who the hell did this?"

"Someone professional," murmured Petra, examining the incision. "It's decent work."

"There's nothing decent about cutting up a kid!" Jonathan grabbed a throw blanket from the other room and wrapped it around Del's shoulders to ward off shock. "Call an ambulance, then go downstairs and get Grace."

Petra's brisk field report to the automated dispatcher reprised the call to April's deathbed: "There's an unconscious teenager with a head wound…"

A door slid open down the hall, and Grace leapt up from the waiting room chair. "Is that Ayodele?"

Jonathan craned his neck toward the emergency surgery ward. "Just an orderly with an empty stretcher."

"But they've been in there for ages."

"Not really." Twisting his watch around, Jonathan showed her how much time had actually passed since the ambulance crew whisked Del into surgery.

Grace spun the dial away and gripped his hand. "Where would anyone get the awful idea to slice themselves open like that?"

"Del showed me some biohacking videos the other day, but I thought it was just another geeky internet trend that caught their attention. I never imagined they'd try it." Jonathan dropped his head back against the wall. Pain shot through the bruise from his fall at the marina. He absorbed it with clenched teeth, thinking of the stitches around Del's ear. "I should have done more to stop it. I'm sorry."

"I don't blame you, Jonathan. I don't even blame Ayodele—they've been so frustrated stuck inside that they'd try any crazy remedy. But whoever sells those gadgets to children, takes their money, cuts their skin? I would hold open the door to hell for them myself." Grace's features hardened into a baleful mask. Another door whined. She looked up again, then slumped back in her seat. "You know I've never been away from them longer than the length of a school day? The sun has never set on my baby without me kissing them goodnight."

"Del's sixteen, Grace. Not a baby anymore."

"They'll always be *my* baby. Do you know what the name Ayodele means? 'Joy has come home.' We tried so hard for them. I'd miscarried five times, because of all the air pollution back in Nigeria. So when breathing damaged those little lungs before they were even old enough to speak..." Grace shook her head, earrings clacking. "We couldn't afford three tickets, so I went first with the baby while my husband kept working. He planned to send money, and meet us here once I'd established our business. But he died in a flood just a few months after I left. I thought about jumping in the harbor and joining him, then and for years after, but that would leave my little one with nobody. I promised myself I'd never let my child be alone, like I was."

"You never told me that part of the story," Jonathan murmured.

"Why would I? You're my baby, too," said Grace, resting her head on his shoulder. "A kid working his way through school didn't need my troubles. He needed a safe apartment to rent and a fridge full of restaurant leftovers."

Jonathan acknowledged the debt with a one-armed hug. "I was lucky to have a backup mom, since the original one crashed."

A punitive slap stung his leg. "How can someone with a heart as big as yours not find room in it to forgive his own parent?"

"Maybe it's at max capacity trying to take care of the one who stuck around."

"Then you need an upgrade." Grace stared when he started laughing. "What's funny?"

"You sound like someone I met the other day."

Slyness shone through the worry in her eyes. "That new lady friend of yours?"

"She's not a friend."

"Who but a friend would have stayed with your father while you came here with us?"

"No one else was available on short notice." Jonathan curled and uncurled his fists in his lap. "Anything was better than dragging him to the hospital—he hates being in here—but I still don't like leaving him with someone I hardly know."

"Well, you'll know her better very soon, because I'm inviting her to dinner when this is all over, to say thank-you. If it hadn't been for her…" Shuddering, Grace hitched up a feeble smile. "Besides, she's much too skinny, and that's one medical problem I do know how to treat."

Orthotic shoes clopped into the waiting area. "Mrs. Njoku?"

Grace jumped up, twisting her hands. "Ayodele…?"

"Is stable and awake. I think they fainted more from low blood pressure than from any effect of that device." Dr. Bhagat gave Jonathan a reluctant nod. "It's fortunate you warned the EMS crew about it, Rowell, or imaging might have ripped it from the skull."

Grace clutched Jonathan's arm so hard that her nails dented flesh. "Did you remove it?"

"Yes, and I don't anticipate any lasting damage. We'll keep Ayodele overnight for observation, but I'm confident they'll recover in a few days with some rest and vitamins." Bhagat led them to a small patient room. Braids fanned across the pillow on one side of Del's head; bandages swathed the other.

"You know the good thing about being stuck in the house all the time?" A woozy grin crossed Del's face. "You can't ground me."

Giggles fractured into grunts as Grace seized their bony shoulders. "What were you thinking, cutting a hole in your head?"

"That I was sick of seeing the world through a window or a computer screen!" Del's fingers furrowed the thin hospital blanket. "What kind of life is that?"

"One where you stay alive!" Grace sank onto the cot and embraced her child.

Del hugged her back. "I'm sorry I scared you, Mama. I thought you'd worry *less* if I could breathe better."

"How on Earth was this supposed to help?" asked Bhagat, pulling a sample container from her coat pocket. A tiny object rattled inside. Jonathan gasped.

That's the same device Petra showed me, the one she found on April! If Biocinium hasn't put them on the market yet, where did Del find another?

Del's voice, tired but adamant, repeated the explanation given to Jonathan a few days earlier: "…Vagus nerve stimulation…control bronchial constriction…"

Jonathan laid a hand on their arm. "There are safe, effective medications for that."

"And if any of them worked, I wouldn't be in the hospital again."

"I noticed that you've been admitted before, for asthma complications." Tapping the bedside computer console, Bhagat pulled up Del's chart. "You even participated in an outpatient clinical study here several years ago, is that correct?"

"Yeah. We all got these smartwatches that measured stuff like breath rate and blood oxygen, and crunched the numbers against air quality data to predict attacks." Del twisted the patient identity band that now adorned their wrist instead. "Mine just went crazy every time I went outside."

Bhagat sniffed. "Good intentions, but poor implementation. Not unlike the resident who set up the program."

April. Jonathan glared at the doctor. "Were you hoping to cancel her along with the study when you took charge?"

"I only hoped to protect our patients from the risks of underdeveloped biomedical technology. Surely even a paramedic can see why," said Bhagat, scowling at the neural chip. "Where did this come from?"

"Three months of restaurant tips." Del extended an upturned palm. "Can I have my property back, please?"

"I'm sorry, but I'm required to turn over all unauthorized bionic products to the police."

"Is Ayodele going to get arrested?" asked Grace, squeezing the teenager's hand until they winced.

"No. We can't report the identities of anyone underage. But there may be follow-up questions about where the device came from, which we can submit anonymously on your behalf."

"I can speak for myself, thanks. And believe me, I've got a lot to say." Del met the doctor's look with limpid fury.

"We'll talk about it before you're discharged tomorrow and you can say all you like," said Bhagat, in a tone that made no promise of listening. But she paused on her way out. "I'll also review your current asthma medications. Perhaps I can recommend some alternatives."

"Which we can't afford," Del muttered when the door shut.

"Oh, but you can spend your tips on this?" Grace fingered the bandages.

"I got a good deal."

Kneeling beside the bed, Jonathan looked Del in the face and asked the question that had been seething in his chest for hours. "Where?"

10. HEAVY METAL POISONING

"You sure can pack it away for such a skinny girl," said Hank, scooping a third helping of leftover jollof rice into Petra's bowl.

"I'm active. I burn a lot of calories." She shoveled her mouth full to distort any traitorous expressions. Fortunately, the old man seemed more amused than suspicious. "Plus, this is delicious. Reminds me of my Dad's dirty rice."

"And my wife's *locrito de pollo*. People like to think they're all different, but no matter where you go in the world, we're all eating chicken and rice." Chuckling, Hank carried the dishes to the sink and doused them with detergent. "Me and Jonathan used to make her recipe every weekend after she died, trying to get it just the way she did. Never quite managed it, but he got to be a pretty good cook. Grace was glad to get him."

"He worked in the diner?"

"Tuition costs a fortune, and scholarships didn't cover everything. I got a good factory job after his mother died, but had to quit when I got sick. Now I can hardly give him anything." The sponge wailed against wet stoneware. "Study all day, service all night…I'm proud of him for going to med school, but I worry about the stress."

Petra grabbed a towel, buying time to craft an ambiguous reply. "Yeah, I can see that he takes a lot on himself." In the past few hours keeping Hank company, she'd sidestepped many such cracks in the old man's reality. *It's like his brain is stuck on an operating system ten years out of date. If that happens to me, I'll be riding the ice with Seventeen forever!* A shiver almost cost her the dripping plate in her hands; she dried it and set it in the rack. "Does he ever have any fun?"

"He used to play guitar—I taught him when he was barely taller than the instrument—but I haven't seen him touch the thing in months." Hank indicated a vintage acoustic-electric model in the corner of the sitting area. "Doubt it's even in tune."

With a nod of permission from her host, Petra picked up the guitar and wiped off a velvet layer of dust. Curved wood cradled her body.

"Been a while since I held one of these," she murmured. Old neural pathways sparked, sliding her left hand up the neck. She plucked a few notes, winced at the slight sourness, and tuned the strings by ear.

"You play?" asked Hank, easing himself into the armchair.

"Not anymore." Petra twisted one of the knobs, winding up her courage with the wire. "I lost a couple of fingers in combat. Prostheses are okay for gripping doorknobs and hairbrushes and beer bottles, but they're not responsive enough for music." She wiggled the gloved digits, demonstrating their stiffness.

"From what I heard the other night, you've still got a fine instrument." Hank rapped his sternum. "Sing something!"

"I'll need backup." Petra settled the tuned guitar in his lap. Tremulous fingers spread across the fretboard. Tentative chords rang through the small apartment. The familiar pattern caught Petra's ears—a rollicking rock classic that had often set the rhythm of her swab on *Wind of Change*. Adjusting her volume for an indoor environment, she jumped into the lyrics. Hank's hands gathered speed and strength as he progressed through the verses.

Get deep enough into the music, and for a few minutes you can forget that you're falling apart. Petra's throat closed, choking off her voice. Her accompanist looked up, puzzled; she danced across the rug to hide her face. The final chorus unraveled into flourishes and laughter.

Quiet applause came across the room. Petra whirled. Jonathan stood in the doorway, wearing a very different expression from when he'd recognized her on the diner's karaoke stage. Heat crept up her neck.

"Is Del okay?" she asked, tugging down her sleeves.

"Yeah. They'll be discharged in the morning."

"Hallelujah," Hank murmured, and plucked out an iconic arpeggio to emphasize the sentiment.

Jonathan stared at the old man's fingers with a disbelieving smile. "That's really good, Dad."

"Might be if my calluses weren't all gone. I won't be much use to Grace in the kitchen tomorrow if my fingertips are more tenderized than the meat." He held out the instrument. "Your turn. Give the girl something she can sing to."

"I don't remember any songs."

Petra laughed. "Just play four chords and leave the rest to me."

"I doubt I can even manage that much." Jonathan flexed his hands and sighed. "I haven't played anything in ages."

"Why not?"

"No time for it. Music doesn't save lives."

"Don't be so sure." Savoring the guitar's glossy wood, Petra returned it to the stand and moved toward the door.

"Can you hang around for a few minutes?" Tension thrummed beneath Jonathan's casual words. "We need to talk."

Hank whistled. "I can take a hint. I'll shuffle off to bed and let you kids have some privacy."

Rolling his eyes, Jonathan herded the old man into the bathroom. Tile smudged their voices into a strange duet, the son's weary directives and the father's muffled replies:

"Did you take your tablets?"

"Poor substitute for an after-dinner mint. They could at least coat them in chocolate."

"Keep making that joke and maybe the pharmaceutical company will—whoa, that's not toothpaste, Dad, that's antibacterial cream."

"Well, you must've left it in the wrong place. Anyone might've grabbed it by mistake."

Home is just a second shift. Doesn't the poor guy ever get a break from taking care of people? Petra fiddled on the guitar, forcing her false fingers into chord shapes until Jonathan emerged from his bedroom. He'd swapped his work uniform for jeans and a plain t-shirt, accessorized with a frown at Petra's startled look.

"What?" he asked, glancing at his fly.

She shook her head. "It's always a little weird the first time you see your shipmates in civvies."

"I didn't want Baltimore City EMS implicated in tomorrow's headline—Man Found Pulverized in Dumpster Outside Cyborg Piercing Parlor."

A wrong note squawked. "You're going to see Steel? Why?"

"Because he's the one who gave Del that implant. They just admitted that instead of going to school today, they visited Heavy Metal." Throwing himself into a chair, Jonathan laced up a pair of worn sneakers. "And that's not all. The device they got installed is just like the one you found on April."

Dizziness smacked Petra again; she clutched the guitar's neck. "Can't be. Steel said he destroyed all the templates. I've got the only device outside of Biocinium's lab."

"I'm going to see about that. Can you geezer-sit a little longer?"

"Not if it means letting you run off to pick a fight with Steel!" Metal creaked, and the A-string snapped under Petra's finger. Her heart faltered. They both stared at the broken wire.

"I'm just going to ask him some questions, not challenge him to a duel," said Jonathan in a soft, startled tone.

"Same thing in his world." Petra set down the instrument and stood. "I'm coming with you."

"Why? From what I saw at the marina, you don't exactly have a way with him."

"No, but I'm a smaller target." Balancing on each foot to pull on her shoes, she hopped in time with a song that drifted through Hank's closed door. "What about your dad?"

"He'll sleep solid for a few hours after staying up so much later than usual. He'll be fine." Furrows in Jonathan's brow as he locked up contradicted his assurances. "Normally Grace and I trade off—she lets Dad help out in the diner while I'm on shift, and I keep an eye on Del when she goes to her night job."

"Sounds like you're practically family." Petra ducked into her car, turning up the stereo to cover a wistful sigh.

"It happens when you see each other every day for a decade. I worked in the restaurant to help cover med school tuition, and the apartment here was cheaper than the dorms. Grace gave me a break on rent for tutoring Del—they were too sick to attend school in-person most of the time, but so damn smart that they got bored with the video classes." Jonathan's smile shrank with the restaurant in the rearview mirror. "After Dad got sick, he crashed with me a lot for easy access to the hospital. Eventually we had to sell his house to cover the medical bills, and things just…stuck."

"The arrangement got stuck, or you did?"

"Both, I guess. The twenty-three-year-old student who moved in would never have believed he'd still be there ten years later."

"Where did he expect to be?"

"Leading a social medicine program to help people in this tidewater swamp deal with climate-related health problems. Government and industry try to downplay the issues, but I've seen what happens when the environment changes, and the way we live in it doesn't." City lights cast shifting patterns across Jonathan's face. "I wanted to do something about it. Not just patch up people who were already sick, but figure out how to keep them well in the first place."

"You wanted to be Mechanic!"

"I wanted to be a lot of things."

"And long-term caregiver wasn't one of them?" Brooding silence confirmed the guess. Petra charted a careful course to her next question. "You said your dad worked at the old Biocinium factory…and Simms told me it went bankrupt when a lot of employees got sick and sued."

"Typical class-action racket where the only winners were the lawyers," muttered Jonathan. "The settlement didn't even cover Dad's medical bills, much less the full-time care he needs now. So I quit school to work and look after him. Or what's left of him."

"Seems like quite a bit, from what I saw. He remembered all the chords to that song."

"But not what year it is, or whether he's taken his medication, or which jar has throat drops versus detergent pods."

"Or how much his son gave up to take care of him." Petra spoke the implied grievance aloud.

Jonathan gave a stiff shrug. "He did it for me."

"So that you could have a good life!"

"Who says I don't?"

"Chasing stolen bionics around Baltimore with an amnesiac vet doesn't exactly scream fulfillment."

"I just don't want anyone else to get hurt."

"There you go again—anyone else." Petra bopped the horn twice, punctuating the last two words as she warned off a jaywalker. "When do you do anything for yourself?"

Reluctant laughter rumbled with the engine. "Whenever I even think about that, life sabotages me. I wanted to take some advanced skills courses at work, but they assigned me a trainee. I wanted to ask April on a real date, but..." Her ghost materialized at the end of the sentence, haunting the space between them. A fiery guitar solo thawed the quiet. "I'd be happy just to pick up my guitar again, but all I shred these days is ambulance tires," said Jonathan, and turned up the volume. Downtown's busy brilliance faded into dark, grilled storefronts. Parking beneath the molten glow of Heavy Metal's neon sign, Petra hammered on the door until it opened.

Steel's gargantuan shadow spilled onto the sidewalk. "Parlor's closed, Rock."

"And the real business just opened." She ducked under his arm and went into the workshop. Last time she'd ignored the row of 3D printers humming on the counter; now she inspected their output. Although half-formed, the device on each stage was unmistakably a knockoff Beat. Heavy footsteps sounded behind her, and she rounded on Steel. "You said Mechanic made you destroy the templates after you finished her chip."

Steel moved her beyond reach of the equipment. "Got new blueprints."

"From who?"

"I know people."

"Like that 'brat' you worked on the night Mechanic died?"

"Tried to work on, you mean. The junky neurostimulator they brought in fell apart when we tried to install it. Mechanic decided it wasn't safe to use." Steel loaded fresh filament in one of the printers. "The kid kept trying to argue about it. Seemed pretty desperate. When I hauled them out of the cabin, they offered me specs for a better piece of gear in exchange for the first copy."

"*Del* gave you the blueprints?" asked Jonathan, storming through the door.

"I never ask my clients' real names. But I remember them all. This one had long braids and short patience."

"So you just gave a teenager a goddamn brain implant?"

"Hey, if someone comes into the parlor and wants a spike through their nipple or a unicorn tattooed on their forehead, it's not my job to tell them it's a bad idea." Stooping, Steel assessed the machines' work with a critical eye. "I just give them what they want. Pure business."

Two steps brought Jonathan within inches of the larger man's nose. "Your 'business' put Del in the hospital."

"That's a user error, not a device malfunction. No one else has reported a bug."

Every muscle in Petra's body tensed. "Who else? You sold more of these things?"

"Mechanic said she'd report me if I did that." A mischievous grin twisted Steel's mouth. "But she never said anything about promotional giveaways. I had to print a couple of test pieces to get hers right. Why waste material? I cleaned 'em up and gave them to some customers as limited-edition exclusives. As-is, of course—use at your own risk, Heavy Metal disclaims all liability."

Petra stared at the printers. Liquid threads seemed to construct a humanoid figure around each device; she blinked, and the metallic army swarmed out toward the street. Words creaked through her dry lips. "These are out in the wild?"

"Relax, it's just a little neurochemical jump-starter. What's the worst that can happen?"

The answer burst across Petra's mind in gory spatters of memory. Panic twitched through her nerves. Her left arm knocked Steel aside and swept the counter. Equipment crashed to the floor, spraying her shoes with titanium alloy.

Rough hands seized her. "What the hell is wrong with you, Rock?"

"Wrong with *me?* I'm not the one distributing untested brain tech!"

"It's not untested—Mechanic did just fine with it. Maybe you oughta try it, too. Tighten up some of those loose screws rattling around in your skull." Steel steered her toward the surgical chair. "Still got her old chip? I'll reconfigure it for you. You want it wired to the amygdala for your anger management problem, or your hippocampus to zap away those old war stories?"

Combat training ignited. Petra broke the hold and spun around to spar with Steel. Even without the exoskeleton, he had advantages: a foot of extra height and at least two hundred pounds. Gravity enhanced his blows. Petra danced between them, landing quick hits to joints and kidneys. Broad knuckles grazed her chin. She staggered back into a more pliant pair of hands.

"Do I need to get Corporal Duke back here with her taser?" Jonathan tried to pull Petra away from the fight, but she launched herself at Steel. Without his suit, he couldn't dodge. She drove her elbow into his gut. Steel stumbled. Leveraging his imbalance, Petra body-slammed him with every ounce of force she could summon. The impact knocked him backward into the surgical chair. She knelt on the padded arms to glower down at him.

"You cannot let these things loose in the city," she snarled. "This isn't some innocent little RFID chip or glucose monitor. It warps people's minds. It's dangerous."

"But valuable." Steel's retort gurgled away when Petra's gloved hand clamped around his collar.

"More so than Del's life? Or April's?" Jonathan asked. Overhead lights turned his eyes into inscrutable hollows. "That's what happened, isn't it? Del offered you the means to make these gadgets again, but you knew April would ruin the racket if she found out. So you went back in the cabin and killed her."

"And leave a body on board for JAG here to find?" Steel tried to shake free of Petra, but she clenched the handful of shirt fabric until its fibers crackled. "There are easier ways to solve personnel problems than murder."

"Like handing out brain grenades?" asked Petra, nodding at the wrecked Beat factory. "Did you sabotage the chip you gave her?"

"After she finally agreed to try an upgrade? Hell, no. That would've been terrible advertising. I was careful to do it right. And she had it for months without a problem. Even you didn't notice. Course, your system seems to be running a little slow these days." A smirk dimpled Steel's fleshy cheeks. Petra shook it off, and he held up his palms in supplication. "Not that I'm much good myself without my suit. We both need repair funds. Tell you what—the merch you just trashed cost about as much as my bail, so let's call it even. I'll crank out some new chips and give you a cut."

"They've cut me enough already." Petra poked a finger into Steel's neck rolls, making him wheeze. "And it'll do the same to a lot more people if it gets around. Once a few of your customers turn up dead, how long do you think biohackers will keep buying parts from you?"

Comprehension shrank Steel's pupils. Vinyl pads groaning beneath him, he sat up and flung aside Petra's arm. Pain seared through her shoulder. She clutched it, hissing.

"That joint still needs to heal," said Jonathan.

"It's fine." Either he believed her, or didn't want to get in striking distance, because he hung back against the wall. *Great. Just when I get him to cooperate, he sees me in a little scrap and thinks I'm a battle droid.*

"If it's giving you a problem, just replace it," said Steel. Opening one of the workshop's large storage lockers, he poked through a rack of secondhand prosthetic arms. "I don't have your size in stock, but I can source one for you."

"Is that your business model? Injure people, then sell them spare parts?" Jonathan slammed the locker shut, just missing Steel's fingers. "Even your excellent public defender would have a hard time explaining that. Tae might be my friend, but I'll still testify against you."

"I'm not worried about one pathetic organic."

"How about a whole jury full of pathetic organics?" said Petra, kneading the shoulder until sensation returned. Aches spread through her entire body. "If anything happens to that kid in the hospital, you can't blame it on Mechanic. You traded the black-market hardware *after* she died."

"What the hell choice did I have, Rock?" Steel sagged against the counter, looking as sore as she felt. He grabbed a power drill and used it to massage his lower back. "I gotta pay my court fees, get a new exoskeleton, and keep this place afloat without charters or Mechanic's referrals. Where am I gonna get the money?"

"Nipple spikes and unicorn tattoos," said Jonathan. Kicking aside the printer wreckage, he stalked out of the workshop.

Steel glared after him. "Why are you running around with that uptight city stooge, Rock?"

"Pure business," she quipped, and limped after Jonathan. Space bent around her. Her eyes, usually sharp even in low light, fought for focus. She dragged a hand along the wall to find the main room.

Jonathan's voice rumbled through the dark. "Give me one reason not to call the cops on him right now."

"Because we might still need him. Nobody on the East Coast has more connections in the bionics black market. And even though he's a greedy, selfish jerk most of the time, I don't think he hurts anyone on purpose."

"He could have killed Del with that contraption!"

"They're the one who gave him the blueprint. If you want the person responsible, we need to find out where Del got it." Petra groped for the door handle and staggered out of the parlor. Streetlights dazzled her eyes with agony. She hid her face against the façade, inhaling the cool scent of brick.

"What's wrong?" Jonathan asked.

"Nothing." Shoving back her cuff, she grimaced at the dark brand on her wrist. *Nothing new, anyway.*

"Just because your shoulder is back in the socket doesn't mean you can start throwing hooks. You need to go to the ER."

"There's nobody left there who can help me." Petra tried to walk away, but her feet had gone numb. The world spun crooked on its axis. Clutching the nearest traffic pole, she slid down to the sidewalk. *Pale squares like ice floes. No matter the latitude, I'm going to die on a cold, hard island.*

But instead of Seventeen's corpse, it was Jonathan who knelt beside her, phone pressed to his cheek.

A robotic voice spoke through the earpiece. "Nine one one, what is your emergency?"

"I said no!" Petra slapped his arm. The phone skittered across the oncoming headlights of a police car. Tires slowed. Dread cleared the fog around Petra's mind. Tipping back her head, she belted out: "Take me home toniiiiight…"

"What are you doing?" Jonathan cast nervous glances at the car.

Brain communication chips would be handy right now! She dug fingernails into his arm and sang the lyric again. The police car rolled down its window.

Jonathan spoke in a loud, exasperated voice. "I tried to take you home three drinks ago, but no, you had to keep partying until the bartender cut you off."

Limp with relief, Petra permitted him to slide an arm beneath her shoulders and hoist her off the ground. Erratic heartbeats slammed against her ribs. "I don't wan-na let you goooo…"

"You'd better not, unless you want to collapse in the gutter. Although a cold bath might do you good."

The police car slid past, seeking more novel prey than a beleaguered wingman and his drunk companion. Both of them exhaled when it turned the corner.

"Nice improvisation," Jonathan murmured.

"Nice harmony. For a second I was afraid you might flag them down for a ride."

"I don't know every officer in Baltimore." Opening the coupe's passenger door, he deposited Petra in the shotgun seat. "There are a few I trust, but most of them look at me a lot differently when I'm not wearing my uniform."

"It's like armor, isn't it?" Petra fingered her sleeve, where a unit patch had once blazed. "Put it on and you're a hero. Without it, you're just…"

"Sub-human." They exchanged grim nods before Jonathan retrieved his phone and dashed off a message. "There's another place we might be able to get you some medical help, but it's…an unconventional setting."

Opening the armrest compartment, Petra took a citrus drop from her stash. The wrapper crackled in her unsteady hands. "I'm an unconventional patient."

11. ALMOST HUMAN

A soprano warbled down the hall, and Petra raised her head from Jonathan's arm.

"Whatdehell izzat?" Delirium thickened her accent.

"Don't worry, it's not the heavenly choir." He adjusted his grip around her waist—she weighed more than he'd expected for her small frame—and helped her limp toward the music. Harsh lights turned the morgue into a bright but empty stage. An opera soared from the computer speakers, serenading an insensate audience.

Petra stared at the body freezers, then shoved Jonathan away. "You're sick!"

"Says someone who just collapsed on the sidewalk." He moved to support her again, but she staggered out of reach, knocking over an equipment cart. Instruments clattered across the floor. The scalpel spun to a stop in the doorway, beside a pair of rainbow-laced sneakers.

Ciro picked up the blade and used it to slice the wrapper of a candy bar. "If I'd have known you were coming, Jonathan, I'd have gotten you something from the vending machine."

"I messaged you."

"Sorry, I silenced my phone. That head doctor from Ripken keeps calling about the final report on April McCormick. She really wants to tie a bow on this body bag. It's stressing me out." He took a bite of chocolate, closing his eyes. When they opened and spotted Petra, he coughed up a mouthful of nougat. "*Dios mio*, is this your idea of a romantic evening? No wonder you haven't had a date in years."

"She needs a doctor, Ciro," said Jonathan, dismissing the bait. "I didn't know where else to take her."

"Not here. Morgues are for dead people."

"Give me a few hours, then." Petra hauled herself belly-first onto the table and twisted around to sit. Her dangling boots reminded Jonathan of the kids who frequented the ER waiting room, silent and stoic. *Too young to be that accustomed to pain.* The edgy, uncomfortable feeling her presence provoked in him softened.

Ciro studied her while he chewed a layer of caramel. "Why can't you go to the hospital? Undocumented?"

"You could say that."

Sympathetic growls rattled in the pathologist's chest, and he grabbed a pair of gloves. "All right, I'll help if I can. What's the problem?"

"Metallosis." The string of syllables seemed to demand all of Petra's breath. "Makes me dizzy, screws up my vision, gives me headaches, eats holes in my memory…"

"Sounds like classic cobalt toxicity, all right. Do you have a joint replacement or some other metal implant?"

"You could say that, too." Petra pulled out one of her omnipresent candies. Citrus perfumed the sterile atmosphere. "Vitamin C takes the edge off the symptoms, but sometimes if I stress the joint, other stuff flakes off the hardware and knocks me on my ass."

"We should check your heavy metals levels. Jonathan, can you grab me a sample kit?" Ciro rolled up Petra's right sleeve while Jonathan prepped a syringe. He frowned at the discolored skin inside her elbow. "Been getting a lot of sticks lately?"

"I promise I'm not a junkie," said Petra. "My last doctor ran regular blood work, and had been trying some IV medicines. I see more needles than my pal who runs a tattoo parlor."

"Well, I don't want to risk blowing the vein. Let's see the other arm."

"No."

Ciro blinked, startled. "If you want me to treat you, I need to test your blood."

"Pass me that scalpel and a bucket."

"You can't even stand up on your own, but you've still got energy to argue?" Jonathan slapped the autopsy table. "Is this why they call you Rock, because you have such a hard damn head?"

Granite glared back, the glaze of illness making Petra's eyes all the more remorseless.

"Look, I don't care what tattoos or scars or injection bruises you've got," Ciro told her. "We'll maintain doctor-patient confidentiality, and the others in here aren't going to talk. I examine bodies for a living. I dare you to shock me."

"I'll take that bet." With quaking fingers, Petra unbuttoned her shirt and cast it aside.

The empty sample tube slipped from Jonathan's hand and shattered. *Oh, that explains* so *much.*

Petra's left collarbone fused to an elaborate bionic arm. Cables wound around an alloy bone, imitating tendons. Artificial muscle sacs pulsed when she wiggled robotic fingers out of their glove. A translucent silicone sheath covered the whole construct; colored light shimmering behind it evoked a bioluminescent marine creature. Metallic tattoos plunged from her throat into the neck of her camisole.

Laboratory machines whirred in the silence.

Ciro cleared his throat. "I can work with the right arm," he said, his voice half an octave higher than it had been before. Grabbing a new vial, he bound a tourniquet around Petra's organic arm and slid in the needle. Dark liquid streamed out.

Petra watched it with dispassionate interest, and caught Jonathan looking, too. "It's blood, not motor oil," she grumbled as Ciro pressed a piece of gauze to the spot and scurried off to the analyzer. "If I could change my fluids that easily, I wouldn't have this problem."

Jonathan swept up the broken glass, avoiding her eyes, her arm, any part of her patchwork body. "You told me it was your fingers. Frostbite."

"That's true. It just didn't stay there. Nerve damage and necrosis ruined the rest of my arm. Same with my leg—the bone shattered when I fell overboard onto the ice, and it went untreated for days. Surgeons couldn't save much." Petra tugged up her right pant cuff. Titanium gleamed beneath the frayed denim. "Or so they told me. I passed out on the seventy-third parallel. Woke up in a hospital, two limbs lighter."

"So they outfitted you with experimental replacements, without your consent?" Jonathan's fingernails dug into his palms. "And now you can't even get medical care without exposing secret military technology?"

Laughter echoed through the morgue. Petra fell back onto the table, cackling until Jonathan worried she would lapse into respiratory arrest. "I'm the opposite of a super-soldier," she gasped at last. "I would have loved some DARPA door prizes, but Dr. Bhagat wouldn't approve anything more than a fancy peg leg."

"But wounded soldiers get advanced prostheses all the time."

"Not if their hearts were trashed by hypothermia." Petra drummed on her bony chest. "Bhagat didn't think I'd survive more surgery—even repairing my heart was too big a risk for her. She prescribed a nice, quiet life puttering between the VA and the VFW."

"Nice and quiet doesn't mean boring and meaningless," said Jonathan. "Some of the most interesting people I've met have been disabled patients. Limitations on some abilities makes them really creative in other ones."

"Maybe so, but I'm not going to outrun the *tuniit* on a mobility scooter. Digging up dirt on *Sedna* might throw me in their way again. If that happens, I need my fight-and-flight equipment fully operational." Goosebumps erupted on Petra's organic arm, and she scrubbed at them with the bionic hand. "Since I'd already beaten the survival odds a few times, I decided to push my luck. Started researching my own treatments, like Del. But biohacking was even more fringe then. It took me months to find these limbs, and a surgeon I could bribe to install them."

"What makes them so special?"

"They operate on signals from my nerves, just like the real ones did. I think about moving, and they move. It makes them sensitive and strong, but a little impulsive." Blue light flashed between shoulder and wrist, and the bionic finger poked Jonathan in the chest. Even weakened, the jab had enough power to make him wince.

You've seen prostheses before. This one is no different—not in basic concept, anyway. Just because she fished it from a prototype scrap pile, and it can throttle a guy Steel's size... Jonathan took a step backward, but Petra shot him a look of such disdain that he turned retreat into retrieval and picked her shirt off the floor.

"How does your heart handle the strain of moving all that heavy hardware?" he asked, draping the garment over her shoulders in a show of clinical bravado.

"A black-market pacemaker. I can adjust it manually if I need to." Petra pulled down her camisole neck. A vertical scar on her sternum formed the axis for a grid of symbols in glittering ink. "But it's crap. It's supposed to charge off ambient sound, but only certain frequencies work well. And when I tried to change the battery a few years ago, it started leaking chromium, which screwed up my vision and hearing."

"Common neurological symptoms of heavy metal toxicity." The all-too-familiar diagnosis slid off Jonathan's tongue.

Petra shot him a penetrating look. "That's what happened to your dad at Biocinium, isn't it? The shaky hands, the messed-up memories...we've got more in common than just old music."

"You seem to have managed better. I'm guessing you added more bionic parts to compensate."

"Lucky for Del." Petra tapped her ear. "Kick-ass aural implant parses frequencies, so I can separate the signals from the noise."

"Feels like I missed all the signals," Jonathan muttered, glancing at the freezers. "The whole time I helped April patch up biohackers in the ER, she turned around and created more!"

"She probably saved you a lot of calls. Not many biohackers are lucky enough to find a real doctor, and the results can get nasty."

"Who did your...procedures?"

"Mostly garage tinkers like Steel or hack surgeons who operate out of trailers across the border." A shiver too strong for mere chill rippled through Petra's shoulders. "After a few experiences like that, I figured it would be better to do it myself. So I tried to install a gadget to improve my vision, and punctured my eyeball. ER staff took one look, branded me a biohacker, and stuck me at the back of the line. If it hadn't been for Mechanic, I'da lost more than the eye."

"She couldn't save it?"

"Not for lack of trying. I think she felt bad, because she scored me a replacement from some friend in clinical research." Petra touched the skinterface on her temple, igniting a scarlet glow deep in her left iris. She chuckled at Jonathan's reaction, then let her hands fall into her lap. "I never meant to have this much hardware, but every problem I fix creates three more."

"Why not just remove the faulty parts? That's the usual treatment for metallosis."

"You sound like Mechanic. She'd been nagging me to do that for months. But the implants are all tangled up in my body systems now. Removing 'em might kill me."

"Leaving them in definitely will," said Jonathan. "Better a shot at life than a slow, inevitable death."

"We've all got a slow, inevitable death. I just need to finish some business first." Petra traced the unit insignia on her organic shoulder. Plain ink contrasted with her skinterface designs. "Upgrades are the only way I'll keep my body running long enough to get justice for my crewmates, but metallosis is melting my memories faster than polar ice."

"There are medications that can help with cognitive decline." Jonathan ticked off his father's attempted treatments on his fingers. "Acetylcholinesterase inhibitors, memantine, a whole new class of experimental nootropics…."

"The ones that can't get regulatory approval because people are afraid they might be used for HPM?" The taunt unraveled in a half-sob. "Mechanic got me what she could, but she worried the pharmacy was getting suspicious, so we had to cut back. I was managing all right until Steel slung me overboard the other day. Must've shredded the rotator cuff and gave me an extra dose of metals I didn't need."

"*¡Ya lo creo!* There's so much metal in your blood, I could turn it in for a deposit," said Ciro, returning with a tablet full of test results. Critical values shone in red.

"I know." Petra held up her wrist. The tattoo she'd tried to hide outside the parlor burned a dark diamond into her skin. Its shape roused old chemistry courses filed deep in Jonathan's brain. *Not a diamond—a cube. The molecular structure of a metal element!*

"Is that a biofeedback indicator?" he asked, recalling the road worker patient.

Petra nodded. "It changes color with the concentration of heavy metals in my veins. The darker, the deadlier."

"This should fade it a bit." Ciro took a package of IV solution from his pocket. "I pinched you some chelation drugs from one of the other suites. It'll help in the short term, but I don't have a license to prescribe for the living. See if you can get this." Grabbing a pad of sticky notes shaped like cupcakes, he jotted down a medicine.

Petra scanned the paper. "I was taking that until my tablets ran out a few days ago. My doctor had promised to get me more, but she died."

"Wait, don't tell me you knew April McCormick, too?"

"Turns out she treated a lot of Baltimore's biohackers off the books," said Jonathan.

Ciro clicked his tongue in comprehension. "I wondered when I saw the wound near her ear."

"She was on a boat in a storm," Petra said quickly. "She hit her head."

"On a knife?" Unlocking one of the body freezers, Ciro pulled out a slab. Jonathan looked away, but not before April's death mask seared into his retinas. "That's not blunt-force trauma. Look at the angles, the neat lines."

Petra raised an eyebrow at Jonathan, and he vouched for his friend's discretion with a curt nod. "She had a neural node implanted."

"Ah, that explains why there's two sets of incisions. See, here's a pattern of well-formed scar tissue—clean, surgical work that looks like it had been healing for months." Ciro pointed out the now-bloodless cuts on the corpse. "But this cluster is fresh, like someone sliced open her skin along the original stitch line."

Forcing his gaze to the cadaver's face, Jonathan willed the pale lips to stir, the lashes to lift. "Then the injury wasn't from putting something in, but from taking it out."

"That would be my guess," said Ciro. "I tested her hair for evidence of long-term propofol abuse. She was clean. I'd say someone drugged her and tried to remove the device. Not sure why they didn't finish the job, since they could obviously handle a scalpel..."

"Like a professional body piercer?" Jonathan asked Petra.

"...And knew how to administer common anesthetics."

"Like an ER supervisor," she retorted.

"Whoever it was, she didn't fight them." Ciro returned April to the freezer. "There's no sign of defensive wounds or physical restraint on her body. Someone injected the drug without a fuss."

"Wouldn't be hard to jump her in close quarters."

"Even then, she probably would have reacted, and left a mark at the injection site." Taking Petra's arm, Ciro indicated the bruises along the vein. "More likely it was someone she trusted to get close."

"That shortens the suspect list." A red star pulsed briefly in Petra's bionic eye. "And I've got a chance to work though it now, thanks to you."

"*De nada.* A live body makes a refreshing change. I'd keep you here for observation, but the only bed I can offer you is refrigerated."

Petra shuddered. "I hate the cold."

"No wonder—there's no insulation on you," said Ciro, sliding a needle into her thin arm.

"Hauling advanced prostheses around is a good workout, and some of my implants borrow from caloric energy. Most days I burn off more than I can eat."

"Well, I don't need a license to prescribe snacks!" Ciro opened the valve and positioned Jonathan's arm as a human IV pole. "Hold this while I run back to the vending machine. We'll get some chocolate and chelation into our patient, and then you're going to drive her home. Doctor's orders."

12. DANCING IN THE DARK

"Easy on the pedals!" The coupe rocketed through the intersection, pressing Petra back in the passenger seat. "I thought EMS knew how to handle non-automated vehicles."

"There's a big difference between a city ambulance and an eighty-year-old pony car." Jonathan's knuckles shone on the wheel; so did the boyish gleam in his eyes when the car executed a neat turn. "Where did you find this crazy thing?"

"On a scrap site, like all my other salvaged machinery." She wiggled the robotic fingers around Ciro's prescribed candy bar. Peeling a wrapper felt like doing push-ups. *I burned too much power fighting Steel, then sat still too long getting that IV treatment. If I don't charge soon, I'll be crawling for days.* "There aren't many vintage models like this around anymore. Seemed a shame to let it rust."

"You restored it yourself?"

"More like rebuilt. The frame was in good shape, but its guts were shot. I installed an electric engine, modern safety features..." Petra tapped the dashboard, and subwoofers buzzed against her legs. "...And a killer sound system."

Jonathan tapped his thumb in time. "Did you learn mechanic skills in the service?"

"Nah, I was practically born with a wrench in my hand. My parents did maintenance on drones for two different armies, and afterwards ran their own mechanic shop. I learned all kinds of engineering tricks. The only contraption I haven't been able to fix is myself." Petra glowered at her face in the wing mirror. Night hollowed out her cheeks, reminiscent of the skulls on the tattoo parlor wall. *'Objects in mirror may be closer than they appear.'* The question smoldering on her tongue since the morgue ignited: "Are you gonna report me?"

Tires thumped a nervous pulse on the pavement. "I'm not legally required to report evidence of biohacking operations unless I'm on duty," said Jonathan, fidgeting against his seat belt.

"Aren't you always? Even off the clock, you're treating patients at home."

"And hauling stubborn sick people in from the street."

"Hey, my aftermarket parts might be faulty, but they're the best treatment I've got. I'm screwed if they get confiscated."

"You think the police are going to impound a limb?"

"I've met biohackers who claim they got carved up right in the prison hospital. One guy swore that the cops busted into his surgery garage and chopped off his bionic fingers with his own hedge clippers." Petra's own hand clenched at the thought and cleaved the candy bar in two. Cursing softly, she crammed half in her mouth.

"That's an urban legend if I ever heard one," said Jonathan. "Healthcare practitioners can't just operate on people without their consent."

"Did you read the actual text of that new HPM bill? It gives medical authorities permission to remove unregulated bionic components at their discretion, in the name of patient safety." Petra ground a peanut between her teeth. "They won't drop a dime to help you power through with a disability, but they'll punish you for finding your own solution."

Jonathan glanced at the indicator on her wrist. "Seems like some solutions damage you more than the original condition."

"They sure as hell will, without Mechanic. Most of Baltimore's biohackers came to her for help. I guarantee you'll see more home-surgery emergencies now that Steel had to cancel the charters."

"Then what are we doing back here?" Jonathan made the final turn she indicated. Headlights skimmed over Henderson's Wharf.

"Ciro told you to drive me home." Infused with sugar, Petra managed to limp down the dock toward *Wind of Change*, leaning on Jonathan's arm more than she liked.

He stared at the vessel rocking in its slip. "You live on April's boat?"

"It was part of the deal she offered me—pilot and maintain the yacht in exchange for accommodation aboard." Petra stepped onto the aft deck and traded Jonathan's elbow for the rail. Body instinct compensated for the boat's motion, easing the dizziness that plagued her on rigid land. "Since most of my veteran's disability pay goes straight to medical bills, I couldn't turn down a free place to crash."

"Doesn't it bother you, after *Sedna*?" asked Jonathan, running a finger over the mounted life preserver.

"I'm from the delta. It doesn't feel like home unless there's water lapping at the foundations." A breath of briny harbor air steadied Petra's hand enough to unlock the salon. Tiny bulbs on the entertainment center flashed beacons through her fog of pain; she followed them to the sofa.

Jonathan hunched awkwardly in the space, as if expecting to hit his head on timbers. "Can I get you anything?"

"Milk." He blinked in surprise, and Petra explained: "Chelation therapy strips calcium from your body along with the toxic metals."

He opened the galley fridge and laughed at the row of half-gallon containers. "Not what most people think of when they self-medicate. Where are your glasses?"

"Just bring me the whole damn thing." Propping her elbow on the sofa's back, Petra slugged down a quarter of the carton. Nutrients seeped through her body. "I'll be fine now. You should get home to your dad."

"Will you be all right by yourself?"

Petra deflected the question with a cavalier smile. "I've been way worse than this. If I were you, I'd be more worried about missing the last bus."

Car keys hit the counter with a gentle clatter. "Okay then, get some rest."

Rest is the last thing I need. Once the door shut, Petra grabbed the stereo remote. Funky chords made the windows buzz. Fortifying herself with another calcium shot, she stood and moved with the music. The bionic knee stalled. She lost her balance and toppled to the deck. Impact rattled her bones.

Rock can't roll. The dark joke twisted her sob into strained laughter. Tears seethed beneath her lashes. Flopping onto her front, she dragged herself on her organic elbow back toward the speakers.

The salon door banged open. Footsteps quivered through the deck, and careful hands slipped under her arms. "What the hell happened?" said Jonathan, lifting her upright. "I heard a crash."

"I'll crash for real if I sit still any longer." Petra resisted his attempt to set her back on the sofa. "My limbs recapture kinetic energy, kinda like a hybrid car. If I don't move, they lose power. I'm like one of those sharks that dies if it stops swimming."

"So you blast old glam metal to keep yourself awake?"

"Hyper-vigilance does that. I never sleep more than a few hours before some damn noise jolts me out of bed, thinking I'm under attack." Shadows seemed less formidable beneath the warm, supple armor of Jonathan's hands, but Petra pulled away and leaned on the stereo cabinet instead.

"You can't move every minute of the day," Jonathan insisted. "What about when you're sick, like right now?"

"Music is my medicine. Remember how I said my pacemaker needs specific frequencies to charge? Classic rock works best, especially on vinyl. Must be something with the electric guitar riffs. Literal power chords!" An exquisite solo coursed lightning through Petra's veins; she pressed her skin against the speakers, absorbing every tremor of sound.

"So that's why you picked that deafening table near the karaoke machine." Jonathan ran a reverent finger along the row of LPs. "Does your insurance consider vintage records a medical expense?"

"I'm on a veteran's healthcare plan—they only cover John Philip Sousa," said Petra wryly. "I bought all these myself. Some cost almost as much as the bionic hardware."

"Then why skip them by flailing around?"

"Since my heart needs music and my limbs need motion, the most efficient way to stay functional is to combine 'em."

"Well, falling on your face won't do it." With a weary sigh, Jonathan placed one arm around her back, supporting most of her weight. His free hand clasped her organic one.

Petra's spine went rigid. "What the hell are you doing?"

"Saving the night crew an ambulance ride." He guided her steps in a geometry that matched the song's tempo.

Is he dancing *with me?* Alarm twitched through Petra's nerves, but her body lacked the energy to resist. *Oh, screw it. If he's gonna report me, I might as well let him power me up to scram!*

She folded hesitant fingers over his. Her cheek just reached his shoulder; fatigue beckoned her head to rest there, but she forced her chin high, looking past his collar. Every inhale carried faint scents of antiseptics and sandalwood. *Damn, I haven't been this close to anyone in a while.*

Judging by Jonathan's tense posture, neither had he. But he shuffled around the salon with unexpected grace.

"Are ballroom lessons a standard part of paramedic training?" Petra teased after a few songs had played through without a word from her partner.

"No, I learned from my mom. She was a D.C. hand dancing queen, until her kidneys started failing."

"She must've been awful young for that!"

"Not for someone who grew up in a neighborhood with bad water," said Jonathan grimly. "Whether it was from drinking the poison that came out of the taps, or the cheap sodas she defaulted to instead, it trashed her kidneys before she turned forty."

"One of those 'downplayed issues' that a certain medical student wanted to treat?" asked Petra, tapping a finger on Jonathan's knuckle.

He nodded. "By the time I was twelve, she needed a transplant, but there wasn't much chance of a donor match. We couldn't afford custom synthetic organs, so she looked for other options." Feet halted mid-song, and a deep breath expanded his ribs until they brushed hers. "I came home from school one day and found her lying on the bathroom floor, in a pile of blood-soaked towels."

Petra hissed. "Biohacking accident?"

"Some crazy hemofiltration device that promised DIY dialysis twenty-four hours a day. Not medically tested, probably not even legal. She tried to insert it using this skinny little fish knife Dad bought for weekends on the Chesapeake. Nicked an artery and bled out on the bath rug." Moonlight through the portholes lent Jonathan's face a somber glow. "I remember all the worthless little details—the bottle of peroxide on the side of the tub, the chips in her nail polish, the phone slipping in my fingers when I tried to call an ambulance—but I can hardly remember her face."

"Brains are dumb about stuff like that, aren't they? Blotting out nightmares to spare us, when sometimes they're the thing we most need to remember." *Like what happened on* Sedna. Petra shut her eyes, giving memory a projection screen, but crucial scenes remained blank.

"You know the worst part?" Jonathan took up the dance again, with the briskness of a soldier dodging enemy fire. "Not long after the funeral, they found a donor. If she'd just waited…"

"She still might not have made it," Petra finished for him. "She saw a chance to get better, and thought you and your dad were worth the gamble."

"Except we were the ones who lost. Dad started working at the Biocinium factory so he could support us on one income. You know the rest." An angry exhale ruffled the top of Petra's hair. "Losing my mom would have been bad enough, but she took my dad and my future with her."

"And you're still mad."

"Not much point being mad at a dead person."

"No, so you take it out on living biohackers instead," said Petra crisply. "I saw how you looked at me in the morgue. Classic Type One reaction!"

"Type One?"

"People who see my upgrades see one of three things." Pushing back to a single-hand hold, Petra attempted a careful walk sequence with a step for each item on her list: "One—an inhuman monster. Two—a bioengineering prototype. Or three—a novelty lay."

"Which of those is accurate?"

"Depends on my mood." She punctuated the statement with a spin, but torpid limbs faltered and she stumbled against Jonathan's chest. His arms tightened to steady her. *Or Type Four, a disabled wreck who can barely stagger through her day. I might need a hand once in a while—or even a whole damn arm—but I sure as hell don't need pity.*

She glared up at him, expecting condescension. Instead his eyes shone with what might have been begrudging respect, or just reflected harbor light. The song's last notes faded. Silence froze their feet; they stood entangled, waiting for a cue. Synchronized breaths replaced the bass line with a quieter rhythm.

Petra's pulse accelerated. *Crappy pacemaker can't keep a beat!* She retreated from the embrace. "Sorry. I got two left feet."

Jonathan hastened to flip the record. "You're not that uncoordinated."

"No, really!" Steadying herself on the sofa arm, Petra tugged off her socks. Native left toes and their artificial counterparts sloped in the same direction. She curled both sets into the floor, correlating detailed sensations from skin with texture signals from sensors. "These prosthetic limbs were a left-sided set. Getting the correct hand, and guaranteed arm-leg compatibility, was worth the hassle of buying mismatched shoes."

"I'd never have guessed. You must've internalized a lot of rhythm on the parade ground." Jonathan nodded at the photo atop the speaker. Faces beamed from the past: Dad's broad Cajun grin, Mom sporting a headscarf printed with tiny anchors, the boys sweet and awkward in collared shirts. All clustered around a young woman whose steel-bright eyes sparkled beneath a new uniform cap.

Emptiness ached in Petra's chest, a void no bionic part could restore. "That was my Coast Guard graduation."

Jonathan extended a hand; she let him draw her back to the floor. "Your parents look proud."

"Ridiculously. At least, until the Arctic conflict heated up and I got packed off to the pole. We'd all figured the Guard would keep me close to home, patrolling oil rigs or rescuing boats from storms." She swallowed hard. "If I'd have been there, maybe they would be, too."

"What do you mean?"

"A hurricane tore through the gulf just a few months after I deployed. The Coast Guard rescued lots of people, but hundreds still died. Including my family. " Salt stung Petra's eyes; she spun herself under Jonathan's arm and wiped the tears surreptitiously on her sleeve. "Nice phone call to get when you're floating at the top of the world."

Fingers on her back softened. "That sounds horribly lonely."

"It would've been, without *Sedna.* My shipmates adopted me. Until I lost them, too." The record crackled to its next track, hissing like sleet on the sea.

"So April really was the closest thing you had to family," Jonathan murmured.

"She and Steel reminded me of my brothers sometimes," said Petra, indicating the photo. "One was full of pepper, always chatting up strangers. The other had non-standard neural wiring—super-smart in the machine shop, but threw his fists around when he got frustrated, although he usually hurt himself more than anyone else."

"That last part doesn't bear much resemblance to Steel." A hesitant finger touched the gap in Petra's misaligned shoulder. "What else does your business partner do when he's angry?"

"He yells and smashes things and stomps off to guzzle a six-pack. He doesn't plot out a cold-blooded surgical murder."

"Unless there's a profitable piece of bionic hardware involved. Steel admitted he was ticked that April wouldn't let him sell it," said Jonathan, maneuvering around the coffee table. "Maybe he decided the device was worth more than the doctor."

"If hardware was the motive, my money's on Kade," said Petra. "Mechanic must've pinched the specs for his Beat. He found out, and wanted them back before a leak spoiled his big launch."

"But he wasn't even on the boat!"

"We don't know that. Steel said one of the passengers was a guy around our age. That description tracks. And we still haven't identified the third person." Gaze locked on the cabin door, Petra projected the murder scene behind it: a syringe descended on Mechanic's turned back, but the figure holding it remained opaque. Dance steps shifted direction, and her vision faded. "Although I have a hunch we've already met her."

An exasperated groan vibrated through Jonathan's chest. "You can't still think Dr. Bhagat is involved."

"How can you still not? She's got a beef with Mechanic, medical training…"

"And no way of knowing April had the Beat implanted."

"Wrong! You found those Biocinium brochures in her office," Petra reminded him. "She could've recognized the device from her military days, just like I did. You know what a stickler she is for rules and regulations. Maybe she saw a security breach and decided to plug it."

"Then why not go after Kade?"

"Maybe he's next." The needle skidded off the record edge, running out of grooves as their speculations ran out of evidence. Petra examined her wrist: perhaps it was a trick of darkness, but the ink seemed a shade lighter.

"Did that help?" asked Jonathan, studying the tattoo.

"Yeah. I should be able to get out of bed tomorrow, and start hunting for these before I end up on the floor again." She pulled Ciro's note from her pocket.

"I thought you knew the local black markets."

"For bionics, not drugs."

Jonathan held out a hand. "I'll see if I can get them at the hospital."

"Why would you do that for me?"

Her own words from the diner echoed back in a low voice: "Mechanic did." Petra studied him a moment, then handed over the paper. Folding it into a tiny square, Jonathan glanced at the microwave clock. "How late do the buses run here?"

"Just take my car. I won't be up to going out early anyway." Petra drained the milk carton. "Give Grace and Del a ride home from the hospital, and bring it back after your shift."

After a moment's hesitation, Jonathan picked up the keys again. "Do you need anything else?"

Sure—a body that isn't disintegrating. People I love back from the dead. Answers to questions buried under fathoms. Nothing much. "Nope, I'm good."

The door clicked shut, and Petra's thoughts crescendoed to fill the silence.

Is he really going to get that medicine, or did I just hand him evidence to turn me in? If I'm out of commission, who's going to track down this implant and stop a citywide Sedna attack? I have to stay functional until then. After that...well, I've got nothing left to stick around for anyway.

She hugged herself until her joints cracked, then changed the record and turned up the speakers as loud as they would go.

13. PERSONAL PROPERTY

"Are you sure you didn't steal this?" Hank asked for the third time, running a finger across the coupe's interior trim.

"You raised me better than that." Jonathan squirmed in the driver's seat, and Ciro's note crinkled an admonition in his pocket. *Chelation drugs aren't thrown around the ER like asthma inhalers. How am I going to get these without looking suspicious? Why did I offer to risk it at all?*

He repeated the reasoning he'd given Petra on the boat: *April would've. Treating her secret patient is a way to honor her memory.* Yet when he'd laid down a few hours ago for a futile nap before his shift, the imaginary eyes watching him from the darkness were not green, but grey. Empathy's rising tide had breached the levee of his disdain. Evans' remark echoed in the back of his mind: *"Once you've seen someone raw like that, you can't help feeling close to them."*

Ridges on the wheel evoked Petra's spine under his hand as they'd swayed around the salon, notches cradling his fingertips like a guitar's fretboard. *An electric guitar, with lots of amp and low sustain. But how's her fidelity?*

An impatient commuter honked behind him. Returning his attention to the road, Jonathan pulled into Ripken's patient pickup area. "Watch the car, okay, Dad?"

"What if I decide to take it for a spin instead?" asked Hank with a roguish grin.

Then every warning sign on I-95 will broadcast an alert for an old geezer in a sports car, traffic cops will hunt you down, and you'll be fuming at me for weeks. Sighing, Jonathan chose a less inflammatory scenario. "Then Grace and Del will have to take the bus and spend an hour chugging around Baltimore instead of resting at home."

"How about after we drop them off?"

"I have to go to work."

"Shame to have a powerful vehicle and just putter to work and back. Machines don't run like that forever." Hank glanced up with an unusually lucid look. Sudden resemblance struck Jonathan hard: his own eyes stared out from sockets hollowed by age and illness. *Is that where all my dull mileage is taking me?* He shook himself and pocketed the keys. "I won't be long."

Discharges and shift changes crowded the hospital's entrance. Jonathan took a back route to Del's room. The wheezy but determined voice grew louder as he neared the door:

"Mama, I can tie my own freaking shoes."

"Don't you curse at me, child! The doctor said to be careful bending down with that gash in your head. What if you get dizzy and fall?"

"What if a piece of flaming space junk crashes through the roof and squashes me in my bed?" Del snatched the sneaker out of Grace's hands. "You can't protect me from everything."

"I have to try, since I can't trust you to look after yourself," said Grace, folding her arms.

"That is so not true!"

"Then prove it, and get dressed before we miss the bus."

"He'll wait for you," said Jonathan from the doorway.

"What are you doing here?" Del looked from him to Grace, eyebrows knit. "You're not going to make me ride home in an ambulance, are you?"

"No, although we could outdo the sirens on the car's big stereo system."

"What car?"

"The one I borrowed to give you a lift home. Come on, I'm parked in the pick-up zone."

The teenager bounced out of bed with a whoop, but Grace fiddled with the discharge papers in her purse, avoiding Jonathan's gaze. "Can you wait a little longer? I'm meeting one of the hospital's financial advisors about billing aid."

Jonathan glanced at his watch and cringed. *Lousy example for Evans if I'm late, especially after hassling her about it the other day!* But he forced a light tone. "No problem. We can always do laps around the block until you're done."

Del followed him out. "Do we have to go straight home, or can we take a ride first? I want to see the city one last time before Mama locks me in the house forever."

"You can't blame her for being worried," said Jonathan.

"I don't. And I'm sorry I scared her, really! But her trying to keep me in bubble wrap is the reason this happened."

"No, this happened because you tried to stick an illegal bionic implant in your brain."

"So what? I bet this place puts dozens of things like that in people's bodies every day."

"Safe ones, not some garbage manufactured in a piercing parlor basement using stolen blueprints."

Sneakers skidded to a halt. "How did you—."

"You first." Taking Del's arm, Jonathan led them outside, where words would dissolve in traffic noise. "How the hell did you get specs for a brain chip, Del?"

A dismissive wave tossed sunlight off purple nail polish. "I told you before. People don't patch their networks."

"That doesn't make it okay to steal data!"

"But it's okay to charge my mom top dollar for something stamped out in a cheap factory overseas? It's okay to poison your dad, then get rich selling him medicine?" Anger radiated from Del like heat from the pavement. "That's why no one does anything about the climate—bad health means big profits. I'm literally sick of it!"

The tirade left Del panting; Jonathan supported their elbow until their breath steadied. "So you decided to download your own cure?"

"Not exactly. Last year I went browsing for new clinical trials, like the one I did here before that meanie doctor shut it down. I ended up on a university message board, where some grad student was venting about how the department didn't approve his neural implant research. It sounded like a cool concept, so I snooped around the school's email servers to see why it got canned. Know what I found?" Del tucked back their braids. "The guy's faculty advisor said the project was too edgy for the school's stuffy donors, but thought it could make a fortune all the same, and offered to arrange human trials in a country that wouldn't ask questions."

Realization knocked Jonathan backward onto a nearby bench. "*You* leaked those emails that started the brain chip scandal?"

"I thought if everyone knew the truth, they'd want the project to get funded. But people are even more selfish and stupid than I thought." Del plopped down beside him. "The school kicked out the *student* for making them look bad, and last I heard, the greedy professor was advising some mega tech company. It's so wrong, Jojo!"

"So is intellectual property violation." He softened the rebuke with a hand on Del's shoulder. Rage and illness shook their frail body, not unlike Petra outside the parlor the night before. "I guess you found that blueprint in one of the student's emails."

"Yeah, but I didn't think much about it until the other night."

"When you went on the screws cruise?" Jonathan held up his palms when Del stammered a retort. "Save your breath. I have it from the technician himself."

"Client confidentiality, my butt." Del chipped at a sidewalk crack with their toe. "Fine. I did go, but the stupid vagus nerve stimulator I ordered didn't work. Steel was kinda smug about it—said that's what I got for buying inferior parts—but the surgeon was nice, even though she was all masked up and I couldn't see her face."

"I bet she was," Jonathan murmured.

"She even asked Steel to make me a better device at a massive discount. They started arguing about prices, and he mentioned something about a blueprint she was keeping secret from him, which reminded me of the emails. When he dragged me out of the cabin for the next patient, I offered to swap him the design for the first copy he made." Del touched the bandage on the side of their head. "He might be a tool, but he's good with electronics. I sent him the stuff as soon as I got home, and he had it ready in just a few days."

"Because he already knew how to make it. That device is...well, it's complicated, but it can hurt people," said Jonathan.

"So can asthma." Plucking a bedraggled pigeon feather from the ground, Del zipped it back into alignment.

"I'm serious, Del. That chip is getting people killed, and you were almost one of them." Jonathan tucked his thumb under their chin and looked into the determined young face as sternly as he could. "Promise me you're not going to mess around with this anymore. No more hacking, of either kind. It's not worth it."

"Maybe not to you, with a body that works the way it's supposed to. But for me, it's my only chance at having a life." Del balanced the feather on a fingertip and sent it drifting on a weak puff of breath. Even that small respiratory effort left them gasping.

Jonathan dug into his pocket for the inhaler he'd finagled from the pharmacy, forgotten amid the crisis. Priming the pump, he pressed it into Del's hand. "At least stay away from bionics until we get to the bottom of this."

"Who's 'we'?" Keen eyes studied him around the mouthpiece, then ignited with glee. Jonathan pressed a finger over Del's lips to keep the medication in their lungs for the prescribed number of seconds before excited commentary burst forth. "That lady from karaoke night? Petra? Is that what you two were talking about in the corner, all secretive? Is she a detective or something?"

"Definitely something." Jonathan pressed the key fob. The coupe's headlights winked.

"*That's* our ride?" Squealing, Del darted over to the car and ran a hand over its sleek curves. "I thought cars like this only existed in old movies! Is this Petra's? She's even cooler than I thought."

Wait until you see the robot limbs. Actually, I'll have to make sure that never happens—the last thing Del needs is a cyborg role model. "You might not like the car so much when you have to tunnel into the back," said Jonathan, folding the driver's seat forward.

"I don't care. It's a million times better than the bus." Del climbed in and settled behind Hank. "Drive it like it's your ambulance!"

"Oh, now you want the ambulance experience." Biting back a smile, Jonathan drove around the parking deck until Grace hurried out a few minutes later. She glanced down the curb and headed toward a battered sedan.

"Mama! Over here!" Del called out the window.

Grace approached the coupe with tentative steps. "Jonathan! Where in the world did you get this car?"

"He says he didn't steal it, but I'm not sure I believe him," said Hank.

"He borrowed it from his new girlfriend," Del snickered, then yelped when Jonathan leaned his seat back against their knees in retaliation.

Grace fingered the hood the way she might test ripeness on a suspect piece of fruit. "I'm not sure which of those is less likely."

"The bus stop is over there," Jonathan told her through gritted teeth.

With an apologetic smile, Grace squeezed in beside Del. They all drove back to Pigtown, speakers thumping.

"Can't we at least go over the bridge?" Del begged when the three passengers piled out in front of the diner.

"No, my shift starts in a few minutes." *And if I walk or take the bus, I'll never get there in time. I'm stuck with this conspicuous car.* Anxious sweat made the steering wheel slide through Jonathan's fingers. He raced down Fleet Street, dodged an SUV pulling toward the curb, and turned into a small lot a block from the station. *Okay, maybe I can stroll around the corner to work without anyone seeing—*

"Jonathan?" He spun. Evans stood behind him, with her thumbs tucked under her backpack straps like a kid just dropped off the school bus. She goggled at the coupe. "You told me you didn't have a car!"

"It's not mine," said Jonathan, turning toward the pay machine to hide his face. "I just borrowed it."

"From who, a drug dealer?" Evans checked her reflection in the shiny paint, and snugged her ponytail tighter. "It looks like the one that woman picked you up in the other night."

"Lots of people are into rebuilding old things." *Of all kinds.* The memory of Petra's recharging dance twitched up a corner of Jonathan's mouth. "Can't leave a gem like that on the scrap heap. The car, I mean."

"That's true. My husband and I have been restoring some old family property. It's way more work than we expected, but satisfying to preserve all that history. Not as much fun as a classic sports car, though!"

"It's the slickest ambulance in Baltimore." Jonathan slapped the receipt onto the dashboard and hurried toward the station. "I had to drive someone to the doctor, then take my landlady and her kid home from the hospital."

"So much for being off work!" Evans trotted after him. "Is everyone okay?"

"Yeah, although the kid had us worried for a bit. Terrible asthma."

Lashes veiled Evans' sideways look. "Is that who you steal the inhalers for?"

Dread clawed Jonathan's chest. He toyed with denials, then sighed. "Yes. Dr. McCormick used to get me extras, but now that she's gone...why didn't you say anything?"

"I'd only been on the job for a few days. Accusing my mentor of pharmacy theft is no way to start. Besides, I figured you must've had a good reason, and it sounds like I was right." Evans hauled open the station door. "Has your neighbor looked into clinical trials? That might be a way to get better treatment for free. I know somebody working on one that might be a good fit—it's cutting-edge biotech."

"No!" Jonathan snapped, and Evans jumped a few inches. Guilt smothered him worse than the muggy morning air. With an apologetic grimace, he slouched into the kitchen. The coffee urn seemed to emit a holy glow. "I see enough biohacking on the job. I don't want it anywhere near my family."

"Guess you don't want this, then," said Evans, plucking the mug from his hands.

"That's not biohacking!"

"It is, if it's not decaf." She returned the cup, and Jonathan sank his nose into the caustic steam. "How is revving up your nervous system with joe fundamentally different than doing it with an embedded electronic device?"

"I'm just trying to stay awake, not be superhuman."

"The biohackers we transported this week didn't seem like mad scientists. They were just sick and scared."

"They should be, putting untested machine parts in their bodies," Jonathan muttered into his drink. The dark liquid reminded him of Petra's metal-laden blood flowing into a test tube. Nauseated, he set down the cup.

"It's that, or keep getting sicker in this out-of-control environment. You have to admit, our standard care for chronic climate health problems is like giving someone painkillers for a broken bone—it might hurt less for a while, but the underlying cause hasn't gone away. We just treat symptoms and ignore the disease!" Evans offered him the omnipresent box of bagels, but lowered it when he stared at her. "What?"

"You sound like someone I used to know." Appetite withered; Jonathan declined breakfast with a wave of his hand. "You might think differently once you see more bio-hacking cases."

"I want to! To learn from, obviously." Evans added quickly, spotting Jonathan's revolted expression. She followed him out to the vehicle bay. "Do we know the most common conditions they're trying to treat? Are there any popular biohacks you see more often than others? What kinds of people are most likely to try them?"

Crackles from the auto-dispatch system cut her off, announcing a new call. Jonathan scanned the data points. "Let's go do a case study."

The Dundalk townhouse wore its sagging porch roof like a ball cap pulled low over grimy glass eyes.

Jonathan climbed down from the ambulance with a sigh. "What did she do this time?"

"You've been here before?" asked Evans.

"A few times. She used to call us when she had seizures or breathing trouble from her diabetes. But the last two times I came out here were different." Grabbing his jump bag, Jonathan strode toward the door. "First she had a wicked cut on her arm that wouldn't stop bleeding—she claimed a bur-rfish sliced her when she threw it back, but it looked awfully deep for the puny fry left in the bay. Then we found her with a finger so infected that she almost went septic. Jabbed with a hook, she said."

"You think she was biohacking?"

"Barbs and spines don't leave chips under the skin." Jonathan knocked on the door, calling the woman's name, but no one replied.

Evans lifted the tape patching one of the window screens and peered inside. "There's someone lying on the kitchen floor!"

"Dammit." Jonathan twisted the knob, a modern chrome fixture at odds with its rickety setting. The door didn't budge. "Is that window unlocked?"

Thumps and grunts returned a negative answer. "No. I'll get the bump key."

"And put it where?" asked Jonathan, showing her the knob's smooth surface, devoid of a key slot. He slapped the small RFID reader installed on the doorframe. "She must've gotten that finger chip to work, and coded it for her house."

"Then how are we supposed to get in?"

"Hack it." Fetching a Halligan bar from the rig, Jonathan fit it to the jamb and pressed with all his weight. Metal brackets squealed, then popped. The door creaked open. Mounted fish trophies goggled from the walls as the paramedics hurried into the kitchen. A middle-aged woman slumped against the cabinets, a gruesome bouquet of blood-drenched dish towels clutched at her waist. The phone in her limp hand still held a connection to the emergency dispatcher, seconds of call time and life time ebbing away. Jonathan swallowed the bilious surge of horror in his throat. *It's not Mom. You can still help this one.*

Evans knelt beside the woman and hooked up the monitors. "Ma'am? Ma'am, can you hear me? What happened?"

"Another DIY surgery fail," Jonathan muttered, examining the sink drainboard. Cutlery and fishing hemostats dripped red trails across the counter. Smeared fingerprints led to a closed drawer, where fast-food seasoning packets almost buried a metal disk smaller than his palm. "She probably tried to hide this before we got here."

Evans took the device. "Looks like one of the implantable insulin pumps they use at the hospital."

"I'm guessing her insurance wouldn't cover the procedure, so she nicked the abdominal aorta trying to put one in herself." Jonathan tore open a pad of hemostatic gauze. "We'll pack the cavity as best we can, and hopefully get enough wound pressure to transport her."

"To where, the morgue? She'll be dead on arrival if we can't control the hemorrhage. Don't we have any vascular clips?"

A pained laugh escaped Jonathan's chest. "We drive an ambulance, not a mobile hospital. Even if we carried that kind of equipment, we aren't trained to use it."

"Maybe you're not." Evans riffled a few drawers and grabbed the hemostats from the sink. "Here, these will do."

"Those aren't medical-grade. They're for tying lures!" Jonathan exclaimed. "She probably used them to manipulate the injector's catheter or knot suture wire."

"They pinch and lock, don't they?" Dousing the tools with antiseptic, Evans pulled on a pair of PPE goggles. "When I tell you, take the towels away."

"Removing pressure will only make her bleed worse! Just get the stretcher. The longer we sit here—."

"—The longer her odds of survival. So don't waste time arguing!" Plastic lenses amplified the flash of her eyes. "If we're going to be partners, you have to trust me, okay? Do it now."

With a curse and a prayer, Jonathan whipped away the dressings. Blood spurted over his gloves.

Evans' fingers plunged into the space and made a few nimble moves. The gushing stopped. "There!" She repacked the wound with coagulant gauze. Blood pressure readings on the monitor crept upward.

Jonathan stared from the screen to his trainee and back again. "I've only ever seen doctors and nurses do that!"

"I started out on a nursing track," Evans confessed, wrapping a wide bandage around the patient's waist.

"You should've stayed, with hands like that. What the hell are you doing out here in the swamp?"

"I discovered that I didn't like snooty doctors and hospital bureaucracies."

Laughing in spite of the mess around his feet, Jonathan went for the stretcher. "You won't escape either one, once Dr. Bhagat sees a patient held together with fishing gear."

But the department head didn't appear when they rolled their patient, weak but stable, into Ripken's ER.

"What happened here?" asked the harried triage nurse.

"Kitchen accident," said Evans, in a guileless tone that left Jonathan too startled to contradict.

Glancing at the stretcher, the nurse clicked his tongue. "Hon, we're going to get you a punch card for repeat visits. Let me see who I can bump to get her into surgery. We're running on a skeleton crew today." He cast a wistful look at a small box on the desk. A sticky note on the lid read *'for pickup - Kade McCormick'.* "Bad enough we lost Dr. Mc-Cormick, but now Dr. Bhagat's been coming in late."

"That doesn't sound like her," said Jonathan.

"Second time this week. She stormed in late the other morning with mud up to her knees, looking ready to perform tracheotomies with her teeth."

"All that rain would put anybody in a bad mood," said Evans.

Especially someone who ran through flooded Fells Point after murdering her colleague on a yacht. Jonathan's fingers itched for his phone. *Petra's going to jump all over this—as soon as she can walk again, anyway. How am I going to get her that medicine?*

"Okay, I can squeeze her into the next open OR, but we'll need to prep her fast." The nurse hustled around the desk. "Follow me."

"You go on. It's hectic enough back there," Jonathan told Evans. Once the stretcher rattled away, he leaned across the counter and poked through the box. The contents of April's staff locker misted his eyes: a name plate she'd never wear again; hair clips still clinging to a few amber strands, and an almost-spent prescription pad. Tearing off a sheet, Jonathan scrawled down Ciro's recommended medication. Anxiety-dampened hands smeared the pen strokes, but it only improved his impersonation of April's handwriting.

"I swear they don't even try. How am I supposed to read these smudges?" The pharmacy assistant grumbled when Jonathan handed over the page. He squinted at the name stamped in the top corner. "Isn't this the doctor who died a few days ago?"

"She wrote it before that happened." Jonathan pointed out where he'd backdated the order. "And she's prescribed chelation tablets before. Look it up."

The assistant checked the computer. "Seems like she's one of the only doctors here who has. But this Petra Arceneaux hasn't been a registered patient for years."

"Dr. McCormick treated her on an outpatient basis," said Jonathan, taking refuge in half-truth.

"It should still be listed."

"I'm sure she just forgot to update the records. The ER is swamped."

"It won't be, if the hospital gets shut down for prescription fraud," the assistant muttered, but entered the order. After a few tense minutes rummaging in the shelves, he produced the medication. "Tell your patient she needs a new doc to sign off on her refill. I can't take scrips from a zombie!"

Nodding, Jonathan spun away and almost collided with the person behind him in line: Evans.

She glanced from the bag to his face. "Sounds like more than extra inhalers."

His insides shriveled. "It's not what you think, it's..." Placing a hand on his trainee's shoulder, he steered her back toward the ER. The few seconds it bought weren't enough for his exhausted brain to generate an excuse. *She's right. I have to trust her.* "It's for Petra, that woman who stopped by the station the other night. She was a...private patient of Dr. McCormick's, and asked me to pick up a prescription for her."

"Why can't she get it herself?" Evans' narrowed eyes flew wide. "She's one of those biohackers, too, isn't she? Running a screws cruise, I should have guessed...but why are you doing favors for someone like that?" She planted an expectant hand on her hip, and the motion drew Jonathan's eye. Ivory poked from her navy blue pants.

"Dirty gloves in your pocket? Even a rookie should know better than that!" Pouncing on the distraction, he snatched the slip of latex. A bloody object bulged inside the glove. He rolled back the cuff to reveal the previous patient's illegal insulin implant. "What the hell are you doing with this?"

"I...I thought the doctors might need to understand how the patient's injury occurred. I just forgot to give it to them. Let me take it over now." Evans swiped for the device, but Jonathan held it out of reach.

"You could have asked me for a sample container from the kit. Why sneak it in your pocket?"

"Maybe because you had your hands very literally full," she snapped. "We had a patient bleeding out, Rowell! I just reacted. We don't get trained on standard operating procedures for biohacking incidents."

"There aren't any." Ducking into the nearest exam room, Jonathan pitched the device into the biohazard container. "But this still has to go in your probation review. We can't have paramedics who ignore basic infection control guidelines, or remove illegal products from a scene."

"What about ones who smuggle drugs for biohackers?" Evans' girlish features hardened, mirroring the expression she'd worn in the blood-smeared kitchen. She blocked the doorway with folded arms.

Jonathan stiffened as the tiny cubicle suddenly became a cell. "Are you blackmailing me?"

"Of course not! I only meant that none of us know how to deal with this stuff yet. We don't have protocols to rely on, only partners." The harsh look melted. "So let's give each other a break, okay? I won't say anything about the prescription. And maybe instead of writing me up, you can assign me some extra study material."

"Well, we still need to submit a formal report on that screws cruise," Jonathan admitted. "The police are asking for it, and I haven't had time."

"I'll do it. Although I don't know much about them," said Evans earnestly. She let Jonathan pass and followed him through the crowded ER. "Maybe you can introduce me to Petra. I could interview her for accurate details about the cruise, and she could give me perspective on biohacking."

"Yeah, all the wrong ways to do it," said Jonathan with an awkward laugh.

"That's exactly what I need to learn about! I can only get so far on academic stuff." Evans jerked a thumb at the bulletin board beside the department doors. Public health pamphlets on heat stroke avoidance and the latest mosquito-borne diseases framed a glossy flyer:

Unnatural Selection: Ethical and Legal Considerations of Human Performance Modification
A Panel Discussion Featuring:
Rachel Ganz, House Office of Legislative Counsel
Steven Simms, CEO of Biocinium Technologies
Dr. April McCormick, Ripken Memorial Hospital

Pain jabbed at Jonathan's ribs. *That must be Tae's panel. Is this how April was linked to Biocinium?* Event details listed a start time later that evening at a posh downtown hotel. "Maybe you should go to that," he told Evans.

"I can't, unfortunately."

"I'll take notes for you, then." Jonathan snapped a photo of the poster and sent it to Petra. The reply buzzed as he climbed into the ambulance, and made him smile enough to draw a curious look from Evans:

Pick me up at 1830. I'll wear my formal leg.

14. BIG TALK

Footsteps sounded on the aft deck, and Petra looked up from the frayed wires in her shoulder. "I'll be right out," she called through the cabin door, and gave the jeweler's screwdriver a final turn. Stripped bolts refused to tighten, leaving her bionic arm slightly askew. She maneuvered it into a shirt; loose sleeves concealed the shoulder's asymmetry, but not its slow, weak movement.

"Try to stay out of fights tonight, okay?" she told the surly woman in the mirror. She cloaked the awkward limb under a trench coat and stepped out into the velvet evening. Jonathan stood at the rail, fiddling with the knot of a faded tie. Creases in his slacks suggested they'd been folded for a long time. The worn-but-dignified look reminded Petra irresistibly of her records, powerful melodies hidden in a frayed sleeve.

He tossed her the car keys, and smiled when she snatched them from midair. "I guess those dance moves helped."

"Especially the chelation agents swinging their molecular metal partners out of my blood." Petra leapt onto the dock unaided. Her leg's gyroscopic system nailed a one-foot landing. Pain rippled through her joints, almost ticklish compared to the previous day's agony, but she took the hint and walked more gingerly to the coupe. "Who says drugs and rock music will kill you?"

"I guess it's a question of degree. Decibels…" Jonathan flicked on the stereo, and under cover of thunderous chords, opened the armrest compartment. "…Or dosage."

Vitamin C drops half-buried a large medicine bottle. Petra extracted it, and tablets rattled with reassuring weight in her palm. "This must be three months' worth, half a year if I split 'em!"

"Hopefully that's enough time to find a new doctor. I won't be able to get you a refill."

"How'd you get any at all?"

"I didn't." One scuffed loafer tapped against the floor. "April did. Call it her last prescription for you."

Questions crowded Petra's tongue, but Jonathan turned to the window, blocking out further conversation. She put away the pills and started the engine. Rearview mirrors reflected the roof; her feet no longer reached the pedals. "What the hell did you do to my car?"

Jonathan chuckled at her annoyed adjustments. "Don't those high-tech limbs of yours have telescopic reach?"

"That would be considered an illegal enhancement, even though it wouldn't give me any more capability than you already get from your genes."

"You should raise that point at the panel."

"Maybe I will." Sliding the seat up several inches, Petra pulled out of the marina. "Someone needs to challenge this anti-HPM bill."

"Why? It's just stricter regulation on biotech products, to stop people selling junk like the piece Del ordered."

"Some lawmakers want more. Harsh criminal penalties for upgrades that aren't medically approved, registration databases for ones that are…the usual dystopian crap. It'll never pass."

"Then why are you so worried about it?"

"Because fear-mongering can have a worse effect than any law." Petra turned up the stereo, drowning further debate in a crash of keyboards. A few songs blasted them downtown to a distinctive red-brick hotel. Gilt shimmered across a lobby ceiling frescoed in elaborate hexagons. Petra craned her neck to admire it. "Looks like a motherboard, with all that gold circuitry."

"It's gaudy," Jonathan muttered.

"It's great! No wonder Baltimore is biohacker central—even the historic hotels have a little metal hidden inside." Winking her bionic eye, Petra followed the event signs to a ballroom. Floor-to-ceiling drapes gave it the impression of a stage, with players acting out social scripts over the refreshments.

"Jonathan! *Gracias a dios.* The lawyers have already driven me through half the dessert tray. How can they serve food like this and expect me to wear a belt?" Ciro, dressed in a lurid club shirt instead of scrubs, bounced over to them with a plate of canapés. He grinned when he spotted Petra. "You didn't tell me it was going to be a double date! How are you feeling, *Piedra*?" Clinical eyes appraised her bionic limbs, then returned to her face with genuine friendliness.

Type Two, but a nice one. Petra helped herself to a tart from his hoard, demonstrating the renewed steadiness of her fingers. "Almost human. I owe you big-time."

"Not at all. Thanks to you, I can have a delightfully controversial opinion on tonight's discussion."

"I'm surprised Tae didn't ask you to sit on the panel," said Jonathan.

"I was the emergency backup—I've done plenty of postmortems on biohackers—but he found some more illustrious token of the medical establishment. Too bad. I'd have had a blast trolling the delegation from Capitol Hill." Ciro waved toward a table at the room's end. A blonde woman occupied the first seat, jabbing a tablet screen with her long pearlescent fingernails.

"Is that the legislative counsel rep?" asked Petra.

"In all her ironic glory. If she's opposed to unnatural human body enhancement, she should write a bill banning those claws." They snared a snicker.

In the next chair, Simms slurped from a glass of white wine. Two empties stood beside his microphone.

Petra nudged Jonathan. "He didn't seem the type to get nervous about a little public speaking. What's got him so wound up?"

"Probably his seat mate," he replied, nodding at the last panelist. Dr. Bhagat surveyed the audience with lips pressed into a thin red paper-cut. "If that's who they got to replace April, this will be a short evening."

"Especially for me!" Petra belted her coat more closely around her body, but it didn't keep out the anxious chill. "Last time we met, I had two missing limbs. If she sees me now, she'll know I've got more upgrades than a legacy computer! I should just tell Tae to meet me at the police station."

"She's not going to call the cops to a hotel ballroom. And if she tries…" Jonathan fidgeted with a loose button on his cuff. "…You can trade her for an accusation of murder. She was late to work the morning April died, and came in covered in mud."

"I'd be suspicious of anyone who *wasn't* muddy after that storm."

"There's more. The day I found her letter of censure about April, I overheard her on the phone with someone, saying she'd tried to cover up some messy problem."

Petra caught her breath. "Why didn't you tell me?"

"It didn't seem important at the time. But now…"

"It's fishier than the Chinese trawler fleets at the pole." Feedback squealed on the sound system, and everyone shuffled toward the seats. "Now I have to hear what she says, even if it's risky."

"She won't recognize you after all this time," Jonathan assured her. "Just keep your eyes down. And your glove on. And your legs still. And—."

"Just sit in front of me," Petra grumbled. She settled in the back corner, nearest to the exit for a quick getaway. Jonathan provided a human shield in the row ahead, while Ciro's shorter figure beside him afforded a window on the speakers. Suits and skirts filed into the rows.

Tae made a few opening remarks, then introduced the panelists. "Ms. Ganz, I'd like to start with an overview of the new legislation you're drafting. What do the congressional sponsors hope it will achieve?"

"I think the objective is right in its name," said Rachel, revealing a smile full of flawless white teeth. "*HARMONY*. The *H*uman *Ar*tificial *Mo*dification *N*eutralit*y* bill will protect Americans' constitutional rights to equality by ensuring that bionics aren't used to obtain unfair physical or mental advantages. How would the alums who hosted this panel have felt about competing with students who used brain chips to enhance memory? Or playing sports against athletes with muscle implants for greater speed?"

"And this is no longer the stuff of science fiction," Tae reminded the audience. "It's real technology with real consequences."

"For our nation and our species." Rachel gave a sanctimonious nod. "Your elected representatives are taking initiative to preserve the balance between science and society."

"What balance?" Simms interjected. "Look at the gaps in disease rates and life expectancy between people who have access to quality care and those who don't. It's never been equal. Products like the ones we're developing at Biocinium promise to democrath—democratiss—democratize medicine." Wine muddled his words, but he turned to Bhagat with a convivial gesture. "I'm sure the good doctor here can speak to the need for that."

"We see patients experimenting on themselves with a range of products, from home inventions to imported biomedical prototypes to pirated military technology." Bhagat's dour expression left no doubt about her opinion on the trend. "Emergencies linked to unregulated bionics have increased exponentially in the past few years, straining our already-overburdened healthcare system. It's clear that public health needs are not being met, or people wouldn't resort to such dangerous alternatives."

"Hey, I'm trying my best," Jonathan hissed under his breath.

"Don't try too hard, or you'll put me out of a job," Ciro whispered back. Their banter thawed the fearful frost in Petra's chest.

"You're right—Biocinium's surveys have identified hundreds of people in Baltimore alone who rely on some kind of biohack." Simms gestured toward the city shimmering beyond the lavish curtains. "But the right bionics reduce both the risk for users and the stress for caregivers. It's the ultimate outpatient solution that will let us get on with life and the pursuit of happiness."

"Or pursuit of profit," Rachel replied, cracking the consonants like a whip. "A key piece of HARMONY is new standards for both products and practitioners, emphasizing patient safety. As with any burgeoning industry, bionics represent a wide range of quality. We don't want corporations exploiting people's illness for their own enrichment."

Overloud laughter squealed in Simms' mic. "That's the foundation of the American healthcare system! And the right bionics will liberate patients from it. That's what really worries you and your lobbyist pals. People won't have to go broke over prescriptions and procedures when they can upgrade their own bodies."

"Human bodies are not disposable commodities that can be traded in for newer models," Bhagat snapped.

"Come on, who wouldn't want to exchange a bum knee and run like a varsity star again, or replace a daily medication with a set-it-and-forget-it smart implant?" Simms raised his hand, and a few more popped up around the room.

"Bionics require additional procedures, which introduce additional complications," Bhagat insisted. "At the current stage of development, they're rarely the best option."

"Shouldn't that be the patient's decision?" Petra called, years of bottled anger seething off her tongue.

Bhagat found her gaze. She stiffened, then spoke with a hard edge in her tone. "Patients are not always in a position to make sound judgments."

"Neither are doctors. Not every condition has a neat test result or an obvious treatment." Petra's bionic fingers dug into her knee. "No one really understands a body except the person inside it. Why should someone else dictate what we do with it?"

"Because these alterations aren't limited to your personal sphere, like a tattoo or a nose job," said Rachel. She peered over the crowd at Petra, coolly curious. "They have the potential to impact the entire community by giving you exceptional abilities."

"We're not talking about superpowers, for godssakes," Simms spluttered. "Just next-generation improvements to healthcare."

"But you just described it as an *upgrade*." A manicured nail rapped on the table. "Are they not intended to enhance a user's physical or mental state?"

"No more than any other assistive medical device."

Rachel gave a silky laugh. "Some of these technologies go far beyond the likes of hearing aids and pacemakers."

"Most biohackers are trying to treat a problem that nothing else has helped," said Petra. Necks strained in the rows ahead, their occupants twisting to look at her. Clammy sweat prickled beneath her coat. "Sure, a few people will try to do more, but no one has stopped making prescription painkillers just because a handful of idiots use them to get high."

"But we do have strict drug regulations, and criminal penalties for abuse."

"Is trying to heal yourself a crime?"

"Against current statues, or against nature?" The lawyer's rosy smirk contrasted Petra's own chapped lips; full curves mocked her leanness; fingers tapered to elegant nails instead of metal bolts.

Nature's not that kind to all of us, sugar. Petra allowed herself a full-bore glare at the other woman. *Why are the people who make laws the ones who'll never have to suffer under them?*

A loud snort in Simms' microphone snapped every head in the room back to him. "We can't stifle innovation that improves human lives just because some conservative pundit thinks we're playing god."

"HARMONY has bipartisan support," said Rachel smugly.

"From puritanical nuts on both ends of the spectrum." Simms raised his glass in a mock toast. "Congratulations, you've found an issue to unite the Bible-thumpers and the granola-munchers."

Affronted murmurs exploded throughout the assembly. The remainder of the hour devolved into a bickering question-and-answer session, despite Tae's efforts to steer productive debate. Rachel spouted polished press statements; Simms blustered about technological progress; and Dr. Bhagat quoted hospital policies, her eyes darting between the clock and Petra.

Just like when I ran drones in the Arctic—I go poking where I shouldn't instead of laying low, and run into trouble. She twisted her hands in her lap until the bionic fingers threatened to dislocate the real ones. *At least this time I'm the only one who has to face the fallout.*

When Tae concluded the panel, Ciro let out a relieved sigh. "I'm amazed that didn't turn into a brawl. Poor Tae— he's too sweet to wrangle a doctor, a drunk, and a demagogue. I'd better make sure he's okay." He squeezed past Jonathan and disappeared.

"That *was* more intense than I expected." Turning, Jonathan directed the words at Petra. She braced for criticism of her argument, but he looked somewhat impressed. "If you want to split, I can talk to Bhagat alone."

"No, you won't be able to read her."

"Why not? I've spent a lot more time around her recently than you have. And you said yourself that I was good at analyzing people."

"Not in the same way as me." Lurching a little as her bionic leg sensed the instinct to flee, Petra approached the table. Each step accelerated her pulse. She grasped for a defiant remark, but the only words her brain could process were from her last conversation with Bhagat:

"Why can't I try these bionic things? I've got nothing to lose."

"Except your life."

"What the hell kind of life can I have like this?*"*

"A very fulfilling one. There are many worthwhile things you could pursue without further damaging your condition."

"Like what, raise money for the Sedna *Survivors Society? There's no one left to help. Take up the guitar again? I'm missing a whole goddamn arm!"*

"I've observed that a patient's attitude can make a significant difference in their recovery. You're not giving yourself any advantages in that regard."

"Do you really expect me to believe that happy thoughts will regrow my leg?"

"That probably has a higher success rate than these ludicrous prototypes you've researched."

"You're making fun of me, just like the command did with my after-action reports. Well, screw you both! I'll get my body back, and I'll use it to find out what really happened to my crew…"

Bhagat's scowl deepened as Petra reached her. "I see you got what you wanted."

"Yeah, a doctor who would actually treat me."

"Dr. McCormick? I assume that's how you two know each other." Bhagat nodded at Jonathan, who'd joined Ciro and Tae nearby. He looked in another direction, but his awkward posture made it evident he had one ear on the women's dialogue. "I knew they had some kind of improper relationship, but I assumed it was just a workplace flirtation, not pharmacy theft for biohackers."

Petra snorted. "I can't picture him stealing kisses *or* drugs."

"No? Then how do you explain Dr. McCormick's habit of falsifying prescriptions?"

"I think it was her terrible addiction to helping people."

"Committing fraud and exposing the hospital to liability helps no one."

"You haven't changed a bit. Still more interested in following procedure than doing any damn good." Impulse twitched down Petra's arm; the rogue left hand slapped the table. Abandoned wine glasses quivered.

Bhagat jumped, staring at the gloved fingers. "I gave Dr. McCormick repeated chances to come clean. I even followed her to the marina after work earlier this week, hoping for a rational conversation that wouldn't be overheard or documented in the hospital. She wouldn't hear me."

"So you got rid of her."

"She left me no choice. I tried to handle the matter discreetly, but she wouldn't see reason."

Brushing back her bangs, Petra tapped the skinterface on her temple. A grid appeared across half of her vision. Indicators tracked subtle movements in the doctor's facial muscles. "You call staging a biohacking accident discreet?"

Bhagat's mouth fell open. "Are you suggesting I was involved in her death? I had no idea she was abetting bio-hackers until she came into my ER with a hole in her skull."

"Awfully convenient that she dies before you have to tell a review committee why you fired her."

"Convenient to lose one of my best doctors when we're critically understaffed, and the city's public health grows worse by the day?" asked Bhagat, glancing at Jonathan and Ciro with an unusual hint of empathy. "If Dr. McCormick would have admitted wrongdoing and stopped the theft, I'd have willingly overlooked the entire affair. The hospital needed her."

"So did the biohackers."

"I see no purpose in revisiting this discussion. You're clearly even more enamored of the concept than you were ten years ago." Bhagat curled her lip at the gloved hand. "There was metal in you long before any bionic implants, Petra Arceneaux. Once you fix on an idea, you are unyielding." Pushing back her chair, she stalked out of the room.

A soft shadow fell over Petra's shoulder. "No, that's not how I got my nickname," she growled before Jonathan could ask.

"And that's not how things were with me and April." He glowered after the doctor. "Improper workplace flirtation? The only steamy thing between us was cafeteria coffee. Bhagat is even more uptight than I thought."

"Maybe because she was at the marina that night," said Petra. "She admitted stalking Mechanic there to harass her. I told you!"

"You also told me she left before you set sail. I doubt she'd admit being there at all if she'd murdered April."

"Well, I'm pretty sure she wasn't telling the whole story." Petra tapped the tattoos again and the grid disappeared from Jonathan's bemused face. "This eye has some basic computer vision capability to detect contractions in facial muscles—a sort of built-in lie detector."

"So that's why you said you were good with micro-expressions!" Jonathan folded his arms. "Have you been using that on me this whole time?"

"Would you have said anything differently if I had?" Grinning at his speechlessness, she turned away.

"Who are you going to inspect now?" he called after her.

"That buffet. I'm still low on fuel after yesterday, and my free-lunch identification algorithm predicts an eighty-six percent likelihood of strawberries."

Peckish professionals thronged the spread. Petra sampled their conversations along with the food:

"…Given the range of natural human abilities, we can't legislate reasonable parameters for what constitutes enhancement…"

"…Elective biomedical procedures? Think of all the medical malpractice suits…"

"…Ooh, is that real cantaloupe?" A manicured hand collided with Petra's glove as she reached for the fruit salad tongs. Rachel Ganz withdrew with a chuckle. "Pardon me! Argumentation always works up my appetite."

"Then you must need the whole bowl," said Petra, relinquishing the utensil. "That panel was on fire."

"And members of the audience were pouring on gasoline." The legislator stacked a pyramid of melon cubes on her plate. "You've got strong opinions on the issue. Are you a healthcare attorney?"

"No, just a veteran who left a few parts in the field."

"In that case, I'd love to hear more. We've had trouble getting insights from the user perspective. Businesspeople are too biased, and biohackers think interviews are some kind of government plot to identify them." Rolling eyes dusted with blue powder, Rachel handed back the tongs. "We need subject matter expertise to inform this bill. Would you be willing to talk with my team? It's a great opportunity to contribute to the country's future."

I've contributed plenty already, for a future that's decided to make me illegal. Petra selected a strawberry with her gloved fingers; it had taken months of practice and a lot of crushed fruit before she'd mastered the artificial hand well enough to grasp anything so delicate. She toyed with it for a moment, then returned the lawyer's razor smile. "I think we'd have lots to talk about."

"Then I look forward to your call." Rachel passed her a business card and sailed off toward an archipelago of expensive suits.

"These things are great for networking, aren't they?" Simms ambled up and helped himself to another glass of wine, glaring over the rim at Rachel's back. "Watch out for that one, though. She pretends to want your input, but she's just looking for weak spots."

"Did she invite Biocinium to talk, too?"

"Earlier this year. I participated in good faith, hoping to clear up mish-under-shtandings about our products and share some of the obsh-tacles to bionics breakthroughs," Simms slurred. "And what happens? Bitch writes a new section into the bill that makes it almost impossible to get approval for clinical trials! I wish Kade could've been here to call her out on that—he'd have had the whole room in tears with his speeches about elevating the human experience. The kid's a shameless idealist, but it goes over well with the morality crowd."

The image of Kade in his cartoon t-shirt, addressing a room full of overdressed professionals, made Petra smile. "Why didn't he come?"

"I don't know. He messaged me five minutes before the panel started and said he had something urgent to take care of at home." Simms took a glum bite of pastry. Crumbs rained on his designer tie. "I could've pulled the boss card on him, but with the company's re-launch riding on the Beat, I can't afford to lose him."

Petra pounced on the segue. "He must be having a tough time right now. When I met him the other day, he told me he'd just lost his sister."

"Yeah, it's a real shame. Unlike most doctors I meet, she was very supportive of bionics."

"You knew her?"

"Not well. She and Mrs. Simms worked on a clinical trial together a while back. She seemed really invested in novel treatments for public health problems, so we enlisted her to help with those surveys I mentioned. I wanted to hire her outright, but she insisted on freelance work so she could keep her hospital gig. Maybe that was for the best." Simms dropped his voice. "I heard she died of a drug overdose. The last thing Biocinium needs is another occupational health scandal. It barely survived the first one."

Neither did your workers. Stoppering the remark with a strawberry, Petra glanced across the ravaged platters at

Jonathan. He looked up from the coffee urn, but his smile faded at the sight of her companion.

"Nice standup routine," he told Simms, stalking over to join them. "I thought the part about Biocinium improving people's health was hilarious."

The CEO stared at him, befuddled. "I'm sorry, do I know you?"

"This is my, ah, colleague, Jonathan Rowell." Petra shifted her bionic foot onto Jonathan's in warning.

"That name sounds familiar. Have we met?" Simms stuck out his free hand, but Jonathan held tight to his mug.

"I probably mentioned him in your office. He specializes in home caregiving for wrecks like me," Petra said quickly.

"Well, if you're looking for a new career opportunity, Mr. Rowell, I hope you'll think of us. We'll need qualified medical staff to pay home visits and ch-*hic*-ck up on participants, once we get our applications past this HARMONY crap. One handshake at a time..." Wiping sugar dust off his fingers, Simms tottered away.

With a punitive twist of her boot, Petra stepped off Jonathan's toes. "This is not the time for chasing revenge!"

"If you have an indicator tattoo for hypocrisy, it's blazing right now." He took an angry sip of coffee. "He won't remember me in the morning anyway. What kind of businessman gets that wasted before a public appearance?"

"A stressed one. He's bet everything on that product launch, and now he's afraid of losing his last dollar, not to mention his boy genius. Kade bailed on this shindig at the last minute." Snatching the last cookie from a pastry display, Petra dunked it in Jonathan's coffee and ate it in two bites. "And I'm going to find out why."

15. BROKEN HOME

"Wait." The crosswalk signal outside the hotel bleated its monosyllable. "Wait. Wait."

"For what, another murder?" Petra waded into the luminous stream of traffic.

Jonathan issued apologetic waves to the startled drivers. "Do you even know where Kade lives?"

"With Mechanic. She invited him to stay while he started his Biocinium job."

"And of course you know her place," he muttered, following her into the parking garage. *I got ten-minute coffee dates in the cafeteria, but the lawbreakers got to hang out at her house. That legislator was right—biohackers* do *get unfair advantages!*

Brooding, he walked straight into Petra; she'd stopped short in front of him. "Something wrong with your leg again?"

"No." She swiveled her head slowly, scanning the shadows. A finger slid up to touch her skinterface.

Jonathan squinted at the darkened cars. Nothing stirred. "What is it?"

"Probably just a pigeon. Let's go."

They climbed into the coupe and pulled up to the fare gate.

"While you were interrogating Dr. Bhagat, I talked to Tae about his panelist selection," said Jonathan, loosening his tie. "Apparently he got April's name from another biohacker he defended. The client tried to pull the same trick as Steel, getting April to sign off on bionics for medical reasons. Tae called her up, heard how passionate she was on the subject, and asked her to participate. Guess who else she recommended as a speaker?"

"Who?" Petra glanced backward while she fiddled with the ticket machine. An impatient SUV rumbled behind them.

"Someone from Biocinium! She said they were the company to watch, setting precedents for community health technology."

"She was probably just boosting her brother, like with those flyers she brought to the hospital."

"Except that Tae planned this panel six months ago, before Kade started the job. So what was the company doing back then that impressed April so much?"

Petra didn't reply. Eyes riveted to the rearview mirror, she drove a loop around the hotel.

"Are you even paying attention to me?"

"Uh-huh. And I'm not the only one." Traffic signals painted her face a tense scarlet. "Someone's following us."

"It's called traffic."

Petra glared at him, then rocketed through a red light. "See?" she crowed.

Flailing for the grab handle, Jonathan twisted around. An SUV hurtled through the intersection after them. "I see an average Maryland driver."

"Who tailed us from the garage. Maybe even from the hotel—I thought I heard steps behind us when we got outside." Petra snaked around the ballpark. "Could be your cop buddies, looking for a bionics bust. No way I'm going to lead them to Mechanic's house."

A luxury hood ornament winked at Jonathan through the coupe's back window. "I've never seen an unmarked car that fancy."

"Or a police tail that amateur." The SUV cut through a parking lot and slipped back into their wake, a conspicuous white whale.

Apprehension tingled in Jonathan's toes, like when he approached an accident scene full of fiery wreckage. "What are you going to do?"

"Evasive maneuvers." Pulling onto the highway, Petra sped toward the Hanover Street Bridge. Swollen clouds over the Patapsco river shuddered with lightning. The speedometer climbed.

"This is insane! Who the hell would care where we go?" Jonathan yelled over the engine's growl. "It's not like we're doing anything secret."

"But they might be. If April's killer saw us together at that panel, or heard all the nosy questions we asked, they might worry we're onto them, and——." Petra broke off in a curse as their pursuer loomed alongside. Tinted windows hid the SUV's occupants. It swerved into the lane ahead of them, clipping the coupe's front bumper. Momentum threw Jonathan sideways. The coupe spun. Petra screamed condemnations, her hands playing wheel and gearshift in a desperate duet. Tires screeched to a stop against the bridge rail.

Jonathan's pulse hammered in his throat. Struggling to breathe through shock and a stuck seat belt, he ran a quick mental scan of his body. *Whiplash? Dislocated shoulder? Another damn concussion?* None of the typical collision injuries emerged.

"Are you all right?" he asked Petra, but she'd already flung open her door. Darting into the lane, she stared after the SUV. Horns brayed. Brakes squealed. Petra planted her boots in the potholes, a statue carved from darkness and halogen.

A stern yank released Jonathan's seat belt. He stumbled out and pulled Petra against him as a car whipped past, close enough to billow the hem of her long jacket. "Are you trying to change your nickname to gravel?"

Ruby reproach glared up at him. "I was trying to get a license plate! If I don't stand really still, my eye's crappy zoom feature can't get a clear shot. But the car was already too far away." She glanced down at the water and shivered. "I've had enough faceless enemies trying to kill me. I want to know what I'm up against."

"If it's any comfort, I don't think there are advanced machines involved this time. No driving algorithm would allow behavior like that," said Jonathan. "That car must be a non-automated model."

"Or the driver is a good enough engineer to hack the safety protocols." Headlights scrolled over Petra's face like a bright, quick chain of thoughts. Pulling from Jonathan's grip, she trotted back to the car. "Come on, hurry."

The low-slung seat no longer looked fun or exotic. Jonathan forced himself to get in anyway. "Where are we going?"

Petra rubbed at a scratch in the paint. "To see if a certain engineer owes me a detail job." Executing an illegal turn, she raced back toward the city.

To Jonathan's intense relief, stop-and-go traffic downtown curtailed their speed all the way to Butcher's Hill. "Did you come to April's place often?"

"Almost every week, before we started running the charters. She'd draw my blood and fix my popped stitches in her kitchen while we watched trash TV."

"Were you her first biohacker case?"

"Patient Zero, you mean? Yeah." Shadows fell across Petra's face. "I guess that makes it my fault she's dead."

"By that logic, it's my fault my dad got sick." Jonathan twisted the loose button on his cuff; it popped free, undone by the evening's anxiety. "You can't think about it that way. It'll just eat you inside."

"Oh, so it's not heavy metals corroding my body, just guilt?"

"It's equally incurable."

Laughing, Petra parked outside a handsome row house. "Well, I won't feel too guilty snooping around the house before Kade gets back."

"He already beat us." Jonathan pointed at a lit window.

"But I don't see that SUV anywhere!"

"Maybe it wasn't him."

"Let's see." Petra climbed out and rang the doorbell. Locks clattered open, revealing a man in his mid-twenties. Resemblance raised hairs on Jonathan's arms: a diamond-shaped face, red-blond hair, and green eyes blinking in disbelief.

"Petra? How did you know where I live?" asked Kade McCormick, opening the door. "This is not a good time."

"I'll say. Your boss just gave a drunk speech on an ethics panel, Congress is determined to ban biohacking products, and you missed a great dessert buffet."

"One crisis at a time!" Glasses magnified the red rims around Kade's eyes. "Let me deal with what happened to my sister, and then I'll worry about the idiots killing the Beat."

"They might not be separate issues," said Jonathan, stepping up beside Petra. "We haven't met, but I knew April at the hospital. I was the one who took her to the ER when she...when she got hurt, and some things about what happened to her just don't add up."

Kade gripped the jamb until his fingernails turned white. "What do you mean? They told me it was an accidental overdose! Oh my god, you don't think she..." Spinning on his novelty socks, he skidded into the house. Petra followed. After a moment's hesitation, Jonathan went after her and shut the door behind him.

A pair of April's shoes nestled beside the umbrella stand, as if she'd just kicked them off. He imagined her curled barefoot on the sofa, wearing sweatpants instead of scrubs; she patted the cushion beside her and smiled. He screwed his eyes shut to erase the fantasy. When they reopened, he was staring at a framed quotation from Hippocrates, hung where April would have seen it on her way to work each day: "*Wherever the art of Medicine is loved, there is also a love of Humanity.*" Pain swelled in his throat.

"What's the matter? You've never been in here before?" asked Petra, pausing in the hall to look back at him.

"No."

A sad smile touched her lips. "Just hoped, huh?"

"These weren't the circumstances I had in mind."

They followed Kade to the kitchen and found him bent over a laptop on the breakfast bar. "I bailed on the panel because I just got this from the family attorney." He showed them the screen, bearing a document with a dignified header. "Turns out April made a will a few months ago. She left me this house, her savings...everything."

"How does someone a few years out of med school have anything except piles of debt?" asked Jonathan.

"Our parents paid our tuition."

"Must be nice."

"Nice? They suffocated us with expectations, even when we were kids. It made us super ambitious, but when we got old enough to realize how screwed up it was, it made us super rebellious, too." Kade slurped from a can beside his computer and coughed; the energy drink's cloying scent didn't disguise a faint whiff of alcohol. "It wasn't intentional, but success became our revenge. Mom and Dad were so proud when April went to medical school, until she switched from neurosurgery to social medicine. They bragged to all the family about my doctoral program in engineering, but cut off my allowance when I left before graduation."

"When you got thrown out, you mean." Jonathan folded his arms. "You were the student in the brain-chip scandal, weren't you? All this HPM uproar started with the Beat."

"How did you...oh, what does it matter?" Kade sighed. "Yeah, the Beat got me expelled. Mom and Dad insisted that I give up the project and redeem myself with something responsible, prestigious, *boring*. When I said no, they pretty much disowned me. I'd be working in an electronics store and sleeping in the park if Biocinium hadn't taken a chance on me."

"You told me April got you an interview there," said Petra, pacing around the kitchen island. "How was she connected with them?"

"I told you. She gave them advice on how bionic products could treat common medical problems."

"Based on her ER experience?" asked Jonathan.

"Dunno. She just said her assessments would improve patients' options over the current technology. Like Petra's arm—if you leave it misaligned like that, it'll grind on the circuitry. Eventually you'll have to replace the whole unit."

Petra's boots squeaked to a stop on the tile. What little color her face had regained since the previous night drained away. "H-how…?"

"I have a degree in biomedical engineering. Between robotics labs and therapeutic rehab programs, I've seen more fake limbs than real ones in the last few years." Kade waggled his own pasty arms in illustration. "Yours is really good, but when you helped clean up the cans in my lab the other day, I noticed a lag in responsiveness compared to your other arm, and the precision of movement is—."

"—Good enough to crush any of your bones if you blab about it," said Petra, pushing back her sleeve. Even prepared for the sight, Jonathan flinched when she unveiled the elaborate prosthesis. He tensed himself to bolt forward if the fragile-looking engineer fainted.

Instead, a smile erased the grief from Kade's face. "Oh, *wow*." He circled Petra, hands hovering over her elbow. "The structural geometry of the muscle actuators is totally novel. And the power recapture system—."

"Can you fix it?" Petra snapped.

"I'll need a closer look. May I?" Fascination lit Kade's eyes. Stiff with alarm, Petra peeled down her collar and let him probe the titanium ring joining the arm to her shoulder. "I can tell you've had this a while. Between five and ten years? Yeah, the hardware's healed in nicely. The socket connections are just a little loose—looks like the bolts got torn out of place. What happened?"

"I smacked around a guy who asked too many personal questions."

"Sorry, I wasn't trying to pry. I've just never seen anything like this! It's incredible."

"Incredibly busted."

"Nah, all you need is a good screw." Silence hung after the statement, and Kade's ears turned crimson. He stepped hastily back. "I mean a quality bolt. You're stripped. Stripped, as in the threads are worn smooth, not like…um… I'll go get my tools." He hurried out of the room.

"Well, I didn't expect that," said Petra, as Kade's footsteps faded on the stairs.

Jonathan smirked. "What, a Type Three?"

"Don't be stupid," she scoffed, but turned away to fold her coat, hiding her expression. "I didn't expect that Kade would have a reason to kill his sister."

"Kill her? He was practically bawling when he opened the door!"

"Maybe with relief that he'd just inherited an expensive house and enough money to fund a start-up for his precious Beat." Petra frowned at the password-locked screen on Kade's laptop. "If Mechanic had told him about her will, he might've been tempted to cash in."

Jonathan shook his head. "How do you get out of bed every morning, believing the worst about humanity?"

"Because being careful with my trust is what keeps me alive to see that sunrise. Not that I had much choice about whether to trust Mechanic at first, but she never gave me any reason to doubt her. Until now." A silicone-tipped finger traced quartz veins across the countertop. "Why didn't she tell me about getting that Beat installed?"

"She didn't tell me, either."

"There's a shocker."

Jonathan bristled at the sarcasm. "Hey, I may not have been her black-market business partner, but we had plenty of troubles to share. Lost patients, burnout, watching Del and my dad shuffle in and out of the hospital…I knew her as long as you did."

"And made it pretty clear the whole time how you felt about biohacking."

"Yeah, by forging a prescription for chelation drugs and lying at the pharmacy to get it filled!" The annoyed confession slipped out before Jonathan could stop it.

Silver eyes widened. "I never asked you to steal anything for me!"

Jonathan sank into one of the dining chairs. A vase on the table quivered, and its wilting peony wept red petals. "It's not just you. I've been filching asthma inhalers for Del for ages. Sometimes I even weasel extra refills for my dad if he racks up a lot of doctors' bills and money gets tight."

A bark of laughter rang on the sleek appliances. "And you busted my ass about illegal healthcare tricks!"

"I don't make a lifestyle out of it. It makes me a little sick every time, but not as much as watching people around me hurt." The petals glistened like bloody bathroom tiles under his mother's body. He swept them under a placemat. "When my mom was sick, I felt useless. I hated that there was nothing I could do to make her better."

"Is that why you went to med school?"

"Yeah, but you know how that ended, so I'm still pretty useless."

"Not to your dad. Or Del. Or me." Petra twisted her fingers, as if wringing each reluctant word from beneath her skin. "With Mechanic gone, I've got nobody to turn to when

I crash. If you hadn't helped me, my only dance would have been the charlie-foxtrot. So. Thanks."

"You can thank me by helping train Evans," said Jonathan with a thin smile. "She wants to ask you about the screws cruise, for her first paperwork assignment."

"Why would she care about my side of things? I thought all you wholesome do-gooders hated biohacking."

"We still have to deal with it. It's better she learns now —we'll see a lot more cases if that HARMONY legislation gets approved and drives more people to kitchen surgeries."

"Hey, that could be a good thing!" Kade returned with a rattling box of electronics equipment. "Now that chips are so much cheaper, we have a chance to make biotech upgrades available to almost everyone. No more being defined by a roll of genetic dice! Bionics are the ultimate equalizer."

"I'm still getting good performance from my base operating system," Jonathan replied.

"When it starts running slow, go see her guy." Kade began tinkering with Petra's shoulder. "This is wicked work. We got demos of similar components in school, but I've never seen them implemented in a fully operational limb!"

"You still haven't," Petra told him. "This one hasn't worked right in days."

"It should now, with the cables properly re-attached. But the joint misalignment will keep pulling them out, unless we replace the main pins holding the whole thing in place." Kade compared two screws, then tossed them back in the chest with a *clunk*. "I don't have the right piece here, but I've got it in my lab. If you want to pop down there, I can have you repaired and rocking in no time."

Opportunity gleamed in Petra's eyes, and her southern accent thickened like smooth coating on a pill. "I'd appreciate that. Is your car big enough for all of us?"

"I'd rather you drove." Kade set his drink can guiltily in the sink. "I'm not big on booze, but after April's will arrived…anyway, I shouldn't get behind the wheel."

"Then you'll have to get behind the front seats of a coupe," said Petra with a thwarted sigh. "Tall guy gets dibs on shotgun."

"Not for long." Jonathan glanced at his watch. "Grace is working her second job tonight, so I have to be around for Dad and Del. I've already left them too long."

"Guard duty again?" asked Petra. "Who fills in when you take an evening off?"

"I don't. Tonight was the first time I'd been to a social event in ages."

"And you picked a bioethics debate?"

"Sounds like a sweet night out to me," said Kade, pulling on a pair of faddish sneakers. "Especially with an afterparty at the bionics lab!"

Petra groaned. "How'd I get mixed up with such a pair of nerds?"

"The robot arm might have something to do with it," Jonathan deadpanned, and grunted when the elbow in question jabbed his ribs.

"At least you can say you were a pioneer." Kade looped a security badge around his neck. "Soon bionics will be like cell phones and smart watches—so common and convenient that we won't believe we ever managed without them. The Beat is our first big leap, I know it."

"You really believe that, don't you? I bet you'll do whatever it takes to make it a success." Petra's unspoken words shot a chill down Jonathan's spine: *even murder your own sister.*

16. NIGHT PROWLER

Once Jonathan disembarked in Pigtown, Kade claimed the front passenger seat. "Your boyfriend seems chill."

Laughter gagged Petra's reply. "He's not my boyfriend. We're just helping each other out for a little while."

"Does he handle the medical stuff for your bionics?"

She started to laugh at that, too, but stopped at the memory of steady hands supporting her through shuffles and spins until she could stand on her own again. "I can't be too picky, now that your sister is gone."

"I still can't believe she didn't tell me about working with biohackers," said Kade, slouching in the faux leather until the seat belt wrapped under his chin. "All these months I've been struggling to land a clinical trial, she could've introduced me to potential candidates!"

"Guinea pigs, you mean."

"I hate that term. Animal experimentation is so mean." Kade patted the evolving ape on his shirt. "And it would be useless for the Beat anyway—none of the species permitted for laboratory studies have brains comparable to humans."

"Then how have you tested it?"

"Computer simulation, like lots of other sophisticated electronics. It functions well above the accepted benchmarks, but piles of data won't win regulators' hearts. I need people's stories."

"Simms seems pretty good at that part."

"Yeah, when he's not lecturing me about deliverables and minimum viable products." A sigh blew Kade's shaggy bangs back over his forehead. "He acts like the company is still stamping out microchips. But a bionic device is more complicated than that. It's a system of systems, embedded in the buggiest system of all—a human body."

"The inhuman parts can be pretty kludgy, too," said Petra, rolling her shoulder.

"I bet, especially when there's no user manual or jiffy repair shop. Who normally fixes your hardware?"

"The guy who broke this. I'll be damned if I ask him for help."

"Hey, I'm happy to be your new maintenance man." The crimson glow in Kade's cheeks didn't fade when the stoplight turned green. "And if you've got friends that need the same kind of help, send them my way."

Heat swelled in the corner of Petra's eye; she blinked it impatiently away. "You sound just like your sister."

"*You* knew her, too?" Kade yelped. "And you didn't tell me?"

"What the hell would I have said? 'Sorry for your loss—so are half the biohackers in Baltimore, who now have no safe resource for medical care.'"

"She was your doctor?"

"And my business partner. We ran medical tourism charters on her yacht."

"Totally not what our parents had in mind when they gave her their old boat. I think they hoped she'd fall in love with some up-and-coming young congressman at a sailing club." Kade gave a weak laugh. "Why'd she keep it a secret from me? We'd have been an awesome team, with her doing all the gooey medical stuff and me handling the electronics."

"After your school incident, she probably figured you'd had enough legal trouble."

"That's my big sis, always looking out for me. I should have been doing the same for her. She'd been stressed lately, but I thought it was just the usual doctor stuff. Y'know, sick people. What if she was really down, and killed herself?" Kade slapped the armrest. "I can't live in her house, or spend her money, if I only got it because I failed her!"

"We don't know that's what happened," said Petra, trying to head off a second wave of tears in his eyes.

"But Jonathan said it wasn't an accident!"

"No. Someone just made it look like one."

"Like, *murdered* her?" Kade's mouth fell open. "Why?"

"You tell me. Was anyone upset with her?"

"Just some uptight admin at the hospital hassling her all the time. April got so many calls after hours that she had to block the number."

Guess that's why Bhagat had to stalk her at the marina the night she died. Petra drummed fingers on the steering wheel. "How about her freelance work for Biocinium?"

"That stopped not long after I got hired. I got the feeling that April didn't leave on great terms. She never talked to me about her work there. Or a lot of other things, apparently." Biting his lip, Kade turned to the window. When he spoke again, his voice was soft and childlike. "They told me she was found on the boat. Were you there, too?"

"I called the ambulance," Petra murmured.

"What really happened to her?"

"Wish I knew. Last I saw her was before we set sail, and she was fine." *Well, that's not entirely true, is it?* Cracked cement thudding beneath the tires echoed her feet on the pilothouse steps, drawn by raised voices on deck. A figure stalked away from the slip; before Petra's bionic eye could focus, a crash belowdecks had sent her dashing into the surgery cabin.

"What the hell, Mechanic? Who were you yelling at out there?"

"Oh...just some old troll complaining that your music is too loud. No big deal."

"Then why are you beating up the bulkhead? I'm the one who gets in fights. You patch up the results."

"For how much longer? The more patients I get, the less I can do for them. The pharmacy crackdown at the hospital...that horrible HARMONY bill the news keeps squawking about...other things...whenever I find a solution, someone tries to shut me down!"

"You wanna know why I started calling you 'mechanic'? Not just a play on your last name. And not just because you treat cyborgs. It's because you tinker with the big societal machine. You're determined to fix the malfunction between biohackers and healthcare, even if you have to break a few parts in the process."

"Sometimes that's the only way, like resetting a crooked bone. You know better than most people how much healing can hurt."

"Having a good caregiver helps."

"I doubt I qualify."

"I don't. You're the only person I trust who isn't buried in the seabed. If you think something needs breaking, I'll hand you the damn hammer. ...Oof, easy, a hug like that will dent even a titanium shoulder!"

"I can replace it for ya, Rock. Got two bags full of top-end refurbished gear here, if you girls wanna quit cuddling and get to work."

"Says the guy who strolls in late! Take one of those metal limbs and stick it, Steel. And I don't mean in the locker...."

"Hey, Petra, we're here." Kade's voice yanked her from the memory. Biocinium headquarters loomed from the darkness; the nimble coupe just made the turn. Petra parked in a far corner of the lot, away from the cameras. Bay breeze wrapped her in familiar scents of dank mud and spilled chemicals.

"Welcome to Biocinium Technologies," chimed the entry screen. "We look forward to upgrading your life during our business hours, starting tomorrow at—."

"Genius never sleeps," said Kade, swiping his badge. Night transformed the lobby's glacial glass to obsidian. Cameras winked in the ceiling corners.

"There's no way to avoid the security cameras," Petra murmured to Kade. "We'll have to come up with a story for Simms about why you let me in after hours."

"Easy. I was showing off all my brilliant inventions to impress a girl." He summoned the elevator and waved her inside with an exaggerated bow. "After you, milady."

She shot him a warning look, and he kept a chastened silence until they reached the basement. Doors grumbled open; Petra put out a single foot and froze.

"What?" Kade asked, but she held up a hand. Faint squeaks filtered into her aural implant.

It could just be the heat system, or a server rack, or... A second sound emerged: an unmistakable, un-mechanical rhythm. *...Footsteps!*

Warm breath tickled her ear. "What is it?"

"Someone's already here. Who else works late?"

"Nobody. Simms is probably still guzzling free drinks at the hotel, I've never seen his wife on-site, and I don't let the business staff into the lab without me. I promise, we've got the whole place to our—." The noise cut off Kade's last syllable. Fear widened his eyes. He retreated into the elevator, clutching Petra's arm, but she pulled away. "What are you doing?"

"Maybe catching a thief." *Or a murderer.* "Stay here."

She tapped a sequence on her skinterface, and night vision illuminated the corridor in a green haze. Sounds of the adversary's movement grew louder as she padded down the hall. So did her heartbeat in her ears.

Just like the old days. Sensors detect an anomaly. Track it down. Defend territorial integrity. She calculated potential force dispersal and engagement strategies, but none of the scenarios left her confident. *Still not a hundred percent recovered from yesterday, still got a screwy shoulder...not exactly fighting fit here, Rock.* The lab door stood open. A lone figure moved within, back turned. *Unless they're tricked out like Steel, I might be able to take them if I move fast.*

Drawing a sharp breath, Petra launched herself into the room and pinned the intruder against a desk. A woman's cry echoed off the equipment. The bin she'd been holding clanged to the floor; cans Petra and Kade had collected clattered away again.

Who steals empty cans? Petra spun her captive around. Adrenaline fizzled. She released the bionic claw. "What are *you* doing here?"

"Tidying one of the few places in Baltimore that hasn't been turned over to janitor robots," said Grace, brushing off her indigo smock. "It's a part-time job to help with Ayodele's doctor bills. What's your excuse?"

Before Petra could respond, Kade darted around her. "Hi, Mrs. N! I thought you were scheduled to come yesterday."

"I was, but I had a family emergency. Mr. Simms was kind enough to let me do the shift tonight instead." Wiping up soda residue from one of the spilled cans, Grace spritzed cleaner on the floor, revealing the source of the squeaks. "He said it was no problem, since you'd both be out of the office, attending an event."

"Yeah, he's still there. I just brought back a client for a follow-on demo," Kade wheedled, beaming a boyish smile.

"Client?" Grace raised her eyebrows at Petra.

"Only if I'm impressed. Kade, why don't you set up while Mrs. N here shows me to the ladies' room?" Taking Grace's arm in one hand and the cart handle in the other, Petra steered both out of the lab before anyone could speak further. She exhaled when the restroom door shut behind them. "Sorry, Grace. I didn't want him to know we'd met before."

Grace stacked her fists atop her ample hips. "Why?"

"Because his pet project is the same device we found in Del's head." Petra held up her hands against the older woman's swell of rage. "I don't know if he's involved or not, but there's definitely some link to this company. Jonathan and I are trying to find it."

"Before more people get hurt." Grace clenched her towel until lavender-scented drops splashed onto her shoes.

"Someone already has—a doctor from Jonathan's hospital. Did you ever meet her? April McCormick?"

"Yes! She ran an asthma treatment program that Ayodele did a few years ago. Always kind and friendly…what happened to her?"

"She was killed recently, and I think it was because of work she did for Biocinium. Did you ever see her here?"

"No, I only started a few weeks ago. I haven't seen any-one, except Kade—he works late a lot. A nice boy." Grace's stricken expression softened a little. "When the buses sus-pended service during that nasty storm a few nights ago, he insisted on driving me home."

Then he couldn't have been on the boat with Mechanic! Petra sagged back against the door, struck with an odd mix of frustration and relief. *But that doesn't mean Biocinium is off the hook.* "Grace, how much of this place can you access?"

"Everything except the factory floor." She held up her security badge.

"Would it cost you too much sleep to look around Simms' office for me?" asked Petra. "I think he's hiding something about Mec—Dr. McCormick, but I can't get in there without ending up on camera."

"Let it roll." Whipping back the curtain on the side of her cart, Grace yanked out the trash bag to reveal a hollow interior compartment. "All it will show is a humble custodi-an, coming in to dust the picture frames, the next best thing to being invisible."

Crouching down, Petra folded herself into the space. Her joints complained, but with knees tucked against her chest, she just fit. "Now I know where Del inherited their guts."

"When you've run into as many closed doors as I have, you learn how to pry open windows." The cloth dropped, concealing Petra from the outside. "But we'll have to be quick, or Kade will wonder where we've gone."

"Can you push this thing with me in it?"

Grace snorted. "Child, I butcher goat haunches with more meat on them than you. Hang on."

Wheels skidded, and Petra braced herself against the sides of the cart as Grace shoved it back down the corridor. One of the axles whined with each rotation; she assigned lyrics to the beat and sang in her head, steeling herself with old rock songs. A swooping sensation in her stomach marked the elevator's rise. Grace hummed nonchalance, strolling down the lobby's smooth expanse. Badge scanners beeped overhead, and the curtain rose on the sterile corporate set of Simms' office.

A hand appeared to pull Petra from the cart. "What are we looking for?"

"Hiring paperwork. Performance reviews. Anything that might tell us what Dr. McCormick did for Biocinium."

Donning a pair of gloves with the precision of a forensics technician, Grace opened the filing cabinet. Petra took the desk. A card reader dashed her hopes of accessing Simms' computer. Ignoring the photos and trophies, she inspected the top drawer: cheap promotional pens stamped with Biocinium's logo, business cards, and antacid tablets. The deeper second drawer held reams of print-outs. Beneath them lay a half-empty fifth of tequila.

"Simms' power lunch?" Snickering, Petra shuffled through the documents. Most were budget projections full of optimistic line graphs. Handwritten minus signs appended to the numbers suggested a less cheerful reality. "Anything, Grace?"

"Just a lot of legal-looking letters, rejecting applications for studies and product approvals."

"I'm starting to think this whole company is bogus." Petra opened the last folder. A note clipped to the inside cover bore the familiar scrawl from her prescriptions:

S -

This is the last batch I can provide. B just keeps demanding more and more, and I can't live with it any longer.
- A

Live with what? Petra studied the folder's contents. Pages rattled in her shaking hands.

"Petra?" Grace's concerned voice drew her back to the room. "Did you find what you wanted?"

"Yes and no." Pulling out her phone, Petra began photographing the pages. "I found the information I was looking for. But it's the last thing I wanted."

17. SILENT PARTNER

Jonathan climbed out of the coupe and cast a loaded glance at Petra. "Let me know how it goes."

"Don't worry, I'm like a medic for machinery," Kade told him, scrambling into the vacated seat. With a wink at Jonathan, Petra zoomed off toward the bridge. He watched the taillights fade, caught between relief and concern.

Glad I had an excuse not to go back to that rotten Biocinium factory! But should I have left Petra alone? No question she can handle herself, but she's still not well, and if Kade really is tied up in April's murder...

A spectral glow behind the diner's upstairs curtains reminded him of other responsibilities. He compacted his worry into an uneasy seed, let it settle in the pit of his stomach with all the others, and climbed the stairs to the Njokus' apartment.

Television flickered across the sofa's motionless occupants. Hank snored softly, chin on his chest, while Del stared at a laptop balanced on pajama-clad knees.

They glanced up and grinned. "How was your date?"

"It wasn't a date." Tucking a throw blanket around his dad, Jonathan sank onto the middle cushion. "We just snooped around a professional event."

"At the Lord Baltimore Hotel?" A few keystrokes filled the screen with a traffic camera image of the building's entrance. "What a waste. When I watched you two go in, I imagined you having drinks at the skybar, not sitting in some stuffy conference room. I thought up your orders and every-thing."

"Oh, yeah? What did we get?"

"Petra had one of those cocktails in the shiny copper mugs—"

To match the hand holding it.

"—You had a diet soda, because you're boring, but you splurged on a crab dip appetizer to share."

"There haven't been crabs in the bay since before you were born."

"Then they were probably available the last time you had a date," said Del tartly. "Let me pretend one of us has a life."

"If anyone's pretending, it's me," Jonathan muttered, plucking at the loose thread in his cuff. *Pretending I don't break the rules as much as April, or maybe even Petra. Pretending old medicine can treat new problems. Pretending I can do more than just shove stretchers and count an old man's pills.*

"What's that supposed to mean?" Del's question yanked him back from his mind's dark precipice.

"It means you can do way better at life than I did, if you don't throw it all away." He peeked under the bandage covering Del's ear. Flakes of dried blood still clung to the sutures, but the wound showed no signs of inflammation. "Dr. Bhagat did a good job. This'll heal nicely."

"Too bad she couldn't stitch up my lungs."

"I thought she was going to recommend new asthma meds?"

"She said I was already on the most powerful stuff available for treating attacks. The best I can do is avoid having them in the first place. Check the air quality reports, wear a mask, or just not go out at all."

"But you already do those things, and it's not helping," said Jonathan, baffled. *No wonder Petra felt desperate enough to try illegal bionic parts after she was wounded. Bhagat's approach is so conservative, it's practically useless!*

"Apparently the best time to treat my asthma was fifty years ago, when there was still a chance at cleaning up the planet," said Del with a snort.

"So she prescribed a time machine?"

"More like nasty-tasting dose of reality. Lots of plants and animals can't survive in this crappy environment any-more—why should we expect humans to be any different? I'm like one of those endangered species preserved in a ter-rarium, watching the world through glass." Del slumped back in their sweatshirt hood and clicked through the video feeds again, hopping intersections like a digital jaywalker. Grainy night time footage reduced Butchers Hill to charcoal smudges. "I lost you when the coupe sped through that inter-section, but picked you up again coming off the bridge. Where'd you go next? Petra's pad?"

"No. A friend's house."

"Liar. You have even fewer friends than I do."

"One of Petra's friends." Jonathan dug his fingers into the sofa foam. *That's true, actually. The more I learn about April, the more it feels like I never really knew her at all.*

"I don't know what's more pathetic—an afterparty for a lecture, or that this guy didn't get an invitation," said Del, magnifying the live feed. A pixellated figure loitered in front of the McCormick house. Climbing the front steps stiffly, he knocked on the door, then tried to peer in the windows. A shifty glance over his shoulder revealed pugnacious features, unmistakable even at a distance.

"That's SoulSteeler!" Del turned narrowed eyes from the screen to Jonathan. "You two have a mutual friend?"

"Yes, and she's dead," he replied, too startled for obfuscation. "So why is he snooping around her house when he knows she's not home?"

Chrome-painted fingernails pounced on the keyboard, and a screen capture appeared in one corner. "Whatever it is, it can't be good...except as a discount on my next upgrade."

"No biohacking, and no blackmail! Send me a copy and I'll see if the police will look into it," said Jonathan. "While you're at it, can you access the cameras around Henderson's Wharf?"

"I can spy on stadiums, concert halls, and police dash cams, and you want to watch a bunch of rich people's bathtub toys?" Sighing with theatrical dismay, Del opened a new window. "What dates do you want footage for?"

"The departure and return of that screws cruise you took last week. I want to see who else was on board. Did you notice anyone?"

"There were two other passengers, but I didn't get a good look at them. We all covered our faces to hide from the city cameras, and sat apart on the boat. No one even talked." Del scrolled through a command line. "Super boring. I just watched videos on my phone until SoulSteeler called me in for surgery."

"So you were the first patient? Then who?"

"A guy who seemed like a repeat customer—he said something about getting an implant adjusted. Pain zoned me out for a bit there, but I kinda woke up when Steel and the doctor started arguing."

Jonathan sat up straighter. "About what?"

"I couldn't hear much. The cabin door was shut, and the storm was getting noisy outside." Del curled their knees in more closely, looking very young; the image of them huddled in the yacht's salon, woozy and alone with waves cracking against the windows, made Jonathan's chest ache. "Steel eventually came out and said we were turning back early because of the weather. He told the third passenger they could rebook, then ran off to the toilet. The person went to talk with the doctor. Rescheduling, I guess."

That passenger might have been the last person to see April alive...or the first one to see her dead. Jonathan took a deep breath to steady his voice. "Did you see the doctor again?"

"No, just a glimpse of the pilot going into the surgery cabin as I was leaving. Why?"

"Because my ambulance took the doctor to the hospital right after that. She didn't make it," said Jonathan, looking away.

Del's eyes went round. "That's horrible! What happened to her?"

"I'm hoping your third passenger knows."

"And you want the marina footage to identify them. Easy." Del entered more code, then uttered a curse that would've made Grace weep. "The marina isn't on the municipal network. It's got a private security system."

Hopes deflated, Jonathan slouched back into the sofa. "Then you can't access archived footage?"

"Of course I can. It'll just take longer. I've got to identify the service they use, locate their server, figure out its vulnerabilities...it might actually keep me entertained for an evening or two. But I expect payment."

Jonathan pulled up the banking app on his phone. "I'll tack it on to the geezer-sitting fee. How much?"

"Money can't buy me freedom!" Plaintive brown eyes met his. "I want a sightseeing tour in Petra's awesome car, one hour for every hour I spend hacking this camera system. Somewhere with scenery other than brick and concrete. You can come, too, but I get shotgun. And full stereo control rights."

Jonathan laughed. "I think she'd agree to that."

Del studied him as if he were an arcane network configuration they itched to enumerate. "Why do you want all this stuff, anyway?"

"Skip the questions, and I'll ask if Petra will let you drive some circles around a parking lot."

With an eager squeal, Del opened a new VPN window, but yanked back their fingers when Jonathan shut the laptop. "Watch the mani! Jeez! I thought you wanted this data?"

"Not as much as I want your incision to heal. The footage can wait until tomorrow. You need rest, and if you're not in bed pretending to be asleep when your mom gets home, she'll put us both in the stew pot." Jonathan chivvied Del off to their room, then shook his father gently awake and repeated the routine downstairs. "What music do you want tonight, Dad?"

"Shuffle 'em. I'll be asleep before the chorus anyway." Hank yawned.

Jonathan picked a random playlist. One of Petra's dance songs rolled out of the speaker. It sounded flat without the richness of vinyl, or the gentle weight of another body leaning into his.

"What is it?" mumbled Hank. "You're smiling."

"Is that bad?"

"No. Just rare." Flashing a grin of his own, the old man rolled over.

Jonathan stepped out and leaned against the closed door. Musical vibrations soaked through the wood. Instead of energizing him, the rhythm lulled his tense muscles. He collapsed on the couch. Imperfect melodies haunted his dreams until a harsh note jarred him awake. Blinking his vision clear, he jolted back in surprise: Petra sat on the rug, winding a fresh string around the guitar peg.

"Sorry." She glanced up through her unruly bangs. "Bionic fingers don't replace strings as easily as they break them. I wanted to surprise you."

"You did," Jonathan muttered. "How did you get here?"

"Grace let me in. I gave her a ride home from Biocinium."

He scrubbed at his eyes, then his ears. "What was she doing there?"

"She's the custodian."

"*That's* her night job?" he squawked. "Stocking fresh toilet paper at the place that almost killed my dad?"

"That, and enabling a little corporate espionage." Setting the guitar aside, Petra handed over her phone. A bleached flash photo showed a note clipped to the inside of a folder.

Jonathan's pulse skipped a few beats: *that's April's handwriting!* "What am I looking at?"

"A pile of papers I found in Steve Simms' desk."

"*The last batch,*" Jonathan read part of the preface aloud. "Who's B?"

"Bhagat, probably. My guess is that Mechanic knew Bhagat was on to her side hustle, and bailed."

"Bailed on what?"

An impatient wave of the glove mimed a swipe. Jonathan scrolled to the next image, showing a typed form. No name appeared at the top, only an identifier number. Check boxes listed different body parts and a number of common conditions. Dated entries going back months recorded assessments of the anonymous patient: *male, mid-40s, wears a modified industrial exoskeleton to alleviate mobility pain from a spinal injury...*

"Is this some kind of medical record for Steel?" asked Jonathan.

"Keep going."

Female, early 30s, numerous bionic components. Two advanced prosthetic limbs. Aural and ocular implants. Mechanical cardiac pacemaker with faulty battery likely responsible for chronic heavy metal toxicity...

He looked up from the screen; Petra's intense gaze awaited his conclusion. "That's you."

"And dozens of other local biohackers I recognize from the descriptions of their hardware." Baleful scarlet flashed in her artificial eye. "The reports go back more than a year. Our health problems, the upgrades we used to treat them, the side effects...she must've taken notes on every secret patient she treated."

"But how did Simms get them? Kade said all April did for the company was medical evals."

"She was evaluating, all right. Us!" Delving into her coat pocket, Petra pulled out a notebook and threw it at Jonathan. "I found that in her bag after she died."

His stomach clenched. "You went through April's things?"

"For clues about who might've killed her. I thought there might be a hint in her notes, but I couldn't decrypt her lousy

handwriting. Until I compared it against the Biocinium papers." Petra began pacing around the coffee table. "And here
I've been hauling her crap around in my car, afraid the cops
might find something in it to incriminate *her*!"

Well-worn pages whispered under Jonathan's thumb.
After a few minutes deciphering April's scrawl, he matched
paragraphs to the transcribed notes Petra had photographed.
"I don't believe she'd do that."

Petra gripped the couch cushions behind Jonathan's
shoulders, enveloping him in her atmosphere of citrus and
salty night air. "Maybe not your fantasy version of her. But
while do-gooder April was batting her eyes at you in the ER,
Mechanic was stitching us up and selling us out!"

"Maybe she was trying to advocate for her biohacker
patients the only way she knew how."

"By turning us into case studies? We don't need that
kind of help," Petra snapped. "If she were really invested in
taking care of us, she wouldn't have let a little pressure from
Bhagat scare her off."

"You don't know that's what happened. B could be
someone else."

"Like who?"

"How about Bukowski?" Grabbing his own phone,
Jonathan pulled up the screenshot Del had taken from the
security camera. "City surveillance caught Steel snooping
around the McCormicks' house, just after we left."

"What the hell?" Petra zoomed the picture in and out.
"He almost never went there, even when Mechanic was
alive. Said it was too risky for them both if anyone linked
her to Heavy Metal. Why would he visit Kade?"

"Leverage?" Jonathan suggested. "Del just told me that Steel argued with April on the yacht. I bet he caught her taking those notes."

Petra's eyes widened. "So that's what they were fighting about."

"You heard them? And you didn't think to mention that?"

"I didn't mention that the wind blew or the tide changed, either—it's just part of the environment. Those two bickered all the time! Besides, I only caught a piece of it, when I got on the crew headset to tell them we were heading back."

"Enough time for Steel to kill April for betraying him. And now that we gave him the link to Biocinium, he's after her brother." Jonathan closed the notebook. "What did Kade say about all this?"

Petra snorted. "He was mad he missed all the fun."

"I can't believe he lived with her and had no idea about her double life."

"Well, he does seem kinda clueless about anything beyond his microscope."

"'Brother' also starts with b."

"Grace saw him at work the night Mechanic died, so he wasn't on the boat." Handing back the phone, Petra turned nervous pivots on the rug: one-two-three-*spin*. "But that just means he didn't hold the knife. Maybe he and Steel were in on it together, somehow."

"Why would Kade extort a sister who's already supporting him?"

"To get *more and more*, just like her note said. If he's committed to his new career, he might've squeezed her for information that would give the company an advantage."

One-two-three-*spin.* "He could've blackmailed her into sharing our medical records, or even testing the Beat for him."

"And bribed Steel with some laboratory leftovers to chop it out again when April stopped cooperating." Jonathan dug his nails into the tattered upholstery.

"You think he operated on her between trips to the head?"

"It wouldn't have taken long to drug April and take a stab at her skull. Propofol works fast."

"And if he were sick, that could explain why he didn't finish the job." Petra grimaced. "It makes sense. We need to find out what Steel was doing at the house."

"I hope Kade made your shoulder indestructible."

She swung her arm like a softball pitcher. "He did a good job, but I'm not going to risk it on another round with Steel. No busting into the workshop this time. We're going to be strategic about it, and get him in a talking mood."

"Is he ever?"

"Yeah, on Sundays, when he drags his butt out of the basement and onto a barstool. Well, not physically. He broke too many and got tired of paying for damages." Picking up the guitar with an apologetic grin, Petra snapped off the excess wire with a flick of her metal fingers. "Anyway, he'll be glued to the football games at his favorite watering hole, halfway through a bucket of beers by the second slate. That usually loosens his lips. Unless his team is losing."

"Then what?"

"Then it'll be a good thing I brought along a paramedic." She set the repaired instrument in his lap and headed for the door.

Jonathan's fingers slid unbidden to the tuning frets. "I should be getting overtime for all the emergencies you drag me into."

"I can probably get you a discount on some upgrades at Steel's parlor," said Petra, pulling on her boots.

"Actually, there is one thing you can do for me."

Her body went as still as a cocked pistol.

"Give Del a spin in your car." Jonathan explained his bargain, and Petra's cautious stance eased into amusement.

"If Del can help us crack this case, I'll sponsor a day trip all along the coast."

"Perfect. I hear the saltwater taffy really lives up to its name since Ocean City sank."

A mischievous slash of hair fell across Petra's eyes. "Your dad wants to jam with me. Your trainee wants to interview me. Now your de facto kid sibling wants to be my co-pilot."

Jonathan plucked one of the new strings. It sang a pure, brassy note. "Must be your magnetism."

"Well, I do keep pointing back toward the north pole! But if those people are drawn to both of us, while we repel each other, you know what that means?" Petra smirked around the closing door. "We're too damn similar."

18. BAD COMPANY

Weapon blades gleamed darkly in the setting sun. Tension etched the soldiers' figures. Arm upraised, their leader waved them forward with a rallying cry:

"Petra!" The hail yanked her from the monument's bronze relief, back to Patterson Park. She whirled. Jonathan trotted up, frowning at her reaction. "I know I'm late, but you shouldn't be that startled to see me."

"Just adrift in war stories."

"You do a lot of cavalry charges in the Arctic Ocean?"

"Just narwhal jousting." She socked his arm, careful to use her organic fist. "What kept you? I thought you were off work today."

"Yeah, but I had to take Dad to the clinic after he accidentally buttered his toast with spackle. He's fine, but…" The rest dissolved in a long exhale. "If Biocinium never sells a single damn Beat and goes under for good, it'll serve them right for what they did to his brain."

"You wanna make that happen? Let's find Mechanic's killer." The park's shade fell away as they merged with dinnertime crowds in Highlandtown. Muffled cheers erupted from bars they passed.

Jonathan cast wary glances around him. "Couldn't we go someplace a little farther from the station? I don't want to run into anyone from work."

"Not my pick. Steel's loyal to his local—he's come here every Sunday for years." Petra opened the door of a pub on the corner. Its brick facade, once painted the jaunty green of pool table felt, had faded to olive under decades of sun and smog. Old event flyers covered most of the window, leaving the shabby interior so dim that her artificial eye shifted to night vision. She navigated the sea of purple jerseys toward a black-and-gold island in the back corner.

"Ugh, off the post!" Steel roared from his usual table, where he filled one entire side of a booth. His gaze hardly moved from the television array when Petra and Jonathan slid in across from him. "Someone needs to calibrate the kicker."

"Or the fans' expectations." Petra ran her finger across a quartet of empty bottles, making them chime. "Whatcha drinking?"

"Not enough." He slugged from a fifth bottle in his fist. "It's only the second quarter and we're already down by twenty."

"Yikes. Better let me buy you another round." Petra beckoned the nearest server. "Another beer for my buddy, please. I'll have a Moscow mule, and..." She turned to Jonathan for his order, but he'd shut his eyes in a fit of silent mirth. "What's funny?"

"Nothing. Guess I have to get a diet Coke."

"And throw in some crab cakes, since she's buying," Steel added as the server scurried away. He dismissed Petra's glare with a seismic shrug. "Hey, I gotta get my meals where I can, now that our charters are all washed up. Half my income came from those trips, and a lot of passengers end up as parlor regulars. It's gonna be lean times without Mechanic bringing 'em in."

"I guess she was good for business, in spite of working for free," said Jonathan acidly.

"Free like those apps that collect your personal data." Poking through a basket of ravaged wings, Steel gnawed an overlooked scrap. "A couple of months ago, I caught her between clients on a cruise, scribbling notes about their health and hardware. She must've been selling the info, 'cuz she begged me to keep it quiet. So I did."

"In exchange for what?"

"Hard-to-get meds for chemical biohacks. Queasy types who can't stomach a knife will pay a pile for pills." Steel drained his beer. "Get the goods on a doctor and it's like having a personal pharmacy on speed dial."

"Until they get caught," said Petra, casting Jonathan a guilty look. "Mechanic's boss was getting ready to can her for being so generous with meds."

"Which would've made April a lot less valuable to you than Del's blueprints." Jonathan crunched a paper napkin in his fist. "So you got rid of her."

"You sure he's an organic, Rock? 'Cuz he seems to be stuck in an endless loop." Steel picked at his teeth with a bone. "I already told you, I didn't kill Mechanic. Even if she was a self-righteous pain in the ass, no one else could deliver on both surgeries and scrips. I hope the junior Mechanic is half so handy."

"You mean Kade?"

"You know him? Figures, she introduced everybody but me. I told her to bring him on board—a bionics engineer with tech company connections would've made us the best biohacking crew on the East Coast!" Emphatic palms slapped the table, rattling bottles. "But she wouldn't let me near him. Wanted him to keep his nose clean and think Baltimore was just a big, sweet Berger cookie."

"Maybe it is, if you've got enough dough." The server returned, and Petra snagged a piece of garnish off the crab cake platter. *At least it's a cheaper bribe than his bail.*

"We might, if I can convince the kid to take his sister's place. I dropped by the house the other night, but he wasn't home." Steel tucked a napkin into his collar, accessorizing his jersey with an absurd paper cravat. "Come with me next time, Rock, and pour on the sweet-tea charm. That's the oldest and most effective biohack in the book."

Petra scoffed and flicked a cardboard coaster at Steel. It bounced off his chest. "Was that what you two bickered about on the boat that night? Recruiting Kade?"

"No. It was those, er, promotional items you saw in the parlor." Leaning forward, Steel continued in a yeasty hush. "The second passenger had one. Idiot thought I hadn't installed it right and wanted the real doctor to take a look. Mechanic freaked when she saw it. She said we'd be hosed if the device ended up in the wrong hands." Beady eyes flicked toward an adjacent table. Petra craned her neck over the booth, following his gaze. Four burly men with the unmistakable air of law enforcement huddled over a bucket of beers.

Jonathan glanced over, too, then snapped back so quickly that Petra's keen ear detected the crack of vertebrae. "Shit! There's Fisher, from work! I told you this was a bad idea. If he recognizes me—."

"—He'll have to eat all his petty jabs about how you never go out," Petra finished coolly, popping a paper straw into his drink. "Relax. There's nothing suspicious about happy hour on game day."

"Except maybe these imitation crab cakes." Steel licked tartar sauce from his fingers. "I don't wanna know what goes in 'em, but it's the most convincing recipe in the state."

"You should be the last person surprised when a fake product outperforms the original." Petra rapped a gloved finger against her mug and sipped, pretending the copper explained the chronic metal taste in her mouth. Over the rim, she caught Jonathan biting back a smile. "Seriously, why is this funny?"

"I thought Southerners liked bourbon, not vodka." Hesitation suggested a quick excuse, but his curious expression seemed genuine.

"My folks were teetotalers—Mom had religious prohibitions, and Dad had an alcoholic father he didn't want to take after—so I didn't drink much until I joined the military. *Sedna* rescued a lot of Russian sailors, who thanked us with cheap vodka that needed a mixer to make it tolerable. Juice was as rare as polar bear piss, but the ship always stocked ginger ale for seasickness, so this became the trendy cocktail for Arctic units. *Za nas!*" She raised the mug in a mock toast.

"What's that, 'cheers' in Russian?"

"More or less. The straight translation is *here we are*—as in, all of us friends drinking together. Or all of us sailors shivering at the top of the world."

"Or all of us wannabe cyborgs, patching our bugs to operate another day," said Steel, tapping his brew against hers. Glass and metal rang a discordant note. He took a long swig, watching television down the bottle like a misplaced telescope, and choked at a bad play. Opposing fans whooped around the bar.

"Your defense has more holes in it than my skeleton," snickered Petra.

"I would've made that tackle. What the hell, a penalty?" Steel fumed at the referees. "He barely touched the guy!"

"That's all it takes with a roster of robotic supermen," a man at Fisher's table grumbled. His mustache mimicked the cartoon mascot on his bottle, only speckled with foam. "There's no value in a fast running back when everyone gets a speed boost, or in a quick defensive end when the quarterback's suit keeps him balanced after a rush. Why'd they have to ruin the game with technology?"

"Safety." Steel patted his spine. "No game is worth getting broken. Trust me, I used to play pro."

"Then you were a damn pansy. Fisher here runs into burning buildings for a living, but you don't see him whining about a few bruises," said Stache, clapping the firefighter on the shoulder.

"No, but a mecha suit to prop up I-beams or carry out more survivors would be awesome." Fisher mimed gargantuan fists with a pair of steins. His other two companions chuckled, but Stache scowled.

"That's what they want, you know. To trick us into making ourselves half-machine, so we can be controlled."

"Y'all got nothing to worry about," said Petra, poisoning her accent with false sweetness. "Sounds like internet conspiracy nuts already control your brain."

Stache slammed down his beer and rounded on her. She rose to meet him, but Jonathan stood with her, blocking her exit from the booth.

"I assume you're coming over to buy this veteran a drink, since you're so appreciative of frontline fighters," he told Stache calmly.

"That can't be Rowell! Not on a school night, and with a chick to boot!" Fisher twisted in his seat, looking toward their table for the first time. His eyes went as round as the coasters, and he immediately turned his back again. "Good to see you out, man. Enjoy the game."

That's not the harassment he usually doles out! Is one of my parts showing? Petra checked her sleeve, but all her artificial components remained concealed. She glanced up at Jonathan for a clue. Befuddlement left his jaw slack.

"Vet, huh?" Stache sneered. "I got a friend who served in the Circle. Told me horror stories about human-enhancement tricks the Russian and Chinese militaries tried on their soldiers...and how the government covered up the same kind of experiments on ours." His eyes scanned Petra's body, and one side of his furred lip twitched in disgust.

Nerve impulses shot through the bionic limbs. Petra surged forward, trying to snake under Jonathan's arm. The impact made him grunt, but he braced himself against the bench and maintained his human barricade.

"Hey, if you can't beat 'em, join 'em." A chuckle echoed inside Steel's bottle. "If your 'robotic supermen' were shooting at me, I'd want a level playing field."

"I'd sooner sleep under the bridge than insult my god-given abilities like that," Stache snapped.

Steel appraised the weedy man with disdain. "God was a little stingy with some of us."

"You play the hand you're dealt! That's what makes you strong, not loading yourself up with gadgets. These so-called biohackers are just a bunch of cowardly cheaters."

"Cheaters, huh?" Wood creaked as Steel got to his feet, towering over his adversary. "Four on one seems like cheating, too. How about your friends ref while we settle this one-on-one?"

A swift uppercut replied.

Steel clamped Stache's wrist mid-swing and hoisted him skyward. "Only chumps play their hand when the game is rigged. If you want to win, you stick an ace up your sleeve." He yanked back his shirt cuff to display a framework of metal and wires.

"You got your suit back?" asked Jonathan, gaping.

"Turns out it's easy to get an operator's license." Steel grinned. "Shoulda done it years ago, but you know I hate giving money to the government. Guess we got something in common after all, pal," he told his captive, and opened his hand.

Stache crumpled, clutching a bent wrist. "Get that bionic bastard," he wailed. Two of his companions leapt at Steel. Their weight tipped him backward like a felled sequoia, crashing through the tabletop. Petra shoved Jonathan out of the booth an instant before it shattered and landed on top of him. Splinters rained around them. Stunned brown eyes stared into hers, so close she could count every lash.

"Why'd you stop me?" she growled.

"Because you barely staggered away from the last fight," Jonathan replied, breathless from the fall. "Did you really want to get involved in another?"

"I'd rather have stopped one rusher than have to deal with the whole team." Disentangling herself, Petra scrambled back toward the wreckage.

Steel lurched to his feet, dangling a man from each elbow like overloaded shopping bags. "You call that a blitz?" he roared, and flung them into the bar. Bone thumped. Beer dumped. Both assailants slid to the floor. Jonathan hurried over and checked their vital signs.

"Black-market hardware spilled on the dock is nothing compared to this kind of exposure! Power down before you get us all arrested!" Petra seized Steel's arm, but he shoved her away. She staggered into Fisher, rising from his defeated table.

He shouldered her aside, alarmingly strong even for a muscular man, and stalked toward Steel. Sweat glistened on his cheeks. "If you want a fair matchup, go against me." A strained whisper just registered in Petra's augmented ear: "Admire your handiwork."

Seizing one of the stools, Steel swung it at the firefighter. Fisher caught it between his hands, wrenched off two legs with a metal squeal, and flung them across the floor.

Rifles skitter across the deck, still clutched in arms ripped from sockets.

Memories paralyzed Petra where she stood. Patrons raced screaming for the exit.

Fall back, fall back, fall—commands dissolve into gurgles from a crushed throat.

Steel hurled the round seat like a discus. Fisher ducked it and charged. Big fists came up to meet him, but he dodged as if he could predict where each punch would fall.

Monsters cut through the boarding party in a blizzard of blades and blood.

Swift hits slipped under Steel's guard, pummeling the soft flesh that bulged between the exoskeleton's frame. For all its increased might, the mechanized suit responded too slowly against a nimble opponent. After a barrage of unanswered hits, Steel faked a spin and caught Fisher face-to-face. Triumph lit his expression. It washed away in a burst of blood as Fisher head-butted him in the nose.

Howling, Steel stumbled into the bar. His massive shoe nearly crushed one of the wounded sidekicks; Jonathan yanked the man aside, then moved to assess Steel's injury.

He held an empty palm towards Fisher's advance. "Okay, you win. That's enough. Let—."

Words shattered with the bottle cracked across his forehead. He dropped. Tossing aside the shards, Fisher snatched a stein off the table and raised it for a vicious blow.

It came down in a sparkling hail on Petra's bionic arm; her prostheses had processed the stimuli before her brain did, planting her between the two men. Fisher blinked in surprise.

Faceless helmet, hard and blank as ice in the midnight sun.

In the instant of advantage, Petra drove her elbow into his solar plexus. The crunch of a rib twisted her stomach. She took a step back, expecting the fight to fizzle, but Fisher leapt right back at her. Clawed fingers raked her throat.

Armored fingers against my neck. Bang. Blood. Bone. Body over the rail.

Terror and rage blinded her. Only the bionic eye transmitted its complex overlays. Fisher became a phantom in monocular vision. He descended again, and she met him with teeth bared. Fists and feet pounded a merciless rhythm, driving him back through a maze of upended chairs. Callused hands lifted her, primed to throw; she locked her metal leg around Fisher's waist. Wheezing, he lost balance.

Free falling fast—crash into cold ice and hot pain.

They collapsed onto a table, shattering plates and Petra's nightmare. She pinned Fisher in a pool of wing sauce and tilted his jaw to one side. A freshly glued incision shone beneath his hair.

He must've gotten one of Steel's prototypes! I'm too late. That damn device is spreading. Slivers of iris shone around the firefighter's dilated pupils, a thin ring of humanity she might still be able to grasp. Snatching a pitcher of ice water,

Petra upended it over Fisher's face. He spluttered, but his frantic breaths calmed a little.

"What does that chip do to you?" Petra demanded.

"Ch-ch-chip?"

"The neural node. The Beat. The devil's jump drive, shoved in your CPU."

"It's just supposed to juice me up. A little extra energy and strength. Double shifts. More money." Jittery words tumbled from his tongue; Petra could almost smell adrenaline on his breath like booze. "But it just makes me mad all the time. I tried to get it taken out, but the hack surgeon wouldn't do brain work on a rocking boat. Since I can't adjust it, I thought a few drinks with the boys might take the edge off." He glanced miserably at Stache, huddled around a broken wrist, and the woozy wingmen counting their bruises. Steel plopped on the floor nearby with a ruby-stained rag clamped over his nose. A few feet away, Jonathan slumped in a thicket of broken bar stools, blood coursing down his face.

Fisher's babbled explanations dimmed amid the hammer of Petra's heart. *Man down! Man down!*

Distracted, she loosened her grip. Fisher rolled free and bolted out through the kitchen, sobbing.

I can't let him run loose with that chip in his head! Petra started after him, but her bionic knee locked and pitched her forward. She caught a chair and stayed upright—barely. The room swam around her. *You're sinking, sailor. You couldn't catch that speedboat in this condition, even if he weren't hopped up on neurochemicals. Come about and rescue your crew instead.*

Slipping fingers beneath her collar, she tapped the skin-terface on her chest. Her pulse slowed to a less dizzying cadence. Steadied, she limped back to the bar and knelt beside

Jonathan. Blood welled from a long gash in his forehead. She gripped his shoulder and he sat up, groaning.

"Del didn't script this part," he muttered.

"What are you talking about? Del's not here." Petra pressed a handful of napkins against the wound. "Must've been a heavy beer to rattle your brain like that."

"M'fine." Jonathan touched the spot and winced. "Might need stitches."

"I can do that for you. On the house for being my o-line," said Steel thickly. Turning to the manager, he added, "same for your next battery change, if you keep this quiet."

The manager sighed and righted the toppled stools. "One of these days, Eddie, I swear I'm gonna call the cops."

"Someone already did," said Petra, cocking her head toward the street. Distant sirens whined.

"Aw, crap. If they find the crab tanks, I'm done for!" The manager dove through the kitchen door.

"Well, I guess the halftime show is over." Steel scooped a few french fries off the floor and crammed them into his mouth. "Let's get off the field before the cheer squad in blue shows up."

Petra wiped at the red smear oozing down Jonathan's cheek. "I don't leave wounded soldiers behind."

Meaty fingers gripped her arm and hauled her away. "You're not the all-American hero anymore, Rock. You're the insurgent. When the troops show up, you disappear to fight another day. Let them have the spies."

"Jonathan's not a spy," she snapped.

"Then why's he so eager to dig up dirt on Mechanic? You know EMS has to report to the cops when they come across biohacking operations, right?"

"He hasn't done that." Petra bit her lip. *At least, I don't think so.*

"Not yet. But Mechanic was a threat to his job, and to his stuffy morals. He should be buying her killer a drink. Or maybe you already did." Steel kicked Jonathan's fallen tumbler, splattering dark, sticky patterns across the floor.

"Bull! There's no way he'd hurt Mechanic. He knew her. Liked her. Loved her, even." The soda trail led Petra's gaze back to Jonathan, probing his brow with practiced hands. *Hands that could use a scalpel, administer a shot of anesthetics, and get close enough to Mechanic to do it all before she suspected a thing.* Bumps erupted on her arms. Sirens crescendoed outside, a voice for the rising panic in her head.

"Last call, Rock," said Steel.

She took one step after him, but her bionic leg rooted to the spot. "I'm staying."

"Fine. But no one's going to give you a medal for going down with this ship." Actuators whined an accusatory chorus as Steel ran off, leaving Petra in the familiar chaos of broken beams and blood.

19. SENSE OF DOUBT

"You're lucky," said the paramedic, applying another butterfly closure to Jonathan's brow. "An inch lower, and the glass might've stabbed you in the eye."

"I hear they've got good bionic replacements these days," he murmured, with a glance across the street. Petra paced the sidewalk, studying the crime scene from a safe distance. Emergency lights tinted her face in alternate pulses of blue and red.

Blue. Moonlight illuminating her silver tattoos as they danced to old rock records on the yacht.

Red. Watching through a haze of blood while she fought Fisher, metal fingers dripping beer froth like rabid jaws.

It looked like she wanted to kill him! How can she go from joking and drinking cocktails to…that?

Petra's own admission whispered in his brain: "*Depends on my mood.*" Jonathan clamped palms over his temples to silence her voice and the ringing in his ears.

"Are you sure you don't want a lift to the ER? Even a minor blow to the head can—."

"—Cause a subdural hematoma. I know. I'll get checked out if the headache gets worse," Jonathan promised, waving his colleague off to treat others. He ran through the checklist of symptoms—*disorientation, irritability, altered breathing patterns, deviated gaze*—and epiphany hit him harder than Fisher's beer bottle. *I've had all those things since Petra bowled me over on the jetty. She dragged me into her cyborg shadow world, just like April. And look how that ended.*

Cold raced up his back, but it might only have been a draught from the pub door behind him. Corporal Duke led the manager out in handcuffs and bundled him into the squad car. Catching sight of Jonathan, she strolled over.

"You're on the wrong side of the stretcher, Rowell." Light words didn't match the concern on her face. "What were you doing in a rough place like this?"

He grasped at Steel's earlier remark for an excuse. "Best imitation crab cakes in Baltimore."

"I hope you're not allergic to shellfish. We caught the manager out back, tipping tanks full of endangered species down the storm drain. Fish and Wildlife will have a field day. Maybe the tech crime unit, too." Duke nodded at the ambulance. The mustached instigator cradled a splinted wrist. Gauze speckled the limbs of his two cronies. "Those men gave statements claiming a biohacker attacked them."

"That's not true!" Petra joined the conversation, arms folded tightly over her chest. "Those jerks started harassing a guy at the next table, and Stache there threw the first punch. He just picked on someone way out of his weight class."

Duke appraised her with narrowed eyes. "You were at the marina last week, weren't you? The description the victims gave sounds an awful lot like your friend with the unregistered exoskeleton. Was he here tonight?"

"It's not a crime to have a few drinks."

"It might be, if it leads to assault. I'm surprised you haven't filed charges, after what he did to your shoulder." Resting a casual hand on her holster, Duke stepped beyond the reach of Petra's arm. "But maybe your memory heals as fast as your body."

Petra pulled down her sleeve, even though the prosthesis remained fully covered. "What can I say? Jonathan's a good first responder."

"That's true." Warmth softened Duke's suspicious smile. "I owe my kid's life to that."

"Not this story again, Latoya." Heat in Jonathan's swollen face intensified, but the corporal had already launched into the episode.

"My son is in the same grade as Jonathan's neighbor, Del, and used to join some of their tutoring sessions. But he always liked storytelling better than subtraction, so when a hurricane blew the top off the trash incinerator smokestack one summer, he bailed on study time for a citizen journalism scoop. His close-ups got too close, and he fell into the flood-ed river. Almost drowned."

"Technically, he did." Jonathan's hands twitched, recall-ing how CPR compressions had slid against the greasy residue of stormwater.

"Technically, you could have, too," Duke shot back. "But you fished him out and got him breathing again. I'll always owe you for that."

"He's got a knack for being there when someone's in trouble," said Petra, smoothing one of the butterfly strips. Even gentle pressure ignited the wound; Jonathan winced, and Petra withdrew like she'd been burned.

Is she hurt, too? Instinctive medical assessment faded when he realized she'd touched him with her bionic hand, and he'd flinched. *Well, she probably is now.*

But something sharper than insult gleamed in the grey eyes. Petra studied him a moment, then stalked away without another word.

Duke indulged a smirk. "I didn't picture that as your type, but I'm glad you're getting out."

"We were following up on a case."

"A case of beer?"

"I'm serious. The doctor that St—er, Eddie Bukowski referred you to helped other biohackers, and I think someone might've killed her for it." He sketched out the argument in a few sentences—a stolen device, research for a biotech company, a mysterious third passenger—until Duke held up a hand.

"I'm going to pretend you didn't just admit to running an unofficial homicide investigation," she said sternly.

"Then make it an official one."

"I'd need more than your circumstantial evidence. If you ever submit that report you owe me on the screws cruise, maybe I can take action. At least I can seize the boat. Forensics will be useless by now, but we can stop them running more charters."

And put Petra on the street. Will she be able to charge her limbs without her records? How will she make it, without a job or a place to stay? She leaned against a lamppost on the opposite corner, one foot tapping a secret melody on the pavement. *Vindicating a dead woman means destroying a live one.*

"Wasn't she the one who called the ambulance that morning?" asked Duke, following his gaze.

"Yeah, so?"

The corporal shrugged and headed back to her car. "When our murder boards get complicated, usually the answer isn't adding new links. It's tracing connections back to the center, because the answer was right in front of us from the start."

Questions lurking in Jonathan's subconscious burst like blood vessels. *Why would Petra want to investigate April's death if she were involved? It wouldn't make any sense. Unless...* Green traffic signals blazed like April's eyes in the ambulance. Her last words echoed in his memory: "don't trust her."

She warned me, right then and there, but I didn't listen! Dizzy, Jonathan stumbled away from the bar. Sunset's last ember smoldered at the end of Eastern Avenue, turning brick the color of dried blood. He fixed his gaze on the glow and tried to outpace the darkness on his heels.

"Wait up, long legs!" Petra appeared at his side. Her bionic limbs lagged slightly, drained in the fight. "Did your cop friend have any other leads?"

Yeah, and one of them is following me.

"How's your head?"

Thinking clearly for the first time all week.

"If you can make it to the marina, I'll drive you home."

Or into the harbor.

"Did that bottle cut out the speech region of your brain?"

"If it did, maybe Fisher is qualified to be your new screws cruise surgeon," muttered Jonathan, sinking onto a bus stop bench. "Bet he could do amputations barehanded."

"Because he had a knockoff Beat! One of Steel's party favors." Petra cast anxious glances up and down the street, as if expecting an assailant to leap from behind a fire hydrant. "When the fists started flying, it must've cranked up his brain chemistry, just like the *tuniit.*"

"So that's why he went postal." *And why she almost killed him—he was just another enhanced enemy, on a different parallel.* Jonathan slid farther down the bench to put extra inches between them.

"And why he tried to get it re-calibrated. He must be the passenger Mechanic and Steel argued about!"

"So what now? Am I supposed to chat him up over coffee and doughnuts at work?" Shards of laughter caught in Jonathan's throat. "Hey, buddy, how about that matchup on Sunday? What a great play, when you tried to lobotomize me with a lager!"

"He might be as much a victim as you are." Petra paced slowly along the curb. "I think we've been looking at this whole thing backwards, because we both wanted Mechanic to be innocent."

"How is she not?"

"She'd worked with Steel long enough to know he'd never sit on those knockoffs. Maybe that's what she was counting on—biohacker patients coming back to her with their Beat prototypes, so she could take notes that would help Kade get his clinical trial."

Pain swelled in Jonathan's skull. "She might have justified collecting medical records, but I don't believe she'd experiment on her own patients."

"But it explains everything!"

"Not why someone would murder her!"

Headlights cast a shifting halo around Petra's silhouette. "Then maybe it wasn't murder."

"What else could it be? No one accidentally gets a huge dose of anesthetics in their bloodstream, and Ciro's tests proved April wasn't a chronic abuser."

"Kade hit on it the other night." Digging in her pocket, Petra pulled out one of her citrus drops. "Bhagat follows Mechanic to the marina and tells her she's fired, thanks to Steel squeezing her for drugs. Her career, and her means of paying the blackmail, is ruined. But her little brother—who she's so determined to support that she'll test his stolen brain chip design herself—finally has a chance to succeed."

Revulsion flooded Jonathan's mouth. "No."

"So she gives him the last, biggest boost she can," Petra plowed on without mercy. "She exposes the chip so Steel or I will find it and keep it out of the cops' paws. Then she puts herself to sleep, knowing Bhagat will cover up her cause of death for appearances, and Kade will get everything."

"April did not commit suicide!" Images of her lively face strafed across Jonathan's mind: asking about his father's health, brushing his finger as she handed him a cup of cafeteria coffee, finding a smile for every patient he rolled into her hectic shifts. "She wouldn't just abandon her patients, or her brother." *Or me.*

"Something Bhagat said could've spooked her. Or maybe the third passenger threatened her—it could've been any local grinder who'd discovered her double deals."

"Like this mysterious B she mentioned in her note?" said Jonathan. "You haven't explained that."

"Maybe B isn't a person at all. It could mean the Beat. You saw what it did to Fisher back there. Mechanic was angry and gloomy before we sailed that night, not like herself at all. I didn't think much about it then, but maybe Steel's knockoff chip was messing with her head."

"She screamed at Dr. Bhagat in the ER that afternoon, too." Each reluctant word weighed on Jonathan's tongue. "I'd never seen her blow up like that before."

"There you go. The Beat must've been driving her mad. She wrote that she couldn't live with it anymore. So she escaped the best way she knew how." Petra cracked the lozenge between her teeth like a bone.

The sound drove a livid spike through Jonathan's head. "That's a crazy goddamn story. Just like the one about Dr. Bhagat murdering April. Or Kade stealing classified military tech. Or robotic yetis slaughtering your icebreaker crew."

Petra slapped the shelter wall behind him, caging his head between her arms. "*Sedna* is not a story!"

"No? Then how about this one?" Jonathan stood and glared down at her. "A paranoid veteran mistakes a new biomedical device for something she dreamed up in a hypothermic state, and kills the person wearing it."

Petra started shaking again—not with toxins, but with rage that seemed to crackle from the wild ends of her hair. "If that were true, why the hell would I call the rescue squad?"

"Cover. Look like a concerned bystander instead of a culprit."

"And then roped you into investigating her death?"

"You still wanted to find out where that chip came from, didn't you?"

Harsh laughter dissolved into the traffic noise. "Wow. You must've gotten hit real hard to dream up a theory like that."

"You haven't denied it," said Jonathan. "If your memory is as bad as you claim, you could even have forgotten that you killed April."

"Don't gaslight me! For all I know, you're the third guy. Maybe you followed Del aboard that night and confronted Mechanic yourself." The intensity of Petra's look transcended their height difference, making Jonathan's back muscles writhe. "What was it that pushed you over the edge? Your perfect ER crush helping us 'transhumanist freaks', or her secret research for the company that messed up your dad?"

"I would never have hurt her." Jonathan's hands curled into fists. "I teamed up with you to find out why she died!"

"Only after Bhagat tried to sweep everything under the rug, rather than investigate." Stabbing a hand into her jacket, Petra pulled out the pill container and rattled April's Beat under his nose. "I ruined your plan to expose Biocinium when I took their prototype off her body. So you let me do your dirty detective work, knowing I'd hunt down this chip if it killed me."

"It almost did, and I risked my ass to help you."

"Repairing your half-human targeting drone," Petra snarled. "The minute you had enough evidence to ruin the company that ruined your life, you'da turned me in."

"At least that would be one less killing machine on the street!" The words spurted out like blood from a stab wound. Scarlet flashed in the artificial eye, but it was the grey one that sliced to Jonathan's core. Breathless, he braced for an attack. Instead, Petra spun away and melted into the busy evening street. No parting shot, no wounded glance over her shoulder. Just vanished, with almost as much unexpected force as when she'd crash-landed in his arms.

Good riddance. Even if she isn't a murderer, she's a maniac. Wet warmth cloaked half of Jonathan's vision; the cut had opened again. He pressed a sleeve against his brow. *I've gotten two head injuries in a week from hanging around her! I can't afford worse—I've got people to look after. Living ones. Whatever April was to me, she's gone, and I can't help her any more than I could help Mom. I never should have even tried. Just stick with what you can handle, Jonathan, and stop pretending you can be anything more.*

Collapsing onto the bench again, he dropped his head to his knees until the smartbus arrived and swept him along its programmed circuit.

20. COME HELL OR HIGH WATER

Rising seas had dampened the Inner Harbor, but not its nightlife. Garrulous crowds wandered the shops and restaurants a block back from the old waterfront. Petra threaded the elbows like so many icebergs blocking her passage.

A lone vessel fighting through a numb sea. I've been chasing Sedna *for so long that I turned into her...or maybe something worse. What if I* did *forget something about the night Mechanic died? Is my brain so buggy that I can't remember committing murder?* Hot tears blurred her vision. Her feet navigated on autopilot until harsh cement softened to the clunk of dock boards. *In any case, I can't deny that my crews keep dying. The only safe thing is a solo voyage. Sorry, Kade, but I need this boat more than you do. I'll sail away someplace warm, earn enough on tourist charters to bribe a doctor for meds, and try to outrun the storms.*

Leaping aboard *Wind of Change*, Petra climbed up to the pilothouse and turned on the music. A song she and Jonathan had danced to blasted a fresh hole in her chest. *He could have left me on the deck in front of the stereo. He could have left me on the sidewalk outside the parlor, for the street-sweeper to suck up with the rest of the trash. He could have just thrown away my number after I ambushed him in the diner. But he didn't. After all that, I thought maybe...no, I should've trusted my instincts. He's a Type One, and I never should have expected anything different.*

She switched tracks and rocketed into the Chesapeake Bay. Old metal tunes blared at decibels that made even her functional eardrum throb; she screamed along to release the pressure in her chest. *You* are *like a hurricane, Rock, destroying everything in your path.*

Urban shorelines faded into a muttering border of trees. Bayou memories beckoned from the sultry darkness. *Okay, one last dip to say goodbye before I take off for the tropics.*

Turning into one of the bay's countless rural tributaries, Petra cut the speakers and the engine. Silence swallowed her. Slowly, the frozen soundscape thawed. Night birds called through the restless leaves. Frogs volleyed their songs between the banks. She crept onto the foredeck and her own soft breathing echoed the tide. Breeze tugged at her clothes.

At least the crawdads don't care what I look like. Petra pulled off her shirt and gloves. Fine hairs stood up on her arms, then relaxed, her skin's relieved exhale at freedom. Shoes and pants came next. The deck leached its last warmth into her sole.

"Oh, what the hell," she murmured, and ditched her underwear, too. Metal became moonlight, transforming her hybrid body into a smooth, luminous figure. The life preserver hung on its peg in the bow; Petra hurled it with practiced ease into the river. It sailed through the air and slapped down on the ripples. Climbing into the prow, she curled her toes around the rail.

"Hit me with your best shot, sea witch," she called, and dove. Flight sent endorphins soaring through her veins. For a heartbeat she zipped through the night like one of her old survey drones, a nimble flying machine. Then she pierced the water, and her hardware became anchors. Enhanced strength couldn't overcome their own weight. She stroked hard with her organic limbs, head barely above the surface. Brackish water covered her mouth and nose. The life preserver floated leagues away. She always threw it just beyond her range, making every swim a fight for survival.

And every time, her fingers grasped the ring just before she sank.

"Not today, huh, Sedna?" Petra panted. Draped over the buoy, she filled her starved lungs. Muddy air rinsed the bitterness of betrayal from her mouth. Rage ebbed with each defiant thump of her heart. Scooping wet hair off her face, she leaned back and surrendered to the current. Familiar constellations winked down at her; adrift on the floe, she'd sung to those stars in a hoarse whisper to keep herself awake. To keep herself alive.

Maybe I'm still on that goddamned ice raft, and this is all a delusion. Petra rolled her head to the side, half-expecting Seventeen's body beside her. Nothing appeared except plastic garbage caught in the tide. *Close enough, comrade—you were just another overpriced gadget thrown away, in spite of all your cutting-edge military tech.* Inspiration blazed across her mind like a comet, and she sat up so abruptly that she almost toppled through the ring. Kicking back to the yacht, she hauled her naked body dripping up the stern ladder. *There's one other person who might be able to tell me where the Beat really came from, if she's willing to talk. And if I'm finally ready to listen.*

Sunrise gilded the cars pulling into hospital staff spots around Petra's coupe. Harried caregivers in scrubs wove between the parked vehicles. Administrators moved at a slower pace, clutching expensive, non-synthetic coffees. At last a neat sedan purred in and a pair of chunky shoes swung from the driver's side door.

"Got a minute to consult, doctor?" Petra called, stepping into the tangerine light.

Bhagat's posture went even more rigid than usual. "You've never valued my medical opinions before."

"I'm more interested in your professional experience. At the lecture the other night, you mentioned pirated military technology." No listeners loitered nearby, but Petra lowered her voice anyway. "That wasn't just an example, was it? It was an accusation. You've seen the Beat before, too."

Bhagat clenched her purse strap. "We should talk in my office," she said, and swept off toward the hospital entrance. Even with fully charged limbs, Petra hurried to keep up. Employees cast curious looks at the pair—the coiffed doctor trailing a pixie-haired, denim-clad familiar—but barked critiques sent them scrambling.

"The waiting room is at least twenty percent fuller than usual for this time of day! I know we're short-staffed, but let's at least stay on top of triage. Don't forget to double-check those samples before sending them to the lab—if we have another mislabeling incident, I'll put everyone through remedial training. Move that empty wheelchair out of the hallway, for goodness' sakes. It's a tripping hazard!"

"You run a tighter ship than my old captain," said Petra.

"I suppose I have been a little snappish lately. It's been a miserable month." Bhagat ushered her into a small office redolent with chai and hand sanitizer.

"You've got a big inspection coming, right?"

"I could manage that. It's the endless parade of annoyances that makes things difficult. A tree branch fell through my roof in the storm last week. My terrified cat escaped through the hole, and I had to retrieve him from a muddy drain the next morning. When I finally got to work, Mc-Cormick turned up on a stretcher. Now we're a doctor short. If that weren't bad enough, the imbecile contractors I hired to fix the roof are not keeping their schedule, and waiting around for them makes me late for my shifts!"

Petra glanced at the framed pet photo on the shelf. *That explains the tardiness, the mud, and the phone call Jonathan overheard. Maybe Bhagat really is innocent—inflexible, but innocent.* "Sounds like civilian healthcare is getting as bad as the military kind," she said, earning a snort of concurrence from the doctor. "Why did you leave, anyway?"

"Ironically, for the same reason you did. I disagreed with the command's decisions about bionics." Bhagat measured a scoop of looseleaf tea into an electric kettle. A red power light on the appliance ignited like a robotic eye.

Petra glared back at it. "Didn't want to glue broken soldiers back together?"

"No, I refused to take them apart. You weren't the only patient brought in from the Arctic on that flight."

Hope shifted the axis of the world; off-balance, Petra gripped the back of the chair. "They told me there were no other survivors!"

"Not from the crew of *Sedna*."

The room settled, and the shadows seemed darker than before. "Seventeen?"

Steam veiled a haunted glance. "That was the only identity we ever established for him, too."

"But I spent days stuck on a slab of ice with him. He was dead." Plastic turned to cadaverous skin under Petra's hands. She wiped her palms on her jeans. "Believe me, I checked."

"His vital signs were too slight to register without medical equipment. The doctors who initially treated you both at the field hospital speculated that his bionic components enabled a sort of hibernation state. It was a practical innovation, minimizing an injured soldier's metabolic functions to buy time until they can be rescued."

Words crumbled on Petra's dry tongue. "He was *alive*?"

"That depends on your definition of the word. He didn't respond to any stimuli, even after we re-installed the neural node you removed. But when we hooked him up to an EEG, his brain activity was far beyond what we'd expect for even a healthy person." Taking a pair of glass tea cups from the shelf, Bhagat rubbed at a nick in one rim. "Seventeen was very much alive, cognitively. Just locked in."

"And the brass thought you could get him out?"

"Well, I *was* leading the premier rehabilitative medicine program in the service." Crisp pours of tea punctuated the statement. "I believed the brain was key to addressing all manner of other physiological ailments. Which, if you'd had the patience to hear me out at the time, was the reason I denied your request for advanced bionics until you'd received adequate psychological counseling."

Petra bristled. "So I had a salvageable body but a shattered mind, while Seventeen had a corpse with a quantum computer trapped inside?"

"You still enjoy your dramatic hyperbole, don't you?" Bhagat set a cup in front of her without sloshing a drop of amber liquid. "I thought the command wanted me to find a way for Seventeen to communicate, so they could interrogate him about the attack. But it quickly became apparent that they only wanted the technology he represented. That device you recovered was just part of an extensive bionic complex. My team was tasked to determine how it all worked."

"And recreate it?"

"Presumably. But I wasn't going to take part in unleashing more fighters capable of the carnage you reported on *Sedna*." An angry flick of Bhagat's head made her earrings glitter like sunlight on melted ice. "I resigned from the program, but doing so stalled my career. After a few years, I left and came here, where I could help heal people instead of disassembling them."

Petra clasped both hands around her cup, but its warmth didn't dispel the memory of frostbite. "What happened to Seventeen?"

"At the time I left, there was talk of bringing in some top neuroscientists from academia to examine him, but you know how quickly military leadership shifts its attention to the next shiny object. That poor young man is probably on life support in some dismal research laboratory, entirely forgotten. However, it seems at least part of him escaped." Unlocking a drawer, Bhagat withdrew a specimen container and laid it on the desk. "I removed this from a patient just a few days ago."

Del's chip! Petra swallowed. "I thought you had to turn in unlicensed bionic parts that come through the hospital."

"Yes, but to whom? The police aren't properly cleared to handle technology like this." A troubled sigh stirred the tea's surface, spiraling vapor around Bhagat's face. "And I certainly can't risk it spreading further."

"Too late." Taking out the jar with Mechanic's chip, Petra set it beside its counterpart.

Sharp breaths flared Bhagat's nostrils. "You got this from April McCormick, didn't you?"

"How did you know?"

She pulled a pamphlet from her desk drawer and slapped it down in disgust. Biocinium's logo shone up from the glossy paper, the same brochure that Simms had presented to Petra in his office. "She brought this in a few months ago, trying to persuade me to let her run a clinical trial on a new biomedical device."

"I'm guessing you said no."

"Not for the reason you think. In reviewing the company's details, I discovered that Dr. McCormick's brother is the chief engineer. If I'd let her lead a trial for his product, the hospital review board would have disciplined her for conflict of interest. But that was the least of my concerns when I recognized this so-called Beat." Bhagat moved items on her tidy bookshelf into imperceptibly neater alignment; the compulsive gesture seemed to calm her more than the tea. "How on Earth did that company obtain such sensitive material? Only a few people in DoD even knew of its existence, and all had special clearances. A leak seems unlikely."

"From our side," Petra murmured.

"Are you suggesting that a disgraced young inventor had access to the adversary source?"

"No, but his sister might have. She did more than just write prescriptions for biohackers—she moonlighted as a surgeon, installing parts for hard-luck scrappers like me." A few taps on the skinterface set Petra's bionic eye to a new light spectrum, exchanging red winks with the kettle. Bhagat gasped and fumbled her cup. The prosthetic hand caught it. "We import hardware from all over the world. She might have come across an original version and tipped it to her brother as a graduate project. When it got him in trouble, she tried to make up for it by getting him a job at Biocinium and testing the prototype."

"Ah, so that *was* the cause of her wound. After we lost her, I looked at the brochure again and wondered if there was some connection." Abandoning the tea, Bhagat took her lab coat from a wall hook. "It's a pity she can't tell me how many more classified surprises should I expect to pop up in my ER."

"Maybe she can." A snowstorm of new information swirled in Petra's mind. She thawed the brain freeze with the rest of her scalding drink and stood. "Thanks for the tea… and for confirming where this chip came from. I'm glad you don't think I'm crazy this time."

"I never thought you were crazy in the first place, just young and distraught." Bhagat straightened the coat's collar. "But perhaps those factors inclined me to give your input less credence than it deserved."

"Likewise." The words came out a little stiff, loosening some long-rusted screw in Petra's chest. For the first time, she let her eyes settle directly on Bhagat's stern ones. "Funny that after all these years, we're on the same side."

The older woman held the door for her with a thin smile. "We always were."

Half-blind with hypotheses, Petra dashed back through the ER and almost collided with the front end of a gurney.

"Sorry!" Jonathan exclaimed from behind it, then blanched when he recognized her. The bandage on his forehead tugged up one eyebrow, heightening his startled expression. Numbness crept through Petra's fingers and toes. She glared at him; his throat worked in silence.

Evans had no such reservations. "You shouldn't run in the corridors, or you'll end up on one of these," she told Petra, gesturing at the stretcher. "Are you all right?"

"I…" Discoveries sparkled on the tip of Petra's tongue. She searched Jonathan's face for a flicker of interest, but he wouldn't look at her. Excitement soured in her throat. "I've got somewhere to be." She shoved past the paramedics before either could reply, and almost sprinted to her car.

For several minutes she just sat in the driver's seat, trembling along with the engine. Once her hands stilled, she took out her phone and reviewed the biohacker medical records Mechanic had supplied to Biocinium. Last time she'd simply skimmed them in angry disbelief. Now she read each patient's description carefully, looking for suggestions of a contraband Beat. Only one patient matched:

Female, early 30s, no bionic enhancements except a subdermal brain stimulation node inserted over the temporal bone…

"So you were a lab rat, too," Petra muttered. "And I bet I'm not the only one who recognized it!

21. LIKE A KNIFE IN THE BACK

"Sorry!" Jonathan began, but his words screeched to a stop with the stretcher. Petra stood in the hall, her face almost as drawn as when he'd taken her home from the morgue. *What the hell is she doing here? Still hassling Dr. Bhagat? Trying to bilk more meds from the pharmacy? Stalking me as her next target? Forget it—I don't even want to know.* He dropped his gaze.

Evans uttered a reprimand, but Petra didn't respond. Her canvas high-tops fidgeted on the tile. After an airless moment, her heels clapped together, prepared to march.

"I've got somewhere to be." She brushed past Jonathan. Static from her bionic arm, real or imagined, shot miniature lightning bolts through his body. He whipped around to speak, but shock and suspicion numbed his tongue. The black storm cloud of her hair disappeared around the corner.

"Last week she picked you up in a sports car, and now she won't even talk to you?" asked Evans, baffled.

"She needs more treatment than I can give," Jonathan muttered, leaning into the gurney. Wheels squeaked and complained. "I don't have time to play therapist for former patients, especially with so many new ones."

"Like you?" Evans tapped her forehead in signal, and Jonathan re-adhered the bandage dangling over his eyebrow. "Did she have something to do with that?"

"It was just an accident." *Like April's death, and me getting dispatched on the call, and getting sucked into Petra's delusion when she said Biocinium was involved. A statistically unlikely amount of accidents.* Factors fired across Jonathan's synapses, intensifying his headache. He rubbed at his cheekbones. *She got in my head better than that damn neural node, and I can't even pry it out.*

"Here, I'll take that." Evans took over the stretcher. Her ponytail swept a path through his fuzzy vision, leading him back to the ambulance. "And you take these." Pills rattled into his palm.

"Thanks." Jonathan collapsed in the cab and downed the aspirin with a swig of thermos coffee. *Now here's a proper partner—covering for me, instead of dragging me into worse trouble.*

Climbing into the driver's seat, Evans cast a worried look across the dashboard. "Are you sure you're fit to work today?"

"Absolutely." Reverb from his own voice made Jonathan wince. "Just give the meds a chance to kick in."

A few calls later, however, the only thing that felt kicked in was his skull. Sirens wailing outside a dilapidated tenement speared his eardrums. "What are the cops doing here?"

Evans checked the auto-dispatcher. "Another domestic disturbance. Those seem even more common than the biohacker cases!"

"It's seasonal. A lot of studies have shown a positive correlation between high temperatures and assaults."

"And it's getting hotter every year? I don't like that math."

"Almost as bad as the math of walk-up apartments," Jonathan grumbled, lugging his gear inside the stuffy building. Paint the color of dead skin flaked off the walls. A child shrieked somewhere overhead. "An average of twelve stairs per level, times three floors, plus two hundred pounds of patient…"

A shout from the landing cut off his calculation, and damp plaster quaked at Corporal Duke's command: "Sir, this is the last time I'm going to ask you. Open this door."

Evans's alarmed eyes shone in the dimness. "We'll be lucky if it's only one patient."

Cursing under his breath, Jonathan took the last flight of steps two at a time. The apartment door hung agape: inside, splinters of cheap pressboard crackled under his feet. Broken furniture littered the room. A young woman huddled on the sofa. Blood trickled down her face, but she didn't wipe it away, keeping both arms around a toddler who clung to her neck. Evans went immediately to them, while Jonathan approached the police clustered around an interior door.

"All right, you've had warning," Corporal Duke told the doorknob. Sweat slithered beneath the straps of her bullet-proof vest.

"What's going on?" Jonathan asked. "You didn't request an ambulance because someone scraped their cheek."

"The lady called us, screaming that her boyfriend had attacked her and the baby. But by the time we got here, he'd locked himself in the bathroom. With a knife."

"He said he was sorry," the woman wailed, pulling away from Evans' attempts to clean her cut. "He said if he took the chip out, everything would be okay again."

The chip—another buggy Beat? Every muscle in Jonathan's body wound tight. "Corporal, that guy might be a biohacker."

"Then he's a brute *and* a criminal. Kick it down, boys."

Jonathan flung an arm across the door. "You can't just bust in on someone attempting self-surgery! One slip of the blade and he bleeds out."

"Better him than them," said Duke, jerking her chin at the woman and child.

"The only person he's endangering right now is himself."

"Until he comes out in a super-suit like the suspect at the pub last night and takes a second swipe at his family. Or my officers. Hugs can't solve every problem, Rowell."

"But tasers can?" Sharp brown eyes flashed a caution not to push their friendship too far. Jonathan held up his jump bag, and a placating palm. "Can we at least try the easy way? Let me go in first. I'll make sure he's medically stable, and try to talk him around. If he's violent, I'll let you take over."

"How generous," Duke sniffed, but stood back.

"Evans, can you bring me the entry kit?" Prizing free the lock, Jonathan put an eye to the door crack. A figure at the sink probed around his ear with a kitchen knife.

"Is he hurt?" Evans whispered.

"Not yet, but if I startle him, he'll stab himself in the temporal lobe." Even a steady, quiet tone felt aggressive in the airless space. "Sir, I'm not a police officer, I'm a para-medic. I'm going to come inside and check on you, all right?"

"I might hurt you." The reply carried less threat than warning.

"I've got enough supplies for both of us," said Jonathan, tossing in humor like a smoke grenade to conceal the tension. He stepped into the bathroom. Red smeared the fixtures. The man glanced around, and his familiar leer set Jonathan's nerves alight. "Fisher?"

"This is your fault," Fisher growled.

"I didn't have anything to do with it," Evans shot back from the doorway.

"Not you. Rowell." Bloodshot eyes glared at Jonathan. "I shouldn't have been home today. I should have been at the station, but they sidelined me with a cracked rib, courtesy of your girlfriend. That was only the second time I got my ass kicked in a bar fight, and the first time by a woman."

Evans' nervous giggles echoed on the tile. "Rowell? Bar? Girlfriend? This is a story I have to hear."

"Go take care of the family. I'll handle this." Jonathan chivvied her out of the room before Fisher could say anything else incriminating.

"Guess I deserved it, though," said Fisher, turning back to the mirror. "I didn't mean to hit you, man. I just got confused. Is your head okay?"

"I'm more worried about yours. Can I take a look?"

"Only if you wanna help me get this thing out." Fisher jabbed a finger at the flap of skin he'd cut around his ear. Bare lightbulbs gleamed on bone and metal.

It is *knockoff Beat! Maybe some of Petra's fighting really was self-defense.* Shaking off a twinge of guilt, Jonathan wiped Fisher's wound clear. "I've gotten a few calls about these. They cause a lot of problems."

"It was supposed to fix them—power me through double shifts, so I can earn enough to take care of her. Instead, I almost killed her!"

"Your partner?"

"No. My daughter." Tears washed trails through the blood on Fisher's cheeks. "She caught that new fever back in the spring, and still hasn't gotten over the after-effects. Cries for hours most nights. Nothing we do seems to help. If I don't sleep at the station, I don't sleep at all—I need something to keep my motor running."

"The station coffee urn is always full," said Jonathan, attempting levity, but Fisher only scowled.

"Caffeine makes me sick. So did the pills and embedded stim injectors I got from a local guy. Guess you know him, since you're drinking buddies."

"Friend of a friend," Jonathan muttered.

"Well, be careful what you get from him. This brain gizmo sounded perfect—uses your natural body chemicals, set it and forget it! Only mine must be set all wrong. Any little poke sets off my adrenaline. Like this morning. The baby screamed until I couldn't take it. I shook her to make her be quiet. I didn't want to, but my hands just moved on their own. My girlfriend stopped me, and I...I *clawed* her. Like some kind of animal." Slick fingers gripped the sink, oozing red down the drain. "I didn't even realize I'd done it until I saw the blood on her face."

"More blood won't help," said Jonathan, opening a sterile bandage. "You could damage yourself taking out the chip that way."

"What choice do I have? I tried to get a doctor to do it— at least she claimed to be a doctor, who knows with these screws cruises?—but a storm came up, and she said it was too dangerous for brain work." Fisher resumed picking at his skull. Blood dripped down his elbow. "Useless. I shoulda let the other lady do it."

"What other lady?"

"On the boat. Seemed to know all about this gadget, like she'd seen it before."

That must have been Petra! Maybe Steel wasn't the only reason Fisher freaked out when he saw our table. Jonathan's mouth went dry. "What did she look like?"

"Hell if I know. She was all covered up and I was kinda seasick. We only talked for a few minutes when I came out of that crummy operating cabin. Steel and the doctor were yelling at each other about my chip. That got her attention, and she asked me some questions about it before going in with the doc." The knife handle slipped in Fisher's wet palm; a new fissure striped his skin, and he swore. "I shoulda done the same thing—gone back inside and made that sketchy sawbones take this thing outta my head!"

"We'll get it out," Jonathan promised. "But this isn't the way to do it." He reached for the knife. Hard fingers clamped around his wrist so tightly that the bone clicked. Fisher spun him against the wall with a snarl. The blade drove toward Jonathan's face, gleaming red and silver. Petra's eyes flashed the same colors in his mind.

Is this what she sees every time she closes those eyes? No wonder she's so damn jumpy. So damn distrustful. So damn brave.

A deafening firework of glass burst behind his head. Mirror shards rained onto the floor. The knife quivered in the medicine cabinet beside Jonathan's ear. Fisher crumpled against his shoulder and sobbed.

"It's okay," Jonathan said shakily, unsure whom he was consoling. He patted Fisher's back. "Your family is fine. You will be, too, once we get you to the hospital and have that thing removed."

Steering Fisher to a seat on the bathtub rim, he dressed the wound, then returned to the living area. Duke was taking the girlfriend's statement while Evans applied steri-strips to her cheek.

Jonathan tapped the rookie's shoulder. "Fisher's all right, but he needs a surgeon. Can you give him something to calm him down a little? We can't have him flipping out like that in the ER." Once she'd shut the bathroom door, he beckoned Duke out of the victim's earshot. "That guy was on the screws cruise with Dr. McCormick. I think he could identify who killed her."

"We already know," said Duke impatiently. "The official autopsy report came through this morning. She died of an anesthetic overdose."

"That doesn't make it suicide!"

"The medical examiner didn't find any defensive wounds, and acknowledged the possibility the drugs may have been self-administered."

The flat words, clearly recited from Ciro's report, punched Jonathan in the gut. "But what if—."

Heavy thuds from the bathroom interrupted his reply. "Wait, don't!" Evans shrieked. A toilet flush washed away her voice.

Vaulting over the sofa, Jonathan flung open the door. Fisher sprawled on the linoleum, his bandage in tatters, while Evans flailed in the empty bathtub. "What the hell? Evans, are you okay?"

"I—I tried to give him a shot, but he shoved me in here," said Evans, disentangling herself from the shower curtain. "He knifed himself in the ear and tossed something down the toilet. Then he just collapsed."

Jonathan pressed fingers to Fisher's neck. No vein stirred. "Dammit, he's gone into cardiac arrest." Evans passed him an epinephrine syringe, but he shoved it away.

"He's got a bionic implant that overloads his adrenaline. You can't give him even more if it's already stopped his heart!"

A scream echoed around them, and Fisher's girlfriend shoved into the bathroom. "Oh my god, what happened?"

Leaping up, Jonathan blocked her entry. "Ma'am, I need you to wait outside."

"I'm always outside, that's the problem!" she wailed. "He never talked about how tired or angry or worried he was. Wouldn't let me help. Wouldn't listen when I said the work was killing him. And now look!"

An electric whine crescendoed behind them. "No!" Jonathan yelled, but the rapid double pop fired before he could turn. Evans knelt beside Fisher with the automated defibrillator in her lap. "What are you doing? I told you it's dangerous to defib biohackers!"

"He can't be a biohacker. He's one of ours!" No pulse registered on the machine; she punched buttons for a second shock. "My City of Baltimore employment contract prohibited illegal bionics. If Fisher had any, he'd be—"

"A scared, desperate person who didn't see any other choice." The words slipped from Jonathan's tongue before his brain fully processed them. For the first time, the biohacker at his feet didn't trigger revulsion or disdain, only pity. Dropping to his knees, he ripped the pads off Fisher's chest and started manual compressions.

Too many of you dying... The time-keeping tune became a duet, with Petra singing softly along in his head. *Everybody thinks we're wrong...*

He continued, verse after verse, but no percussion beat beneath his palms. Outside, the baby started crying again.

The ambulance parked itself in the bay, and Jonathan sank into the engine's silence. "It wasn't your fault. Defib is standard protocol. You did what you were trained to do. The training just hasn't kept up with reality."

Evans tucked a fingernail between her teeth, staring silently at the dashboard.

"We're lucky he didn't hurt you." Jonathan rubbed the bridge of his nose. "I guess I didn't talk him down as well as I thought."

"You're not doing anything as well as you think. I've watched you all week—the ups and downs, the distractions. It's more than just a late night or a bump on the head." Sniffling, Evans fixed him with a pained look. "You aren't the first person in the field to fall into drugs."

Jonathan blinked at her. "Excuse me?"

"If it were just you having a problem, I'd cover for you while you got help. But stealing them? Selling them? Dr. McCormick was obviously running a prescription drug racket, and when she died, her dealer Petra recruited you instead." Nervous words accelerated, not leaving room for rebuke. "I'm guessing she deals in stuff that people like poor Fisher use to give them a boost. That's how you knew he was a biohacker, wasn't it? You were both customers, and being mean to you was just an act, so nobody would guess you had a connection."

"That's—." Jonathan spluttered. *That's ridiculous, but the truth sounds even crazier.*

"Rowell, please. You're a nice guy, and I know you don't have it easy at home. I'm not judging you." Evans chewed her lip a moment before she went on. "But I can't let you put our patients at risk. I think it's best if you resign."

Jonathan's lungs deflated. "Resign?"

"Otherwise I'll have to report you and get you removed. Then it all goes on your city employment record, which might ruin your chances of another job once you're clean. Neither of us wants that."

"Evans, you've got this all wrong. I'm not dealing drugs!"

"Is that what the records will say if I tell Dr. Bhagat to audit the pharmacy?"

Arguments withered. *She's right. The evidence will condemn me, no matter why I did it. And with a mark like that against me, I'll never work in healthcare again.* Truth billowed in Jonathan's chest like a breath held too long underwater, bursting for release: *I can explain everything. There's a stolen military brain chip loose in Baltimore, and I've been investigating a murder with a malfunctioning cyborg veteran who's got a vendetta and a killer mezzo…*

Instead he heard his own distant voice whisper: "I'll put in my notice tonight. There's just one thing I need to do first." Gravity seemed to have doubled; the tablet weighed a ton as Jonathan pulled up an Illegal Activity Notification form. He scrolled through the dropdown menu of offenses for 'Human Performance Modification'. "I promised BPD that I'd finish the screws cruise report."

Evans took the tablet gently from his hands. "I'll do it. The only paperwork you need to worry about is the resignation letter."

With a hesitant pat on his shoulder, she climbed into the back of the rig. Jonathan punched the time clock and wandered outside.

Serves me right. Pinching medicine, snooping around, playing detective...I abused my position. I deserve to get canned. But what the hell do I do now?

Thick grey clouds promised rain.

I could apply with one of those private ambulance services...but Evans would probably report me if I turned up too soon.

Wind off the harbor crackled with ions.

Grace would let me work in the restaurant again...but I can't impose on her any more than I already have.

A distant peal of thunder echoed like a cosmic gavel over his head.

Maybe I can land some scholarships and go back to med school...but then how will I pay for Dad's treatments?

Consumed in bleak prospects, he went a block past the diner without realizing it. His feet longed to walk until the problems faded in the smog behind him. But duty's lodestone hung heavy in his chest, and he turned reluctantly back.

"You're earlier than usual, Jonathan!" Grace greeted him, placing a stack of fresh menus on the counter while Hank set tables for the dinner rush. Her broad smile inverted. "Another bad day?"

"I'd rather not talk about it right now."

She steered him onto a stool. "Ayodele! Peppersoup!"

Jonathan rested his forehead on the bar's worn edge and stared at the floor.

Glittery sneakers appeared in his downcast vision. "You look like you got run over by your own ambulance," said Del, setting a bowl at his elbow. Only a sliver of bandage showed beneath their cleverly styled braids.

"That might've been a better solution."

"Hey, I don't even say stuff like that, and I'm the one who's housebound! Besides, I've got something that will cheer you up—the footage you asked for." Del tapped their rhinestone-encased phone against Jonathan's utilitarian one. Files transferred with a smug chime. Transaction complete, Del pulled up a navigation app. "Now, about my payment. I've mapped out the whole drive. Saturday's weather looks nice—is Petra available then?"

Heat stung Jonathan's eyes. He shoved the bowl and its spicy steam away from his face. "Petra's not coming around anymore."

Del gaped. "She dumped you already?"

"No."

"You dumped *her?* Are you an *idiot?* Wait, I just answered my own question."

"No one got dumped because we were never a thing." Jonathan slapped the bar, making the spoon jump. "Why is everyone so obsessed with that insane idea?"

"We just want you to have someone in your life," said Del consolingly.

"My life is full of someones! My dad. You and your mom. Ciro, Tae, Latoya…" He caught himself before he said *April.* But for the first time since her death, her name didn't stab; the other names buffered him, emotional gauze over a wound. "I've got everything I need." *But I went chasing a fantasy anyway, and now everyone who depends on me will suffer.*

"Everything, except a tissue." Del dabbed his face with a corner of their apron, then wrapped him in a fierce hug. "I thought teenagers were supposed to be the weepy ones, not the adults!"

"That's why it's good to have all those someones. We take care of each other," said Jonathan, dredging up a smile. *Although without a damn job, I can't take care of anybody at home.*

Home. Care.

Recalled words poured a cocktail of hope and dread through his veins. When Del moved off to wait tables, he opened a browser on his phone. Search history pulled up the site he wanted almost immediately. *I don't need a Beat for a device to read my mind.* He studied the page, tapping an anxious rhythm with his spoon.

"Everything okay, son?" asked Hank, shuffling past.

"It will be, dad." Familial titles brought Jonathan a bittersweet smile. *Feels like we've switched places. Now I understand why he put up with it. If he did it for me, I can do it for him.* Draining the soup to fortify himself, he called the number.

22. VICTIM OF CIRCUMSTANCE

"Wonderful to see you again, Ms. Arcenaux, but I'm afraid you caught me at a bad time," said Simms, pumping Petra's hand. "I'm about to conduct a job interview."

"Well, I'm not here to interrupt. I have an appointment with your chief engineer," Petra replied. The elevator pinged on cue, and Kade's sneakers chirped across Biocinium's polished lobby floor. "Follow-up questions about your Beat."

"Yeah, sorry I couldn't fit you in yesterday." Kade beamed at her. "Simms and I had to meet with some regulatory people about our latest trial application. I think it might actually go through this time."

"Really?" Petra purred, feigning curiosity. "What made the difference?"

"Oh, we just presented more compelling medical use cases for the product," said Simms airily. "At any rate, I'm confident enough to start recruiting support staff, and it'll send the wrong message if I'm late!" Excusing himself with a toothy smile, he ducked back into his office.

"So you're going to test the Beat on humans?" Petra asked Kade, following him to the elevator. Her stomach churned even before the car dropped.

"You make it sound like a supervillain science experiment. It's no different than, say, an advanced prosthetic arm." He studied her sideways in the mirror. When the doors opened at basement level, he murmured beneath their rumble: "Speaking of which, how's your shoulder?"

"Better than it's been in years. Even the finger dexterity has improved—I restrung a guitar with this hand the other day." *Not that I'll ever hear it played.* Faint notes drifted through Petra's mind: Jonathan's hands skimming the taut metal to check its tune. She shrugged away the memory of those fingers curled around her shoulder blade. "Maybe you should inherit your sister's nickname."

"I'm just glad the repair held," said Kade, badging open the laboratory. "I'd never seen tech like that before, so it took some guesswork to figure out its subtleties."

"Kind of like the Beat?"

"What do you mean?"

"It's not really your design."

"Yes, it is! I mean, sure, I borrowed some foundational work from open sources…"

"That's the first place I saw it, too." Petra backed the engineer against the wall. His slouched posture left him barely taller than her; she glared at her reflection in his glasses. "The *source* was an enemy soldier's *open* skull."

Mouth quivering, Kade wilted. "Remember when I joked that it came to me in a dream? That's the closest thing that makes sense. I wanted to do something radical for my graduate project—something with public health, to support April's work—but it seemed like everything had already been done. If I couldn't come up with something, I'd wash out of the program. One night while I was lying awake agonizing, I got an email. No subject, no message, just an attachment of a partial device blueprint."

"Who sent it?"

"I don't know. I got a friend in campus IT to look at it, but the address was an anonymous burner account. I figured it was a professor who supported my goals and wanted to give me a little inspiration."

Of course—some elite egghead the military contracted to work on Seventeen, like Bhagat said. They would've hated the idea of keeping such novel tech classified, so they tried to leak it through a desperate student. Petra's organic knee trembled. Shoving away from Kade, she gripped a counter. "So you took credit for a mystery machine?"

"No. I took credit for developing an abstract design fragment into a functional biomedical device." Kade placed a prototype in the micro-manipulator and beckoned Petra to look. Bracing herself with a breath, she peered into the eyepieces. A tiny gasp escaped her throat. For an instant she stood on *Sedna*'s deck again, surrounded not by carnage, but swirls of ethereal white powder.

"Haven't you seen snow before, Rock?"

"Only in movies and Christmas cards, sir."

"Wait 'till you taste it. Go give the railing a lick…"

She'd been too mesmerized to take the bait, marveling at the delicate architecture of the flakes in her palm. The Beat featured similarly exquisite detail in electronics rather than ice, more refined than the bloody shard she'd pried from Seventeen. "It does look different than the one I saw."

"It's different than anything the industry has ever seen!" said Kade. "My faculty advisor told me it was a total game-changer. But when I wanted to run clinical trials and make something actually *useful,* then it was too edgy, too high a risk to the school's prestigious reputation."

And to the sensitive military side project they were running in the basement. Petra drew back from the lenses. After-images of the Beat teased her organic eye. "So they tried to shut down your research."

"I fought them on it, and somehow the exchanges got out. Before I knew it, the idea was getting condemned by cable news pundits." Kade toyed with the lanyard of his employee badge, scowling at his own miniature photo. "I ended up with nothing except a kickass-but-controversial product."

"And a sister who'd do anything for you." Petra pulled Mechanic's chip from her pocket. "Even beta-test the device."

A sharp inhale hissed through Kade's teeth. "How did you get that?"

"I didn't. Your sister did. I found it sticking out of her head right before she died."

Kade backed away as if the jar held a live scorpion. "No way!"

"You said yourself she was always looking out for you. When she couldn't use her hospital connections to finagle you a clinical trial, she decided to do a one-patient study." Pretending to tuck back a stray lock of hair, Petra tapped her skinterface. The detection grid measured every twitch of Kade's features, but she didn't need it to interpret his expression. *He's legitimately shocked. He didn't know.*

"How could she even have gotten a copy?" he rasped. "Every one of my prototypes is accounted for. They're all here—I just checked this morning. The Beat has never left this lab."

"Maybe not a physical one. She got the schematics and had a biohacker friend make her a copy." Petra placed the chip onto the stage beside its authorized cousin and compared them at magnification. Steel's version looked rougher, but the essential components matched.

"But she wouldn't have had access to those files." Kade sank onto a stool, shaking hard enough to rattle its legs against the floor. "I told you, she left Biocinium around the time I started. She never set foot down here."

"She probably pulled them off your personal computer."

He shook his head until his glasses slid down his nose. "I'm not allowed to work on proprietary material at home—too many cybersecurity risks. Whoever gave her that version of the design could only have gotten it from inside Biocinium's corporate network. And none of us would leak the big project! There's too much at stake."

"I think that's exactly why they did it." Pulling out her phone, Petra displayed the patient record where April had described herself.

Kade paled until his face matched his lab coat. "Where did that come from?"

"Simms' desk. The so-called medical evaluations April did for Biocinium were dirt on the biohackers she treated in secret. Including herself, after she had your Beat installed."

He stared at the document, then at the two Beats displayed on his workbench. Jumping up, he ran out of the lab.

"Where are you going?" Petra called, but Kade was already in the elevator. *Dammit, I should've guessed he was a loose cannon after that tantrum with the recycling bin! I'm not going to let anyone else get hurt over this, even a dick like Simms.* She trotted up the fire stairs. Bruises from the bar fight clawed deep into her muscles. Shoving through the soreness, she burst into the lobby just as Kade hammered on the office door.

The CEO's ruddy face appeared in the gap. "Can't this wait? I'm in the middle of an interview."

"Hiring new lab animals to replace my sister?" Kade twisted away when Petra tried to catch his arm. "Now I know why she had enough leverage to get me a job here."

He shoved his boss in the chest. Too startled to resist, Simms stumbled backward into the desk, scattering picture frames. His visitor jumped away from the avalanche.

Petra's pulse, piqued from the stairs, leapt even higher. "What the hell are you doing here?" she demanded.

Jonathan stared at her, then at the same scuffed loafers he'd worn to the bioethics panel. "Applying for a job."

"Don't bother. You won't get to keep it long, once everyone finds out what this tool is doing." Kade brandished a cut-crystal business award at Simms. "They should've shut this place down years ago, after all those employees got sick. Yeah, I read about Biocinium's shady history. I was stupid to think things would change."

Petra prized the bludgeon from his grip. "Hang on. You don't know the whole story yet."

"I don't even have the executive summary," Simms blustered. "I have no idea what you're talking abou-owwwt!" He broke off in a yowl as Kade opened a desk drawer into his knees. Papers flew.

"This!" Kade shook a fistful of Mechanic's notes. "April was reporting to you on biohacker health issues."

"Yes, to inform our market strategy."

"And our clinical trial applications! These are the case studies from the presentation you gave yesterday, all the patients you said the Beat could help. I thought they were just random people that Mrs. S. interviewed for her surveys. Not test subjects. Not my own *sister!*" Flinging the documents away, Kade dropped his face into his hands and sobbed. Pages drifted down around him.

Like a green recruit who's had all the training, but falls apart the first time under fire. Petra patted Kade's shoulder. He flung his arms around her neck and cried into her collar.

The unexpected contact fired panic signals in her nerves; her bionic arm nearly pitched him across the room. She cast a desperate look at Jonathan, hoping to transfer her distraught charge to a professional, but he had his hands full of scattered documents.

"That is a ridiculous accusation!" spluttered Simms, massaging his bruised shin.

"Maybe not." Jonathan handed him April's record.

Simms' complexion turned chalky. "I never, *ever* authorized that! Illegal human modification experiments?! Oh, we're screwed. Totally screwed." Diving back into the drawer, he pulled out the tequila. His hands shook so much that he couldn't unscrew the cap.

Petra ducked out of Kade's embrace, opened the bottle with a flick of bionic fingers, and poured a dram into one of the Biocinium logo mugs.

Simms held it for a moment, then offered it to Kade. "I swear, I didn't know April was submitting medical data on herself. I would never have risked our one viable product on an unofficial test like that. I only wanted case studies on existing biohacks, so we could demonstrate to the regulators how many poorly managed conditions the Beat could treat." Liberating his bottle from Petra, he took a long slug. "Instead, it's ruined us. What am I going to tell Beth?"

"Beth?" asked Jonathan, frowning.

"My wife." Simms waved at the scattered photos. Picking them up, Petra replaced them on the desk:

Gowned graduates posed outside a university building.

Relatives in a staged wedding portrait surrounded tuxedo-clad Simms and a woman in a frothy white gown.

A printed article from the local business news, headlined *Baltimore Chipmaker Gets New Management, New Mission,* showed an inset photo of the company's previous owner.

Jonathan's hand reached around Petra and seized one of the frames. His mouth pressed into a thin line. "Thanks for your time, Mr. Simms, but I don't think I'm the right person for this position," he said with frigid cordiality. Slapping the photo facedown on the desk, he stalked out of the office.

"Me, either." Simms swiveled morosely in his chair. "I wanted a nice tech company gig with a window office and a fat travel budget, but no, she wanted us to make something out of this worthless old factory."

Petra snatched up the photo and analyzed every feature, the way she'd once assessed images from recon drones. Pattern recognition seared her eyes. "*Al'ama!*"

"What does that mean?" Kade sniffled.

"That we've been totally blind." She tossed the frame into Simms' lap and dashed out of the building. Tepid drizzle blurred the figure vanishing across the lot. Pain in Petra's knee warned that she wouldn't catch him on foot. She leapt for her car and stopped short. The adjacent staff space, which she'd ignored on her determined march inside, held a white luxury SUV. She ran a hand over the hood. Dark streaks marring the finish matched the paint on her coupe.

It was here the first time I visited, too! The answer has been right in front of us the whole time…and now that we finally see it, he's going to just walk away?

Petra slung herself into the driver's seat. Tires squealed on the wet pavement. The coupe rocketed past Jonathan and spun to a halt in his path, pinning him in a brilliant fork of headlights. Eyes locked through the glass, a look so intense that it threatened to puncture the windshield. But the wipers danced on. Petra's bionic finger, preempting her thoughts as usual, unlocked the door.

The click made Jonathan jump. He shook himself, squinted up at the thickening rain, and ducked cautiously into the passenger seat. Sandalwood mingled with citrus in the air vents. They sat amid the soft fizzle of drops on the roof, staring at Biocinium.

"How did we both miss it?" asked Jonathan at last.

"Because we thought we knew the answers already. You thought it had to be a biohacking crime, and I couldn't look past my old service demons. We couldn't see what was right in front of us." *The bad, or the good.* Petra stole a sideways look at him. "But you must've suspected something, if you went in undercover."

"That wasn't a sting operation. It was a real interview. I called up Simms and asked about the jobs he'd mentioned at the panel. I have to find something, since my *partner* forced me to resign." Jonathan almost spat the word.

"Because of me? And Mechanic?"

Hollow laughter confirmed her guess. "Totally backward, isn't it? But there's nothing I can do. I've got no excuse, and she's got...proof!" Scrabbling for his phone, he pulled up a video clip. "I was so worried about the job that I completely forgot Del's footage!"

Petra leaned closer to watch; instead of shying away, Jonathan angled the screen toward her. Shadows crept through the marina in grainy night-vision. The first moved with Del's unmistakable air of defiance. Fisher's muscular silhouette hurried down the dock shortly after. And finally, wrapped in layers that obscured any unique outlines, came passenger number three.

"They're all walking away from the camera! What good is that for identification?" Jonathan fumed.

"Do you have any images from when we got back?"

He pulled up a second set of files, time-stamped from early the next morning. Tidal surge lapped over the dock. Boats yawed at their ropes, and *Wind of Change* careened into its slip. A petite form stepped down from the pilothouse.

"That you?" asked Jonathan.

"At the helm the whole damn trip, like I told you." Before her avatar reached the deck, someone charged out of the salon and bolted toward the street. Wind blew back the runner's hood. Petra stabbed the pause button. "There's your murderer. Send this to your cop friends!"

"They can't do anything with it." Jonathan dumped the phone in the cupholder. "It's inadmissible evidence, and circumstantial to boot."

"Then we'll need something undeniable." Petra watched the video again, pumping her heel against the footrest. "You up for a crazy CONOP?"

"A what?"

"Concept of operations. A battle plan. I think there's a way to smoke out this sucker...but it'll need to be an allied offensive." Anxious bionic fingers clutched the wheel until it creaked.

Jonathan glanced at her hand with a tentative smile. "You do have a knack for getting unusual combinations to work."

Laughing, Petra explained her idea. Rain picked up its tempo in time with her heartbeat. "Well?"

Jonathan traced circles on the armrest until it seemed he might leave a permanent groove. At last he dialed his phone. "Hey, Latoya. About that screws cruise..."

23. DEAD END JUSTICE

"I thought you were resigning!" Evans exclaimed the moment she stepped into the station, completely bypassing *good morning.*

Jonathan didn't look up from his equipment. "They couldn't get coverage on such short notice, so you'll have to put up with me for one more shift."

"Oh. I don't mind. Honestly, I'll be sorry to lose you as a mentor." She leaned against the ambulance door, pouting. "I wish it didn't have to come to this."

"Me, either." Jonathan kept ticking imaginary boxes on his completed list. An alert pinged from the cab, and he spun eagerly toward the dispatch screen. "Play the call," he told the computer.

A familiar voice rumbled out of the speaker: "Yeah, uh…there's an unconscious woman at Henderson's Wharf. I don't know what happened, but she doesn't look good. Boat's called *Wind of Change.*"

Evans scrolled through the incident database. "Isn't that the screws cruise yacht from last week?"

"Yeah. The caller sounds like that big guy who tried to run from the cops." *Dammit! If Steel is involved…* Jonathan pushed away the rest of the thought and jumped into the cab. Butterfly closures still held the corner of his eye partially shut, so he set the ambulance to autopilot. "Think he chucked someone overboard again?" he asked Evans, hoping a joke would relieve the tension in his chest. It didn't. Each block accelerated his heart rate until the rig squealed into the marina. Clutching his bag, he ran along the slips and jumped onto *Wind of Change*'s aft deck. The unlocked door slid back at his touch.

Evans glanced around the empty salon. "Where's the caller?"

"Guess he split. Didn't seem too keen to deal with city services last time."

"I'm surprised he called at all."

"He probably wants to score some good citizen points before his court date." Jonathan peeked into the master stateroom. Tangled blankets spilled off the double bunk, as if the occupant had tumbled out of a nightmare. *Or into one.* Swallowing hard, he opened the surgery cabin.

Gruesome deja-vu gripped him. A woman sprawled on the operating table. Red rivulets oozed over the metallic tattoos on her temple.

Two long steps brought Jonathan to her side. "Petra? Petra, can you hear me?" The headset around her neck rattled when he shook her, but she didn't respond. He hooked her up to the vital signs monitor, making sure to place the pulse clip and cuff on her organic arm.

Evans frowned at the readout. "Blood pressure looks pretty good for someone with a gash in her head."

"She's got a lot of bionic compensation," said Jonathan, probing Petra's blood-matted hair. Glitter caught his eye; he gripped it with a pair of tweezers and plucked out a shard.

"What is that?" asked Evans sharply. "A bullet? A broken knife tip?"

Tentacular filaments quivered in the light. "It's some kind of chip."

"Like the one from the doctor we found in here the other week?"

Tearing his gaze from the Beat, Jonathan fixed his probie with a curious look. "We didn't find any foreign bodies on that patient."

Evans turned almost as pale as Petra. "I read the autopsy report. It described surgical scarring in that same area, probably from a biohacker implant. I've been studying."

"Well, the ER staff can study this once she's stable." Clamping gauze over Petra's ear, Jonathan wound a bandage to hold it in place, but his fingers fumbled with the knot.

Evans took the material—and the chip—carefully from him. "Are you all right?"

"Yeah, it's just…two people I know, one right after the other…" He turned away so she couldn't read his face.

"It's okay." Grim confidence hardened her voice. "Go get the stretcher. I'll finish her."

Nodding, Jonathan hastened out of the cabin. His pulse pounded so furiously that it dimmed his vision at the edges. Tremors rattled his knees. Instead of heading to the rig, he leaned against the bulkhead just beside the door. Sounds illustrated the scene in his mind: the snarl of a velcro cuff, the diagnostic computer's pings, rattling objects as Evans opened a drawer.

A curse. A yelp. A crash. Jonathan bolted back inside. Petra, so alert she seemed electrified, pinned Evans to the floor. Blood dripping from the ends of her hair painted gory constellations on the rookie's chest.

"She's gonna finish me, all right—with a lethal injection, just like Mechanic." Petra pried a hypodermic needle from Evans' fist and hurled it across the deck. "Is this a drug paramedics typically use?"

"No, but it would be very familiar to a nurse who went undercover with EMS." Jonathan crouched down to look his erstwhile trainee in the face. "Unofficial market research to save Biocinium, the 'old family property' of Elizabeth Evans Simms."

Resigned anger colored her cheeks. "Did Steve let it slip?"

"Almost. He said my name sounded familiar when we met a few days ago, but he was too drunk to place it." Jonathan gave Petra a nod and she rocked back, allowing Evans to scramble into a corner. "I thought he recognized it from my dad's lawsuit, but you probably mentioned it, telling him all about your new partner who was too dumb to realize you were a fake."

"I'm not a fake! I did a rescue squad ride-along program while I was a nursing student. It was easy to renew those credentials. Emergency medicine hasn't changed much," said Evans, kicking the discarded monitor. "But everything else in the field has. After a few years running clinical trials for biomedical companies, I noticed that the most promising new treatments weren't drugs. They were devices. When Dad died and left me Biocinium, it felt like an opportunity to rebuild his legacy. I hoped making Steve the public face would distance us from the company's history."

"Then he should choose more discreet pictures for his office. The founder in the press photo is the father of the bride in the wedding portrait. I almost didn't recognize you in the makeup and tiara." Prompted, Petra wiped goat's blood from her cheek. "Too bad your corporate makeover was just as shallow. The new management is as exploitive as the old one, using biohackers for a city-sized clinical study!"

"Was it your idea, or April's?" Jonathan asked Evans.

"Both. We kind of bonded in anger when Ripken's new ER head canned the asthma trial we had worked on together. April was determined to keep finding better treatments for her patients. After I acquired Biocinium, I reached out to her for advice on what market niche we could fill. She started sharing patient data, and encouraged me to make my own observations in the field." Evans smoothed her mussed uniform. "But playing stupid about biohacking and pocketing hardware samples was never going to get me the information I really needed."

"So you experimented on us," Petra snapped, holding up the decoy Beat she'd planted in her hair.

"You're already experimenting on yourselves. All I did was circulate another prototype."

"A deadly one!"

"That's a fixable technical error. I had to remove some features from the blueprints I gave April—I couldn't risk some greedy biohacker pirating our full design! Maybe I missed something."

"Like the fact that April would never experiment on her patients without their consent." Jonathan folded his arms over a resurgent ache in his chest.

"She thought she could fool me by testing it herself and submitting an anonymous record. Once I called her out on it, she stopped contacting me. Booking one of these stupid cruises was the only way I could talk to her." Evans glared around the cabin. "I told her that if she wasn't going to partner with us, she'd have to return Biocinium's intellectual property."

"And she refused."

"No, she handed me a scalpel and told me to remove the Beat on the spot. She said my feature-limited version didn't function correctly without Kade's app. Our underground study wouldn't be fair to him, or the patients."

"But you don't really care about either of those," Petra spat. "You figured if her biohacker partners found the device in her corpse, we'd replicate it and distribute it across Baltimore."

"Where you could keep tabs on all the cases that rolled through the ER." Disgust roiled in Jonathan's blood until every muscle shivered. "Like that poor bastard Fisher. Did you shoot him full of epinephrine and chop out his implant because he was a failed test, or because you were afraid he'd recognize you from the boat?"

"Both—either one could spoil my research. Just like April if she'd tipped off her patients about it. Drugs solved all those problems. I guess that makes this kind of a funny ending." Lunging across the floor, Evans snatched up the fallen syringe and tore back her own sleeve.

"Don't!" Jonathan hurried forward. Evans' hand shook too hard to land the needle. Crouching beside her, he reached out to take it. "No one else needs to die. Let me have that, okay?"

"Okay." A whip-quick movement hooked her arm around his neck, pressing the syringe barrel against his throat. Impatient words tickled his ear. "You really are a nice guy, Rowell—too nice. Anyone can sucker you in with a scrape or a sniffle. She certainly did." Evans snapped at Petra, who'd taken an aggressive step toward them. "Get back in the corner and face the wall."

The bionic eye flickered, calculating distances and speeds. Evans raised her elbow, prepared to jab, and Petra's hands went up. She backed away with a tormented look at Jonathan.

Keeping the needle an inch from his flesh, Evans marched him back through the salon. "I wanted to keep you out of this, but I realized you were nosing into things when I picked up Steve from that bioethics panel and saw you there with Petra."

"So that's why you tried to run us off the bridge," said Jonathan. "Petra recognized your car outside the factory when she went back there."

"I just wanted to scare you. But you couldn't take a hint, and when you tipped off the police in Fisher's apartment—."

"That had nothing to do with you," said Jonathan. "If you hadn't tried to force me out of my job to keep me quiet, I'd never have guessed you were involved at all. Although I should have. When April told me *don't trust her,* she didn't mean Petra. She meant you."

"One more reason I had to stop her from jeopardizing my work." Evans linked her arm with his, a perverted gesture of companionship to prevent him from fleeing as they stepped onto the dock. "I was afraid I might have to deal with you the same way. No one would question the overdose of a stressed-out paramedic with a history of forging prescriptions."

"I take medicine for patients who have no other way to get it. It's wrong, I know, but I can't watch people suffer."

"Then help me to help them! You need a new job, don't you? Take April's. We'll set you up on a private squad somewhere, and you can report to me on all the biohacking trends in Baltimore." Yanking open the ambulance door, Evans prodded Jonathan into the driver's seat and climbed up after him. "You told me that biohacking is a major health problem in this city, but that's only because we don't have the means to do it right. April said it best—we can't keep treating symptoms and ignore the disease!"

"You're right. We should treat the disease." Setting his teeth, Jonathan flicked the manual override switch and stomped on the accelerator. Velocity flung Evans backward; she hadn't yet settled into her seat. She dropped the syringe to brace herself. Jonathan veered down a dead-end alley. Rubber screamed. He swerved against the wall, shearing off the passenger wing mirror with a crunch. A hard brake sent Evans flying again. Before she could recover, Jonathan flung off his safety belt and tumbled out of the cab.

"The disease is people like you, who think others are expendable," he growled, slamming the door. Metal quivered against his back as Evans kicked the inside; he'd parked the passenger door tight against the brick. "Better get used to being locked in a tiny space, because once the police get here —hey!"

Evans climbed through the cab divider into the ambulance's rear. Jonathan leapt to intercept her. One of the double doors swung wide and met him in a full-body collision.

Shockwaves tore through his skeleton. He staggered backward. Liquid trickled into his eye from the reopened cut, painting the world in a binary haze. On the red side, Evans jumped from the vehicle and took off toward the street, her ponytail a mad pendulum.

A silhouette materialized in the alley's mouth to block her exit. "Jonathan?" Petra's bark demanded a *yes, ma'am,* but his dazed brain struggled to reply.

"He's fine," said Evans, halting just out of Petra's reach. "But you're not, are you? I read about you in April's files. You're running out of parts to replace, and you just keep getting sicker."

"That's not your problem."

"It could be, if you work with me. You can offer better insight than any survey into what people need from bionics. And Biocinium could provide bespoke products for your needs, instead of homemade copies and secondhand junk." Evans waved a disdainful hand toward the yacht.

Fists curled at Petra's sides. "Why would I help you, after you killed my friend?"

"April traded your private information behind your back, and refused to share a new device that could help you! What kind of friend is that?" Careful, circling steps brought Evans closer to the street, closer to escape. She reached out a tentative hand. Petra's spine stiffened, stony as her namesake city. "You must be tired of bribing doctors and enduring backroom surgeries. Don't you want someone who cares about your welfare, not just your wallet? If Biocinium succeeds, I can help you get proper treatment. Maybe even cure you for good."

The rock crumbled. Head drooping, Petra clasped the proffered hand. Evans raised her chin in triumph...then gasped as Petra yanked her forward in a bionic vise.

"No drug or device can heal what hurts me the most," Petra hissed. "But I'll feel better knowing that this time, I won't let the killers escape."

"Me, either." Drawing back her free hand, Evans drove the deadly needle into Petra's arm. Jonathan yelled something that his ringing ears rendered only as dismay. Petra stared at the syringe bobbing obscenely from her sleeve. A wry smile flickered across her lips. Evans tried to wrestle free, but Petra's repaired shoulder held even as she sank to the ground, anchoring the other woman in place. Jonathan stumbled toward them. Brick walls distorted around him.

Sirens in his head burst into reality: a patrol car raced along the waterfront, lights blazing.

Corporal Duke jogged down the dock to meet her reinforcements. The pilot's headset from *Wind of Change* bounced on her shoulders. "You didn't tell me this plan featured a car chase, Rowell," she panted. Separating the two women on the ground, she cuffed Evans' wrists.

"It wasn't supposed to feature a second murder, either." Half blind, Jonathan dropped to his knees beside Petra.

She opened her eyes and grinned. "Nice improvisation."

"Nice harmony." He let out a relieved breath. "I thought she had you."

"Luckily Mechanic's reports didn't specify *which* limbs were prosthetic." Plucking out the needle like a pesky splinter, Petra pushed back her left sleeve to inspect the arm beneath. "Dammit, she nicked the silicone!"

"See? She's the criminal, not me!" Evans nodded frantically at Petra. "You can't believe the word of a paranoid veteran loaded with illegal bionics."

"Then we'll have to take yours," said Duke. Pulling the phone from her belt, she stopped recording from Petra's headset. Two swipes brought up the marina surveillance clip Jonathan had sent to secure her help: Evans sprinting away from the yacht in a burst of muddy stormwater. "We've got consensual monitoring on everything you just admitted in the cabin, but I should remind you that anything you say can and will be used against you in a court of law…"

Tuning out the rest of the familiar speech, Jonathan slumped back onto the pavement.

"Does Steel need to call another ambulance for you?" asked Petra, dabbing her cuff over his sticky brow.

"I feel about as good as you look."

"Hey, at least this blood isn't mine." She wiped more offal from her hair. "Playing dead with a goat-meat perm might turn me vegetarian."

"Not until you try Grace's egusi stew. After chopping up extra for your stage makeup there, she'll have to cook a double batch. She wants to invite you for dinner as a thank-you for helping Del. And I bet Dad would love jamming with you again."

The uncanny eye probed Jonathan's face for sincerity. "Do I have to eat in the kitchen with the dishwasher, the toaster, and the other machines?"

He studied his shoes. Laces flopped on either side of his foot. "I'm sorry I said that. I wish I could say I didn't mean it, but in that moment, I think I did. Everything hurt too much to process, and blame is an easy band-aid."

"Frontier dive bars taught me not to credit anything someone says after getting hit in the head with a beer bottle." One side of Petra's mouth quirked upward in a self-critical smile. "And maybe I did come off a little shady. I wasn't exactly straight with you about things."

"That's no excuse." Jonathan retied his shoes, marveling at how easily his careful knots had unravelled. "I guess it just scares me how fast technology is evolving people into organisms I don't understand."

"You understand them way too well. I don't have many sore spots, but you still found one to poke." Petra twisted a finger of her glove. "I'm made of more metal than meat. Sometimes I wonder how much I can replace before I'm not me. Or not even human."

A smile radiated pain through Jonathan's facial muscles, but somehow felt good anyway. "If you still worry about stuff like that, I don't think you're in any danger."

"That's not true." Petra scowled at Evans, now ducking into the back of a patrol car. "She was right about one thing —I'm getting worse. I'll need more upgrades eventually. Who knows what they'll do to me?"

"It must've been tempting to side with her and get help."

Leaning back onto her elbows, Petra stared across the harbor's greasy ripples. "You wanna know why they called me Rock? Military nicknames are ironic. When I started out as a drone operator, I was terrified to work with such sophisticated equipment. My hands always shook on the controls, so my smart-ass watch officer would say things like 'get rock-steady over there to reconnoiter that unflagged ship'. "

"I guess that got shortened."

"And it stuck, even after I got confident. But it took on a different tone." Petra turned back to Jonathan with eyes like fresh-forged steel. "Because no matter how much I wavered, I always got my target. Every damn time."

24. ELECTRIC FUNERAL

Autumn breeze meandered through the hospital's rooftop garden, shaking the last blooms from the summersweet. White petals speckled a stone newly embedded in the mulch. Petra brushed them off, tracing the carved plaque: *In Memory of Dr. April McCormick.*

"The landscape crew wouldn't plant anything new this time of year." Dr. Bhagat sniffed in disapproval. "But come spring, I'll insist on a nice perennial to accompany the stone."

"Minerals last longer than organic material," Petra reminded her, twisting a fallen leaf in her gloved fingers.

"But the latter has the capacity to heal and grow." A brief spark in the doctor's eye might have been amusement, or just a trick of late afternoon sun. "Combining the two makes an appropriate memorial for her."

"It's cool, but her real legacy will be way more impressive than any flower or rock," Kade chimed in. He'd thrown a blazer over his cartoon t-shirt in an effort to dress up for the occasion, exuding the style of a roguish entrepreneur.

Not a bad look for Biocinium's new leader. Petra shot him a teasing grin. "You mean that note in her will, asking you to let me keep *Wind of Change*?"

"No, although I'm glad to get it off my hands. I get seasick just riding the bus." Kade shuddered. "I meant her legacy in healthcare. All those records she compiled on her biohacker patients are evidence of a serious public health gap the Beat could fill. I think that's what clinched my Humanitarian Device Exemption."

"You finally got approval?"

"It's not a full-scale trial. Just an exploratory study," said Bhagat, nudging one of the garden's border bricks with her toe to align it with the others. "There will only be a handful of participants, all of whom haven't responded to conventional treatments."

Kade smiled shyly at Petra. "I'd like to start with April's patients, if you'd help me get in touch with them. They deserve to be the first people offered this opportunity."

"First dibs on last hopes?" Petra paced around the garden, summoning courage for her next question. "You said the Beat might be able to treat memory loss, right?"

"Sure, we just configure the nodes to target the hippocampus, and—."

"I know someone who might take you up on that." She pivoted to hide whatever thrill or trepidation her expression might betray. "What about asthma?"

"If that's the patient I think you're referencing, they would be an excellent candidate," said Bhagat, settling onto a bench.

"After you removed one device, you're prescribing another?"

"A legal one, administered by a doctor with a historically cautious approach to bionic medicine." A smirk played around Bhagat's thin mouth.

Petra skidded to a stop on the path. "Are you joking?"

"I never gave much credence to the therapeutic value of laughter."

"Nope, you're all about data and protocols, which makes you freaking perfect to oversee this study!" said Kade, beaming. "I'm stoked that you agreed. April said you were a total hard-ass, but I think she respected your thoroughness. That's exactly what we need to convince regulators that the Beat is safe and effective."

Conflicting responses tangled in Petra's nerves; her bionic limbs twitched, unsure which signal to follow. "So you'll basically be my case manager again?"

Bhagat nodded. "Yes, but this time our goals and our methods are both in concert."

"No more creative differences?" Petra extended her hand, and the doctor—with only a moment's hesitation—clasped it. "What the hell, let's try a reunion tour."

"Where do I buy tickets?" asked Jonathan, striding toward them from the door. "Sorry I'm late. The calls just didn't stop coming today, and the new trainee is already overwhelmed."

"Good thing you didn't actually resign," said Petra.

"Sometimes I wish I had. Every season brings another trending health crisis. We're going to miss April around here." Kneeling, he laid a bouquet of yellow roses at the base of the stone.

Yellow—not romance, just friendship and remembrance. Petra smiled. *Looks like at least one of us has a shot at recovering from all this.*

Bhagat appraised Jonathan with a critical eye. "If you want a change of pace, one of the recommendations from our otherwise-satisfactory ER inspection was hiring some paramedics to help out in the trauma bay. With your experience, I think you'd be highly competitive for the position. You spent some time in medical school, is that correct?"

"Yeah, but I never finished."

"Well, as a member of the hospital staff, you'd be eligible for educational programs, if you were interested in further training."

A slow, stunned smile blossomed across Jonathan's face. "That would be great."

"Come by my office after the service and we'll discuss it." Bhagat frowned at the hospital chaplain hurrying across the flagstones. Other co-workers followed in twos and threes, snatching a few moments to honor a lost teammate. As a group formed, Petra withdrew. The sinuous path carried her to the roof's edge, and she leaned over the rail. Miniaturized people bustled around the street below.

Seventeen could be down there right now—coming out of that shop, or getting into that cab, or jaywalking across that intersection. He could be anywhere. Or, if his hardware keeps spreading, everywhere. The sun dipped beneath the skyline, plunging her into shadow.

"The main event of a memorial service is, y'know, the service." Jonathan's voice made her jump. Behind him, the group dispersed back inside the hospital. "That was actually one of the better ones I've been to."

"Nondenominational?"

"Short."

"Even that's too much for me. I had two versions of god in my house growing up, and neither one gave me a damn bit of help."

"That's how I felt after my mom died. I resented every minute Dad made me spend in church with him, except for playing guitar in the youth group band." Hands in his pockets, Jonathan gazed up at the purpling clouds. "Music reminded me that transient experiences—a song, or a life—can still have meaning."

"We're all commercial jingles, brief but memorable." Petra hummed a few notes from the latest ubiquitous advertisement.

Jonathan chuckled. "More like four-chord songs, writing our own lyrics over the same basic structures."

"Speaking of which, have you practiced?"

He held out a hand in reply. Fresh calluses etched his fingertips.

"I miss these," Petra murmured, inspecting the toughened skin. "Although they must smart like hell after just a few weeks back on the strings."

"Yeah, but it feels better than anything I've done in ages. Like rehab after an injury. It hurts because it's healing."

"And you said music didn't save lives." Petra spun herself under Jonathan's arm, a playful ghost of their dance, then let go and turned back toward the city. "I might need more than that, though. Kade invited me to join his new trial for the Beat, but I'm not sure I want that thing in my head."

"Why, because it came from a dead adversary?"

"I'm not sure he is dead." Hugging herself against the wind, Petra related Bhagat's admission about Seventeen. In the hectic weeks since Evans' arrest, she hadn't had an opportunity to share the discovery. *Or maybe I was just hoping that it wasn't true.*

"Are you afraid he'll come after you?" Jonathan asked when she'd finished.

"He doesn't scare me. His tech does."

"Is it really his tech anymore? Kade developed it in a totally different direction from the original, and it might help a lot of people. Including you."

Petra searched his face for sarcasm, but the brownstone expression stayed sturdy as ever, only now a hint of welcome shone behind its windows. "Since when do you support bionics? Or anything to do with Biocinium?"

"The chip and the company have changed a lot from what you and I knew. Maybe we both need to update our mental operating systems," said Jonathan with a faint smile.

"And if we end up with a city full of Seventeens?" Petra shivered.

Warm fingers patted her shoulder. "If that does happen, no one's better placed than we are to see it and stop it."

"What are we, Baltimore's unofficial bionic crimes investigative squad?"

"Someone should be."

Petra rubbed her skinterface, and the analytic grid appeared over Jonathan's features. *Damn, he's serious!* She grinned. "Well, the partnership will get its first test tonight."

"This one's for my *esposo hermoso!*" Alcohol mangled the Spanish words, but Tae gripped the mic fearlessly and belted an upbeat Latin love song across the weeknight crowd at Dapọ Diner.

Petra winced at the off-key notes. "I'm guessing he's not as big on opera as you are," she told Ciro, lounging in the seat beside her.

"Nope, he's completely tone deaf. Can't carry a tune in a body bag." He drummed cheerfully along on the table. "That's what makes it so adorable when he tries anyway, just for me."

"At least he looks more comfortable with a mic now than he did at the bioethics debate."

"He'll get familiar with that topic soon enough." Ciro cast her a worried look over the rim of his cocktail. "With the HARMONY bill going up for a vote soon, I suspect both Tae and I will be getting a lot of new biohacker clients."

"Not if I can help it," said Kade, setting down his soda with the crisp finality of an exclamation point. "With the money April left me, I'm going to evolve Biocinium from another cheap tech manufacturer into a safe space for bio-hackers. At least, as long as no one else steals my designs." He glowered across the table.

"Hey, I never technically stole anything," Steel muttered around a kebab. He occupied two chairs, and twice as many plates, opposite the wiry engineer. "Your sister gave me all that stuff. But after what happened to that poor firefighter bastard, brain tech is too big a liability. I'll stick with re-placement body parts. You can have everything from the neck up."

"It doesn't have to be a turf war. We can support each other. If your clients need neural work, send them my way, and I'll refer my study participants to you for those amazing skinterfaces," said Kade, with an admiring glance at Petra.

Flipping his skewer onto the miniature log pile in front of him, Steel held out his beer. Kade toasted it, and both men swigged on the deal.

Petra sighed into her copper mug. "Good thing Mechan-ic isn't here to see this."

"Why? It's exactly what she wanted—biohackers and the healthcare establishment working together." Rueful edges softened Kade's smile. "And me getting out of the lab for that party she never got to throw me."

"You'd better do a song for her."

"Forget it! I don't sing." Disco lights sparkled across his glasses. "Unless you want to do it with me."

Petra shook her head. "I'm already stuck in a duet."

"I hope you're better than the opening act," said Steel as Tae staggered down from the stage into his husband's arms.

"That was…unforgettable, *cariño,*" said Ciro, laughing.

"Yeah, if you'd have sung my defense in court, they'd have cleared my fines just to make you stop," Steel told him.

"And yet you're here, and not in prison." Tae loosened his tie. "Shall we celebrate with a group rendition of *I Fought The Law*?"

"You'll have to get me way drunker than this."

The lawyer's hand flew up to hail the server. "Could we trouble you for another round?"

Del bounced over, and Steel shrank in his chair. He'd nearly balked at the diner door when Del had shown the party a table; although the teen had coolly pretended not to recognize him, he'd treated them with a careful courtesy Petra hadn't known he possessed. *I bet he leaves a tip equivalent to the price of a knockoff Beat.*

"The same again, or are we trying something new?" Del plugged orders into a tablet. "What do you want, Petra?"

"My accompanist. Where is he?"

"Right here," Jonathan spoke behind her, maneuvering his guitar through the close-packed chairs. Freshly polished wood glowed in the warm light.

"About time! I was starting to think you got cold feet."

"Just cold fingers—had to play a bit downstairs and get them loose. What about you, are you warmed up?"

Petra knocked back her drink. "I am now."

"You know alcohol is a muscle relaxant, right? It lessens your control of your vocal cords and makes you sing worse."

"Then get me a few more until I'm as bad as your guita—aah!" She yelped as Jonathan drew out her chair and tipped her onto her feet.

"Let's see if you can live up to your nickname, Rock."

"People call you *Rock*?" Del clapped their hands and cackled. "Oh, that's amazing."

"Why?" asked Petra, but the kid had already seized the karaoke mic.

"Hi, everyone! We've got a special live act for you tonight. Introducing for their debut performance..." Del glanced back at the table with a smirk that outshone the mirrorball. "...*Rock and Rowell.*"

Jonathan groaned. "Please tell me I didn't hear that."

"Just be glad your last name isn't Bottom," said Petra, stepping onto the platform. She took the first mic from the stand and lowered the second level with Jonathan's guitar.

"I still think this is a crazy idea," he whispered.

"So was investigating a murder on nothing but a hunch, but we pulled that off."

"There weren't fifty people watching."

"Just one who mattered." Petra raised the mic to her lips, so the preface rang through the restaurant. "We've never played together before, but teamed up in tribute to a friend we recently lost. We'll try to make her proud."

"I hope we already did," Jonathan murmured, and strummed the opening chord. Energy resonated through Petra's bones. Their unlikely crew of companions clapped along. Behind the bar, Hank offered Grace a courtly bow, and they turned a few jive steps around the register. Jonathan glanced up from the fretboard, lights dancing in his eyes.

Whaddya know—it is *the perfect rhythm for a heartbeat.* Turning briefly to the wall, Petra slid a finger along the skinterface on her sternum. Her blood shifted to match the song's tempo. Rhythm pulsed through her body until even the bionic parts fused into one vibrant whole. *Machines can't feel music like this. As long as I'm still rocking, I'm still Rock.*

Sound soaring through her veins, Petra spun back to the room and sang.

AFTERWORD

My body is a time bomb. Is that ache in my hip a benign sports strain, or did the labrum finally snap? Is this headache simply dehydration, or the onset of my nervous system unraveling? I don't know what will break, or when, but my genes smolder with the destructive potential of hypermobility spectrum disorder (HSD).

"Hypermobility?" people ask, goggling at my hyperextended elbows (great for volleyball, lousy for bowling.) "Isn't being flexible a good thing?"

Not when it's internal. HSD affects connective tissue, which is present throughout our bodies. Excessive elasticity causes manifold problems. Joints and ribs dislocate at the slightest provocation. Sprains occur just getting out of bed. Digestive organs malfunction. Circulation fails, and can cause sudden blackouts. Short-circuited neurological systems trigger migraines, anxiety, and neuropathies. If humans are "meat machines," we HSD cases are walking cascade failures.

Our constellations of seemingly unrelated symptoms make HSD easy to misdiagnose. It's impossible to project its unique manifestation in an individual. So far, my problems have been minor. If I'm lucky, I might follow the trajectory of my mother, who didn't discover she had the condition until middle age, and mostly manages well. Or a twist of DNA could destine me for physiological collapse, like my younger sister.

My sister—let's call her Alice—suffered years of mysterious ailments and inconclusive medical evaluations before she was diagnosed with Ehlers-Danlos Syndrome (EDS), a condition at the extreme end of the hypermobility spectrum. Her condition deteriorated rapidly in her late twenties. Two complex surgeries forced her to resign from her work in healthcare, just a year shy of qualification for disability payments. Despite the surgeries, EDS left Alice completely disabled. Chronic pain continues to defy every treatment. Once a dancer, swimmer, and weightlifter, she now sometimes needs a walker to get around the house.

Yet Alice adapts. Tinnitus plagues her for months at a time, so she listens to audiobooks constantly to drown out the ringing in her ears. Mysteries are her favorite. When she suggested I write one, I hybridized it with elements of my beloved science fiction. Reimagining cyborgs through the lens of disability helped me come to terms with my condition. More importantly, it reconnected me with my sister.

Alice and I had had a rocky relationship since our teens. A decade of mutual maturation gave us a tenuous new start in our thirties, but it wasn't until she offered feedback on *Beat in Her Blood* that I really got to know her as an adult. Her incisive observations on mystery craft proved invaluable as I ventured into a new genre. She also volunteered candid insights on life with disability. Physical challenges are only part of the ordeal. As if battling EDS weren't enough, Alice must also battle the healthcare system.

Many specialists don't take insurance. If they do, the company often denies simple prescriptions and routine procedures. Appointments, claims, and approvals generate so much administrative work that Alice often quips: "being disabled is a full-time job." These themes resonate through *Beat in Her Blood.* Patients like Petra seek dubious alternatives. Secondary effects fall on people like Jonathan, who forfeit their dreams to tend sick family members. Meanwhile, corporations reap profits from pain. The COVID-19 pandemic exposed cracks in the system's foundation, but an even greater test creeps closer every season.

The American Medical Association declared climate change a public health crisis in June 2022. The World Health Organization expects it to cause approximately a quarter million additional deaths per year between 2030 and 2050, and that's just from malnutrition, malaria, diarrhea, and heat stress. Numerous other problems will rise along with the mercury, including arthropod-borne pathogens, respiratory ailments, renal disease, and mental health issues. We made the planet sick, and now it's reciprocating.

If we cannot preserve our habitat, we'll have to improve our capacity to survive in it. Is transhumanism the solution? At the time I wrote *Beat in Her Blood*, most of the bionic enhancements featured in the story existed, at least in research. Sophisticated biomedical technologies are increasingly available as consumer electronics. Equipped with gadgets that optimize our physical rhythms, and continuously connected via smartphones, we're already proto-cyborgs. We just haven't yet put the hardware under our skin.

Alice is ahead of the trend. EDS caused her vertebrae to torsion until the weight of her own head impaled her brain on her spinal column, resulting in brain stem injury and irreversible neurological damage. Surgery fixed her skull in position with titanium plates. This heavy metal "upgrade" probably saved her life. For a recovery gift, I gave her a sweatshirt that showed stages of human evolution from hominids to giant robots. (The garment makes a cameo appearance in this novel.)

If that progression is our species' path to survival, it won't be a smooth road. Societal change can be as traumatic as Alice's surgeries, a painful but necessary alteration of the body politic. Rather than depict bionics as a panacea, *Beat in Her Blood* explores its emergence from a disability perspective. My guiding questions, inspired by experiences with HSD, may soon demand answers of us all as Earth declines:

How do we cope with what cannot be cured?

What would we risk to keep ourselves intact?

What happens when chronic health problems afflict not only a marginalized few, but the majority of the population?

How many of us are as strong as Alice?